Praise for
Indigo Christmas
by Jeanne M. Dams
Agatha Award Winner

ᴖ

"The novel has a suspenseful story, but as usual, it's the characters and setting (rendered in precise but not obtrusive detail) that really capture our interest."

—*Booklist*

"Readers…should admire the author's grasp of period and locale, not just in superficial details but in social attitudes and preoccupations."

—*Ellery Queen's Mystery Magazine*

"Delightful… series fans will be well satisfied."

—*Publishers Weekly*

"The believable nuances of class and attitude are what make this series a standout, as well as the unusual setting of South Bend, Indiana…. The book is a pleasant delight."

—*Aunt Agatha's Newsletter*

"*Indigo Christmas* is a historical snapshot of an early America where immigrants may clash in culture, religion, and food, but the immigrant drive to overcome adversity shines in Hilda's abilities to keep the peace in her new family as well as to solve injustice. It stands on its own as a story with never a dull moment. Eagerly recommended."

—*Historical Novels Review*

HILDA JOHANSSON MYSTERY
7

MURDER IN BURNT ORANGE

Also by Jeanne M. Dams

Murder in Burnt Orange

A Hilda Johansson Mystery

Jeanne M. Dams

PERSEVERANCE PRESS / JOHN DANIEL & COMPANY
PALO ALTO / MCKINLEYVILLE, CALIFORNIA / MMXI

Printed in the United States of America

A Perseverance Press Book
Published by John Daniel & Company
A division of Daniel & Daniel, Publishers, Inc.
Post Office Box 2790
McKinleyville, California 95519
www.danielpublishing.com/perseverance

Distributed by SCB Distributors (800) 729-6423

Book design by Eric Larson, Studio E Books, Santa Barbara, www.studio-e-books.com

Cover painting by Linda Weatherly S.

10 9 8 7 6 5 4 3 2 1

LIBRARY OF CONGRESS CATALOGING-IN-PUBLICATION DATA
Dams, Jeanne M.
  Murder in burnt orange : a Hilda Johansson book / by Jeanne M. Dams.
    p. cm.
  ISBN 978-1-56474-503-3 (pbk. : alk. paper)
  1. Johansson, Hilda (Fictitious character)—Fiction. 2. Women private investigators—Fiction. 3. Swedish Americans—Fiction. 4. South Bend (Ind.)—Fiction. I. Title.
  PS3554.A498M87 2011
  813'.54--dc22
                        2011005175

MURDER IN BURNT ORANGE

MOTHERS ARE HELPED
*Happiness of Thousands of Woman Due to
Lydia E. Pinkham's Vegetable Compound
and Mrs. Pinkham's Advice* (adv't)

—South Bend *Times,* 1905

1

Hilda pushed her plate away, ham and eggs untouched.

Patrick put down the *Tribune.* "Are you not feelin' well, darlin'?" he asked cautiously. "I thought young Kevin was givin' you less trouble these days."

"Kristina is behaving well," said Hilda, frowning. "Except for kicking me every night. I am not ill. It is too hot to eat."

If Patrick sighed, he did it inwardly. "You've got to eat, me love. Don't forget you're feedin' two. Eileen could bring you some ice cream, or some strawberries and cream, or—"

"I do not want to eat, Patrick!" Hilda pushed her chair back and rose from the table, with some difficulty. She felt, and was sure she looked, enormous. She grasped the back of the chair while she found her balance. "I am hot and tired and my back hurts, and I do not want to do anything. I will go upstairs and lie down in front of the fan."

Patrick got up to help her, but she fixed him with such a glare that he subsided. His sigh this time, as she left the room, was audible.

Eileen, when she came into the dining room to clear the table, looked at Hilda's plate with a frown. "Sick again this morning, Mr. Patrick?"

"She said not, just hot and out of sorts. She's gone back to bed. You'd best look in on her later in the mornin' and see if you can get her to eat somethin'."

"It's starvin' the babe, she is!" Eileen was near tears. "I could see why she didn't want to eat while she was bein' sick every day, but now she's better, Mrs. O'Rourke and me, we cook things we're sure she'll like, her favorites—used to be, anyway—and she won't so much as taste them. She doesn't eat, barrin' outlandish things like sauerkraut and sardines, and them pretzels she can't get enough of. And I'm sure she hasn't spoken a good word to me since—well, for months, and her who used to be so nice to me!" The tears were very close to the surface now.

Patrick rose and patted her on the arm. "Now, Eileen, it's nothin' personal. She's uncomfortable and doesn't quite know what to do with herself, this bein' her first and all. And it is hot, right enough. This is a bad summer to be havin' a baby."

There had been heat waves throughout the Midwest that June of 1905, after record cold the preceding winter. Hilda hadn't minded the cold so much. She was Swedish, after all, born on a farm in Dalarna, where the winters were bitterly cold and dark. Northern Indiana seemed almost tropical by comparison. In any case, the cold lessened her nausea. The heat was a different matter. If Dalarna had ever been really hot and humid in summertime, Hilda claimed she could not remember it. And even if it had, she had not been pregnant at the time.

"It's bound to cool off soon," Patrick continued. "It can't stay this hot forever. She'll feel better once we get some rain."

Eileen sniffed. "I hope so, sir."

So did Patrick.

∾

"You look tired, me boy," said Mr. Malloy when Patrick walked into the office on the top floor of Malloy's Dry Goods.

Patrick took out a handkerchief and wiped his brow. "Not nine o'clock yet, and it must be ninety in the shade. And I didn't get much sleep last night."

"Hilda a bit restless, is she?"

Patrick mopped his brow again. "Restless isn't the word, Uncle Dan. Downright fratchety, she is. Nothin' suits her. First she was sick. Then she was sick and her—well, she felt sore. Then she started feelin' better, but the baby started kickin' her and wakin' her up. Now the baby kicks harder, and gets hiccups, and it all wakes her up. And when Hilda's awake, I'm awake. She's hot and tired all the time, and her back aches, and she can't find food to suit her, and Uncle Dan, I'm about to lose me mind! I don't remember me mam actin' like this with me brothers and sisters."

"By the time you were old enough to notice, your mother had other children to keep her busy, Pat. You got to remember, no woman knows how to do it the first time. Hilda's likely scared, too."

"Hilda? She's never scared of anything."

"She's never faced anything before that she thought she couldn't get out of. Even when those villains kidnapped her, while she was working to save my hide, she reckoned she could get away—and she did. But there's no escaping this predicament *you* got her into. She doesn't know what to expect, and I'm sure she's heard all the horror stories. That's a rare spunky woman you've been lucky enough to marry, Pat, but of course she's scared, though she'd never admit it."

Patrick licked his lips. They were salty with sweat. "To tell the truth, I'm scared, too. Women do die havin' babies, sometimes."

Dan Malloy acknowledged the fact with a nod. "They do. But not often nowadays, not when they're strong, healthy specimens like Hilda. Stop worrying, boy. You'll forget all about the nuisances once the baby's here."

"I don't know, Uncle Dan. Seems as if the Hilda I married has changed into somebody else. I'm not so sure I even know her anymore."

The day grew even hotter under a relentless sun. There were few customers in the store. The ladies who might have been interested in new ribbons or laces or handkerchiefs or parasols were sitting on their porches sipping lemonade, and the men who might have bought these things for their wives or lady friends were sweltering at their jobs. All the windows in the store were open wide to catch the least hint of a breeze, but there was no breeze. Several electric fans produced a good deal of noise, but little relief. Upstairs, the offices seemed so airless it was hard to breathe, and even harder to concentrate on work. By noon, Patrick's collar was so damp and limp he had to go home to exchange it for another.

He found Hilda in the parlor, reclining on the couch, fanning herself. She was wearing the silk kimono Aunt Molly had given her, and (Patrick strongly suspected) nothing whatever under it. He was a little shocked. A lady simply did not appear downstairs nearly naked.

"Do you not want to be upstairs, with the electric fan?" he said, after he had kissed her.

"It is too hot upstairs. And the fan buzzes so, it makes my head ache." She sought a more comfortable position, allowing the kimono to slip a trifle and confirm Patrick's suspicions.

"Then I'll bring you somethin' to eat, and we'll have our lunch together."

"I am not hungry."

Patrick said nothing, but stalked out of the room.

He returned shortly with a tray. Eileen followed, carrying a small table that she set down in front of the couch.

"Patrick! I said I was not hungry."

"I know what you said." He put the tray down. It contained a large bowl of jellied consommé, a green salad, some bread and cheese, and a tall glass of iced lemonade. "You will eat this."

"I do not want it."

"But you will eat it." Patrick had an Irish temper, and it had finally broken its restraints. "I'm not havin' our child suffer because you're not comfortable. Eat." His voice was not loud, but it was pure steel.

He pulled the chair away from the writing desk in the corner, sat astride it, and glared at his wife.

Hilda glared back. Patrick's jaw set even more firmly.

Hilda had a temper of her own, even when she was not pregnant and perishing with heat. For a long moment she considered throwing the consommé at him, but the parlor carpet was new. Even in her fury, her housewifely thrift couldn't quite allow her to ruin a fine piece of Axminster. Moreover, she knew that when his anger reached this stage, she was not going to win.

She scowled, sat up, and took a tiny spoonful of soup. Once she began, she found that she was, after all, ravenously hungry. She ate everything on the tray, while Patrick kept a vigilant eye on her, now and then taking a bite of the large ham sandwich Eileen had provided for him.

"I hope you are happy now," she said acidly when she had finished. She was not going to allow him the satisfaction of knowing she had enjoyed her meal.

"I will be happy when you have eaten your ice cream," he said sternly. He was not going to allow her the satisfaction of knowing he had softened. Not yet.

When Eileen had brought in bowls of strawberry ice cream and they had both eaten their fill, he came and sat beside her. Taking her hands, he said, "Darlin' girl, I'm sorry I had to go all hardhearted like that. But I have to make you look after yourself. You were starvin' yerself and little Kevin before me very eyes."

"I am not starving K-Kristina," said Hilda in a wobbly voice, and suddenly burst into tears. "It is just that I am so fat, and I am so hot and tired, and I want this to be o-over!"

Once more bewildered and apologetic, Patrick patted and soothed and finally rang for Eileen. "Mrs. Cavanaugh is tired, Eileen. Can you help her up to bed? And turn on the fan, unless it will keep her awake."

"I will give her a cool bath, sir. That'll make her more comfortable. Up you get, ma'am."

Still sobbing, Hilda allowed herself to be helped off the couch and up the stairs. Patrick stood irresolute, wondering whether his presence upstairs would make matters better or worse, until the clanging of fire bells interrupted his thoughts. Once a fireman, he still responded to the summons like an old fire horse. This hot summer the sound was all too familiar. Fires started easily and spread quickly from one building to the next. He started out the front door to see if he could figure out where the fire wagon was going, but a shout from Eileen called him back.

"You can't go back to the store lookin' like that, Mr. Patrick!"
She tossed a fresh collar down to him from the landing, and
grinned. "Don't fret, now! She's had a good meal, and a good cry,
and she'll sleep as soon as I've cooled her off a bit. And it's only
another two or three months!"

Patrick crossed himself and raised his eyes to heaven. "May
the blessed saints be praised, and may we all survive it, Eileen."

2

THE HEAT CONTINUED. A thunderstorm two nights later served only to increase the humidity without bringing cooler air. The rain helped douse a few small house fires, but others were more serious. A local bank was nearly destroyed. The general feeling was that arson might have caused that fire, since the bank was rumored to be on the verge of collapse, but with the bank records destroyed, nothing could be proved.

Hilda's temper did not improve, nor did her appetite. Doctor Clark, when he had examined her, came downstairs with a grave face.

"She's fretting, lad," he said when Patrick had seated him in the parlor. "No, thanks, no whiskey. I've other calls to make, and anyway whiskey warms me. I wouldn't say no to some lemonade."

Patrick rang the bell. "But is the baby all right?"

"Baby seems fine. Good strong heartbeat, and growing like a weed. I take it you are forcing her to eat?"

Patrick frowned. "I'll not say I'm forcin' her. But—well, what's a man to do? I'll allow I've lost me temper a time or two and pushed her a bit."

"Good for you. Keep it up. She's on the thin side, herself, though the baby's just fine—a bit big for this stage, if anything. The body will see to that, you know. If there's not enough food for both mother and baby, the baby gets the lion's share. But it's not her nutrition I'm worried about, so much as her nerves. They're in a bad state."

Patrick nodded dolefully. "She's fair drivin' me to distraction, and that's the truth. I don't know what to do for her. I don't mind tellin' you there's times I'd like to take her and shake some sense into her. Nothin' I say or do is any help, unless I downright lose me temper, and then she cries."

"Hmm. I don't suppose you've talked to her mother?"

Patrick snorted. "Her mother and me, we're not on speakin' terms these days. I was beginnin' to talk her around, make her think the Irish weren't all bad, and maybe I was good enough for her precious daughter. But now Hilda's takin' this baby so hard, Mrs. Johansson thinks I'm the devil himself to get her into this state. She won't even come to see Hilda if I'm here."

Doctor Clark nodded. He knew all about the acrimony between Hilda's Swedish family and Patrick's Irish people. "Your mother, then. Or your aunt. Hilda needs a sensible woman to talk to."

Patrick brightened. "My mother doesn't like Hilda any more than her mother likes me. But Aunt Molly, now…"

The next day, June 22, the first day of real summer, brought with it increased heat, a horrifying newspaper headline, and a visitor. Eileen was serving breakfast, and Aunt Molly, after the barest tap on the screen door, let herself in and marched into the dining room.

"Don't be silly, my dear," she said to Eileen's stammered apologies. "You were busy, and I'm family. Do get me a cup of coffee, there's a good girl. Hilda, how are you?"

Hilda muttered something and bit the tiniest possible corner off her piece of toast.

Molly Malloy was not a person to be ignored. "Perhaps you didn't hear me, Hilda. I asked how you were."

"I am well, Aunt Molly." It was the merest murmur of a reply, meant to satisfy courtesy, not to convey meaning.

"You don't look it," retorted Molly. "Your hair looks like it's housed a nestful of mice, and what are you doing downstairs in a kimono?"

"You gave it to me," said Hilda, a tiny hint of anger touching her voice.

"I did that, but not to wear down to breakfast. But never mind. Patrick, have you seen this headline?"

She thrust the front page of the *Tribune* under his nose. He pointed to the copy folded beside his plate. OPEN SWITCH HURLS TWENTIETH CENTURY FLYER FROM THE TRACK read the two-column head. Datelined Cleveland, Ohio, the story included gruesome details of the number of dead and injured, the fire that burned many of the wooden cars, the last statements of the dying. Patrick was not the sort of husband who forbade his wife to read the paper, but he had already decided to keep this one from Hilda's eyes if he could. In his opinion it was the sort of thing that could mark an unborn child.

"Yes," he said to Aunt Molly, with a significant glance toward Hilda.

"And what do you propose to do about it?" demanded Molly.

"Do? What do you mean? What can I do about a train wreck?"

"A *deliberate* train wreck, Patrick. Have you read the story? The switch was left open on purpose. Those twenty-one people were murdered, Patrick Cavanaugh, and Mr. Malloy was very nearly on that train!"

"Uncle Dan? But he's in Chicago."

"He is, but he was to have left yesterday evening for New York. But for the grace of God, he would have been in one of those sleeping cars that burned." Molly crossed herself.

"What happened?" asked Hilda. Patrick and Molly turned to her like puppets on a single string.

"Nothin' you need concern yourself with, darlin' girl," said Patrick at the same moment that Molly said, "An accident, but an accident-on-purpose. You'd be interested."

"Molly!" said Patrick. Molly and Hilda ignored him.

"It's just the sort of mystery you like to solve, Hilda," said Molly, accepting a cup of coffee from Eileen and sitting down at the table. "No clues at all, and a great deal at stake. You know, of course, that there have been a great many train wrecks of late, and even the Pinkertons haven't any clues to who's behind them."

"I did not know," said Hilda. "I have not felt well enough to read the newspaper."

"Nonsense! You're expecting a baby. It's a perfectly normal state of affairs, not an illness. The trouble is, you have nothing to do but feel sorry for yourself. You need a task, something to interest you."

"But I can do nothing! I cannot go out in this condition, only to church. I cannot even have guests in. Polite society—"

"Pooh to polite society! When have you ever cared about such a thing, Hilda Cavanaugh, you who come down to breakfast in a kimono? You flouted all the rules by marrying my nephew, and the more I love you for it. Now you're making him unhappy, because you're neglecting yourself and your child, and I won't have it. It's time you pulled yourself together, young woman!"

The doorbell rang. Eileen, who had stayed just outside the dining room to listen, went to see who was calling at an hour when there should be no visitors, let alone two.

"But Aunt Molly!" Patrick managed to get a word in. "Hilda hasn't been at all well. I don't want her overworkin' herself."

"Overworking! May Jesus, Mary, and Joseph defend us! She's been doing nothing for six months, and it's time she bestirred herself. I was working in the back of the shop alongside Mr. Malloy right up until the pains started with my first, and never felt better in my life."

The discussion was interrupted by the entrance of a tall woman who looked strikingly like Hilda, though her coronet-braided hair showed silver mixed with the gold. She strode ahead of Eileen, ignored the other people in the room, and unleashed a torrent of Swedish directed at Hilda.

"Du, Hilda! Lyssna på mig! Ingen gott kommer från att du sitter där hela tiden och tycker synd om dig själv! Du är—"

"Mama! Speak English!"

For the first time, Mrs. Johansson noticed Mrs. Malloy. Mrs. Malloy smiled, without much hope of the smile being returned. Mrs. Johansson nodded, stiffly. Neither held out a hand.

"I am sorry to—to break in," said Mrs. Johansson in her halting English. "I yoost said, I must speak to Hilda. It is about the train crash."

This time Aunt Molly's smile was warmly genuine. "Why, Mrs. Johansson! That's why I came, too. Hilda's so good at solving problems, and the train wrecks are a big problem."

Mama looked surprised, but unbent a trifle. "Yes, and my son, Sven, he goes on the train sometimes, for Mr. Studebaker, and it would be very bad if he would be hurt. And Hilda, she sits and does nothing—"

"Now if that isn't just what I've been saying! Mr. Malloy travels by train a good deal, by that very train that was wrecked last night that he would have been on if it hadn't been for a meeting that went way past its time, and what I think—" she paused for breath "—what I think is that Hilda needs something to take her mind off her—er—discomfort, and this would be the very thing. Now sit down, do, and let's talk Hilda into it."

Eileen brought fresh coffee for everyone, and they talked, Mama breaking from time to time into agitated Swedish that Hilda had to translate.

Hilda argued vehemently that she didn't want to get involved in anything as dangerous as hunting for a train wrecker, that it might be harmful for the baby, that in any case she was prohibited by her condition from being seen in public. While she argued she ate cold ham and boiled eggs and toast and jam, and drank coffee with thick cream in it, without noticing what she was doing. Patrick noticed, and winked at Eileen.

"You wouldn't have to go out, child," said Aunt Molly. "Not that it would hurt you any if you did. Gracious, women have been having babies since time began, and there's nothing indecent about it."

"You are right, Mrs. Malloy," said Mama. "It is foolish to say that a woman carrying a child must not be seen."

"Mama, most of the rules of society are foolish. But they are rules, and the real ladies in South Bend are not friendly with me anyway. They would like me even less if I broke the rule."

Aunt Molly shook her head. "My dear girl, the *real* ladies, ladies like Mrs. Studebaker and young Mrs. Oliver, admire you greatly. It's only the social upstarts and those who don't know you who turn up their noses. Let them, I say."

But Hilda shook her head just as firmly. "No. The rule is foolish, but I will not break it. When little Kristina grows up, she will be a society lady, and I do not want people to turn their noses up at her."

"Then," said Molly, "use your boys, your 'Baker Street Irregulars.' They'll have heard more about what's going on than the police, or I don't know boys."

"Yes," said Mama, "and Erik, he is not in school, it is summer, and his yob—*job*—does not take all his time, only the afternoons. He can ask questions for you."

"And Mr. Malloy can talk to the businessmen in town, find out what the gossip is among the railroad men."

"And I can ask around among the servants," put in Eileen from the corner, and then blushed. "Sorry, ma'am. I didn't ought to've been listening."

Suddenly Hilda grinned. "Why should you not? I always did, when I worked at Tippecanoe Place. What is the good of being a maid if you cannot hear and learn interesting things?"

"Then it's settled," said Aunt Molly. "You will organize our search, tell us what you need to know, and we will be your eyes and ears while you provide the brains."

"Now, hold your horses a minute!" Patrick, not quite sure how things had spiraled out of control, looked at the women warily. "It's all very well, you two wantin' Hilda's help over this business. But Hilda's right, it's foolish to think that she could do anythin' about a criminal like a wrecker. If the police and the

Pinkertons haven't found out who it is, is it likely that one woman can do anythin' at all? Especially a woman who's—a woman in her condition? And it could be dangerous, besides. I'll not have her gettin' into trouble and maybe hurtin' herself and my son."

Three women began to talk at once. Patrick finally put his hands over his ears. "All right. All *right!* Aunt Molly, you were sayin'?"

"I don't think, Patrick dear, that it could do any harm for Hilda to put her excellent mind to work on the problem. She need not involve herself beyond that. Who knows? She might come up with an idea or two that would be of help to the official investigators."

Mama nodded energetically. "That is what I say, too. She is young and strong. It will not hurt her to t'ink about it."

Patrick looked at Hilda.

"I will decide," she said briefly, and reached for a cinnamon bun. "Eileen, is there more coffee?"

Patrick showed the two guests out. "Mind you," he said in a low voice as he opened the screen door, "I'm still not sure this isn't a fool idea. But I don't want you to think I'm not obliged to the both of you for givin' Hilda somethin' to think about. That's the best meal she's had in weeks, and there's a sparkle back in her eye. Not that she shouldn't have had that right along. I can't understand why she's been so down in the dumps."

The two women looked at him pityingly. "A man would not understand," said Mama, and Aunt Molly nodded agreement. "You have never borne a child."

Patrick couldn't argue with that.

Aunt Molly's carriage was waiting on the street. She turned to Mama. "May I take you home? It's far too hot to walk anywhere."

"Thank you, but I go to work." Mama straightened her back and lifted her chin.

"Then I'll take you to work, and we can talk on the way." Molly tucked Mama's hand into the crook of her arm. "Wilson's, isn't it? I hope they're managing to keep the place more or less comfortable in the heat. Mr. Malloy's store is well-nigh unbearable these days."

Patrick watched as the two climbed into the carriage and clattered away down the brick pavement. He shook his head in awe. If Molly had begun to bring Mrs. Johansson around toward a truce, it was almost a miracle. And Hilda's revived energy—well, he might have to think again about their wild scheme.

3

HILDA SAT AT the breakfast table after everyone had left, thoughtfully nibbling at another cinnamon bun and drinking coffee. She was hot and uncomfortable, and the baby seemed to be dancing a jig. She had every excuse for going back to bed.

On the other hand…

She put down her coffee cup and rang the bell. "Eileen, is there a cool dress I can still wear?"

Eileen nodded eagerly. "I let out the bodice of your white lawn, ma'am, and put gussets in the waist. It'll fit you still, and it's lovely and cool."

"No corset," said Hilda decidedly. "And as little underneath as is decent. And Eileen, before you help me dress, ask Mr. O'Rourke to take the carriage and find Erik and bring him to me. He is probably still at home and in bed."

"Yes, ma'am." Eileen fairly danced out of the room. This was more like the mistress she knew and loved.

It took Mr. O'Rourke a while to find Erik. He had not been in bed. Too hot to sleep, he had risen at dawn and gone to the river to fish. That was fun, but cleaning the fish afterward was not. So he was happy to postpone that chore, leave his catch on ice at home, and go with Hilda's coachman.

"You smell of fish," was his loving sister's greeting when he walked in her door. "And your feet are dirty. Why do you not wear shoes?"

"It's too hot. And I was fishing—what do you expect me to

smell like? Anyway, Mr. O'Rourke told me you wanted to see me right away. I thought maybe something was wrong."

"Nothing is wrong. Please go to the scullery and wash your feet. I do not want mud on my new carpet."

Resentfully, Erik went, and returned in a fever of curiosity. "So what did you want me for?"

Hilda chose her words carefully, having given the matter some thought. "Mama and Aunt Molly have asked me to try to learn what I can about the train wrecks that have happened in the past weeks, especially the one yesterday."

Erik nodded. "The Twentieth Century Flyer. Goin' seventy-five miles an hour, she was, and hit an open switch. She flew, all right—off the track and into a ditch, engine and cars and all. Then the engine caught fire, and—"

"That is enough, Erik. I have read the newspaper. It was horrible. The police and the Pinkertons are working to find the man who did this, and I am sure that I cannot be of any real help to them."

"Why not? You've helped 'em before, haven't you? Solved cases for 'em when they didn't have no idea where to look."

"Did not have any idea," Hilda corrected automatically. "But that was when I could get about and talk to people. Now I cannot."

"Why not? You can still walk, can't you?"

Hilda winced. A farm boy knew all about obstetrics, at least with regard to cows and sheep and horses, but at fourteen, and the youngest in his family, Erik was perhaps unaware of social prohibitions. Obviously he didn't understand that pregnancy was not to be discussed.

"It is expected that I stay home for the next few months, except to go to church," she said, and changed the subject. "That is why I need your help. If I am to please Mama and Aunt Molly, I must at least pretend to seek information about the wrecks. Have you and your friends talked about them?"

"O' course! Nothin' much else goin' on here when it's so durned hot."

"Erik! Your language!"

Erik grinned. "Patrick says 'damned hot.' I heard him."

Hilda gritted her teeth. "Then he should not. And anyway what a grown man says and what you may say are different things. But what have you heard about the train wrecks?"

"There's a lot o' talk, but none of it means much. Some say it's hoboes doin' it, makin' trouble 'cause they get thrown off the trains."

Hilda frowned. "That does not sound reasonable. Most hoboes are peaceable men. And they know how to stay away from the train guards, so they will not be caught."

Erik nodded. "That's what I say, too. Nice guys, hoboes. They only steal when they have to."

Erik knew something about hoboes, for they had once saved his life. They were not, perhaps, the most suitable companions for a respectable boy, but she shared his opinion that most of them were "nice guys," though she would never have expressed it in that slangy way. "What else do your friends say?"

"Stupid stuff, mostly. One of 'em—well, Ben, you know him—he says his father says it's probably the railroad men doin' it themselves, to collect on the insurance."

"Oh! But that is a wicked idea! To kill so many people, just for money!"

"Yeah, and stupid. Them railroad men—"

"*Those* railroad men."

"—those railroad men are rich as kings. They don't need the insurance money. Now, Andy, he says he's heard talk it's anakiss—antikris—"

"Anarchists?"

"Yeah, like the ones in Russia. You know, blowin' stuff up and killin' kings and stuff like that."

Hilda hadn't read the newspapers carefully of late, but she had the notion that Erik's summary was somewhat less than accurate. However... "Why would they want to destroy trains? I believe what they want is to have a better government in Russia. What does that have to do with American trains?"

Erik shrugged. "Dunno. That's what Andy's heard, though."

"From guests at the hotel?" Hilda knew Andy well. He was a bellboy at the Oliver Hotel, the finest in town, and often overheard interesting conversations.

"Guests, and town people who come to the hotel for dinner. Important people."

"Hmm." Hilda thought for a moment. "Erik, when does Andy get off work, do you know?"

"Supper time, or thereabouts."

"And you will be at work yourself then. Do you think you could leave for a few minutes and go and ask Andy to come and see me on his way home?"

"Sure. The firehouse is only a couple of blocks from the hotel, and the horses won't miss me for five minutes. But can't I come, too?"

"No, you must not leave your work for so long. But if you come back tomorrow morning, I will tell you what Andy tells me, and we can make some plans."

"Okay, I guess. Well, I reckon I better get back and clean my fish before I go to work." Then he brightened. "Say, Hilda, can Mr. O'Rourke take me home? And I saw them cinnamon buns in the kitchen. They look awful good. Can I have one?"

When Patrick came home for lunch, he found Hilda in the parlor, dressed and with her hair braided properly. She was sitting in an overstuffed chair, surrounded by a pile of newspapers.

"Patrick! You are home. Good. What do we do with old newspapers?"

"Here, now! Do I get a kiss, darlin' girl?"

He bent over her and got a perfunctory kiss before she questioned him again. "Newspapers, Patrick. I can find them only as far back as two weeks ago."

"Blessed if I know what we do with 'em. Use 'em to light the fires, I suppose, or in summer to wrap the garbage. Why?"

"I am looking for the accounts of the uprisings in Russia, but I cannot find anything."

"And why the sudden interest in Russia?"

"Andy says—you know, Erik's friend Andy—he says there is talk that Russian anarchists are behind the train wrecks. It does not seem likely to me, but I want to read about the uprisings before I talk to Andy, and he is coming to see me this afternoon."

"So you're serious about this train wreck business? Hilda, I told you, it's maybe dangerous!"

Hilda's eyes flashed. "You told me also that it was foolish for me to think I could do anything. I am smart, Patrick. You know I am. I can sometimes find out things other people cannot. And how can there be danger when I never leave the house? Be sensible, Patrick! And find me those newspapers. There would be copies at the *Tribune* and *Times* offices, would there not, if we do not have them?"

Patrick sat down, heavily. He was extremely dubious about this whole endeavor. But—here was his Hilda back, the eager, bright-eyed, strong-willed woman he adored, ordering him about in her usual imperious fashion, looking healthier and happier than she had since January.

He sighed. "I'll see what I can do about the papers, darlin'. Now what about me lunch?"

Patrick called in at both newspaper offices on his way back to the store. He was finding it useful, in more ways than one, to have money. Patrick Cavanaugh, fireman, might have received scant attention at the busy offices. Patrick Cavanaugh, partner in a prosperous business concern that advertised heavily, was shown every courtesy. Certainly there were extra copies of papers, back several months. Would Mr. Cavanaugh like to take them with him? Oh, of course. Well, then, a newsboy would be dispatched to the Cavanaugh home as soon as the relevant issues were compiled. No trouble at all, sir. Thank you, sir.

The papers arrived, several pounds of them going all the way back to January, and Hilda settled down to learn about unrest in Russia.

There was a good deal to learn, none of it agreeable. It seemed, at least at first, to have much more to do with labor unrest than with anarchism. A massive strike in St. Petersburg in

early January had led to a fearful bloodbath, when thousands of
striking workers and their families, presenting a petition to the
czar, were attacked by the Russian army. Hilda read in horror
about screaming men—and women and children—in the thousands, trying to flee gunfire and the murderous hooves of cavalry
horses.

With a shudder, Hilda read on. It came as no surprise to
learn that, on February 4, the Grand Duke Sergius, uncle to the
czar, had been assassinated, blown to bits by a bomb placed in
his carriage in Moscow. Spurred on, perhaps, by this success, the
strike movement grew, spreading to rural districts and causing
great disorder.

After that, the situation in Russia seemed to calm down for
a while, or at least the unrest ceased to inspire the editors of the
South Bend *Tribune* and *Times*, who moved other news to the
front page. Russia's ongoing war with Japan took pride of place
in the foreign news columns, the tide turning now to favor one
country, now the other.

Hilda wasn't interested in a war on the other side of the
world. She leafed quickly through several issues, making a face
as she looked at the pictures of gorgeous spring and summer
fashions. She could afford that sort of clothes now. If only she
could wear them!

There was a bright side, however. Those lovely dresses absolutely required a corset, and Hilda had, at least for a while, the
perfect excuse for not wearing the detested garment.

Reluctantly she turned back to the news columns, and when
she came to May—oh, dear! How could she have been so unaware of what was going on in the world! For in May the strike
violence broke out in America, and not only in America, but in
Chicago!

Chicago was only a few hours from South Bend by train.
Uncle Dan went to Chicago all the time, and Sven sometimes, to
the Studebaker Repository on Michigan Avenue. Violence there
was violence close to home, far too close for comfort. Surely it
couldn't spread here—not in such terrible form, at least.

The trouble this time, she read, had begun with a strike by garment workers at Montgomery Ward, the big mail-order company. In sympathy, the big, powerful Teamsters' Union refused to haul goods for Montgomery Ward. Hilda found herself unable to follow the confusing details, but the accounts sounded as though matters had got entirely out of control. Teamsters stopped their wagons in the middle of intersections, bringing all traffic to a halt. Policemen tried to bring order, but rocks were thrown and clubs came out and—*Herre Gud!* thought Hilda. It was as bad as St. Petersburg, or nearly, and right there in Chicago. She put down the papers, sick from the details, but she couldn't help remembering other episodes, violent ones, in the past.

The fact was, labor unrest was nothing new. Neither was anarchist sentiment, the anarchists often making use of the strikers' legitimate grievances to further their own ends. Only a few years ago the anarchist Leon Czolgosz had come to South Bend, shortly before he assassinated President McKinley. John Bolton, coachman at the Studebaker family's Tippecanoe Place where Hilda had worked at the time, had met him, and so had some of Hilda's friends. And the next year, the Anthracite Coal Strike had gone on for months and had brought great suffering to much of the country.

Hilda was, generally speaking, on the side of the workers. She knew about poverty; her family had been desperately poor on their farm in Sweden. She knew, too, that America, where immigrants had thought to find gold in the streets, had its own brand of dreadful poverty. Friends had told her about brutally long working hours in filthy, unsafe conditions, about children working for a few pennies a day in near-starvation while their bosses lived in fine houses and grew fat on luxurious food.

Hilda and her family were some of the fortunate ones. They hadn't experienced those terrible conditions once they came to America. The Studebakers, by whom several of them were or had been employed, were fair to their people, and the Wilson Shirt Factory, where Mama worked, was at least clean and the management humane. But even in South Bend, Hilda knew, some men and women, yes, and children, too, lived in great poverty. She had seen some of their homes, not very far away from her own. Hilda could understand the fierce compulsion to better one's lot in life, to force employers into treating their workers like human beings.

Now, of course, having married Patrick, with his good job and fine paycheck, Hilda had no money worries. She even had servants of her own.

A thought struck her. She took a damp handkerchief out of her sleeve, wiped her brow, and reached for the bell-pull. When Eileen appeared, Hilda gestured for her to sit down.

Warily, Eileen sat, on the very edge of a hard chair.

"Eileen, do you get enough to eat?"

"Yes, ma'am." The girl's voice was questioning.

"And does Mrs. O'Rourke let you get enough sleep?" The cook, Hilda knew, was something of a tyrant.

"Yes, ma'am. 'Cept these last few nights, it's been too hot to sleep."

Hilda slapped the arm of the chair. "Hot! Of course! I should have thought. I will ask Mr. Cavanaugh to buy another electric fan and put it in your room."

"There's no need for that, ma'am. I'm ascared o' them electric contraptions."

"They are quite safe, Eileen, although they are noisy. But if you put cotton in your ears, you can sleep well. And you must get your sleep. You work very hard. Is the work too hard, Eileen? Do you need help?"

"I can do the work, ma'am! Is Mrs. O'Rourke sayin' I'm shirkin'? 'Cause it's a lie, if she is." Color was rising in the maid's face.

Hilda realized she had gone about this the wrong way. "No, Eileen. I am sorry. I did not mean to worry you. It is just that I have been reading about all these strikes, and I wondered if I am good enough to the people who work here. I know what it is to be a servant."

Eileen's anxiety found relief in tears. "Oh, ma'am, you're the best mistress in town. Leastways, now you're back to yourself.

You took me away from that awful job I had before, and you treat me like I was your own daughter, and I'd niver want to go noplace else."

"Anyplace else, Eileen. Well, then, bring some lemonade for both of us. I want to talk to you about these strikes."

"Mrs. O'Rourke needs me, ma'am, to do the vegetables. But I'll bring you the lemonade, and welcome."

"Very well. But tell Mrs. O'Rourke—ask Mrs. O'Rourke to come in for a minute when she can."

Time was when Hilda would have marched into the kitchen to get her own lemonade and speak to the cook. She knew better now. Mrs. O'Rourke was an excellent cook and housekeeper, but was very protective of her domain. The master and mistress of the house invaded it at their peril.

Hilda sat and waited for the lemonade and the cook to arrive.

Y ES, MA'AM?" Mrs. O'Rourke's face wore what was nearly a scowl, and her voice said clearly what her words did not: that she was in the middle of preparations for supper, that the kitchen was hot and she was tired, and that she certainly had no time for a talk with the lady of the house.

Hilda heard all of the unspoken dialogue. "Mrs. O'Rourke, I know you are busy, and I am sorry to take you away from your work. I wanted to ask, would you and Mr. O'Rourke like an electric fan in your bedroom? And perhaps in the kitchen? I will ask Mr. Cavanaugh to get them, if you wish."

The cook hesitated. She disliked accepting favors from Hilda, who was, in her opinion, still just a housemaid pretending to be a grand lady. But this heat wave had gone on forever, it seemed. The kitchen was hot and she, Mrs. O'Rourke, was neither as young nor as thin as she used to be. "Not in the bedroom, ma'am. Mr. O'Rourke can't abide a draft. But in the kitchen, now…"

"Good. You will have it tomorrow. And would you please send Eileen to me as soon as she is free after supper? Thank you, Mrs. O'Rourke."

Having thus assuaged her conscience and staved off, she hoped, any threat of rebellion and uprising in her own household, Hilda sat back with her cool drink to wait for Andy.

Andy had been one of Hilda's chief sources of information for some time, now. A little older than Erik, he had worked at the grand Oliver Hotel since it opened, to help support his family.

Although he had but little formal schooling, he was bright and had taught himself to read and write. He and his friends at the hotel were Hilda's "Baker Street Irregulars," her eyes and ears on the world. Especially now that she was confined to her home, Hilda needed Andy's help.

He arrived just as Hilda was beginning to look for Patrick's return. The day was at its hottest, and Hilda was lying on the couch in a fitful nap when Eileen came in and spoke softly to her. "He's here, ma'am. That boy. He *says* you want to see him."

One day, Hilda thought drowsily, she would ask Eileen why she disliked Andy. "That is fine, Eileen. Show him in. And would you bring us a fresh pitcher of lemonade, please?"

Eileen sniffed, but did as she was told.

Andy came warily into the parlor. It was nothing like as grand as the lobby of the Oliver, but the hotel was Andy's domain. There he wore a snappy uniform and had some status. Here he was only a poor boy in shabby clothes, calling on a lady. No matter that she had been a servant. She was a lady now, and an obviously pregnant lady at that, and Andy felt shy. He was still more uneasy when Eileen returned with a tray with lemonade and fine glasses and a plate of cookies. He wasn't used to being waited on.

"Sit down, Andy. Do you have time to stay for a few minutes?"

"I got to get home soon, ma'am. Ma'll be needin' me."

"I will give you some lemonade then, to cool you, and I will be quick. Andy—what is your last name? I have never known it."

"Mueller, ma'am." He stood, twisting his frayed cap in his hands.

That explained Eileen's attitude, then. The Irish and the Germans in South Bend didn't mix. Hilda would have to talk to her about that. Later.

"Andy, I need your help. Did Erik tell you what I am doing?"

"He says you're lookin' into the train wrecks, ma'am, and

what I say is, you hadn't better. Sorry if I'm not bein' perlite, but that's no business for a lady to get herself mixed up in."

"Sit *down,* Andy, and have a cool drink. You are not impolite, and it is kind of you to want to protect me, but what harm can come to me here in my own home? And I need to find out what I can, because my mother and Mr. Cavanaugh's aunt have both asked me to. Now, I want to know what you have heard."

Reluctantly, Andy sat and accepted a glass. "Ma'am, I've heard enough to know this is pretty risky business, no doubt about it. Some men was talkin' in the lounge just last week. They never pay me no mind, just like I didn't have ears or somethin'."

Hilda nodded. "I know. It was like that for me, too, when I was a servant. It made me very angry, but it was sometimes useful. What did these men say?"

"They'd been drinkin', see, and they wasn't watchin' their words. One of 'em, he says, 'It'll do the trick, you mark my words. Every railroad man in the state'll sign on soon as they hear of it.'"

Hilda frowned. "That does not make sense to me. What did they mean?"

Andy squirmed in his chair. "It's not for me to say, ma'am."

"Andy! This is me, Hilda! Why will you not talk to me? You used to tell me everything. Are you no longer my friend?"

"Well, see, it's like this, miss. I ain't forgotten how good you've been to me. But these men—they're nasty. I seen a lot of men, in and out of the hotel, what you'd call gentlemen, and the other kind. And these guys, they give me the willies. I reckon they're gangsters, or the next thing to it, and I don't want nothin' to do with 'em. Nor I don't want you havin' nothin' to do with 'em."

Hilda looked at him thoughtfully. He was as pale as his sunburned complexion would allow. "You are frightened."

"You bet I am! And I ain't usually scared of nothin', you know that."

"I know you are brave. Can you tell me why these men frighten you?"

"It's nothin' you can put your finger on, miss—ma'am."

"Call me 'miss,' Andy, as you used to. It is more friendly."

"Yes, miss. These guys—it's just sort of the way they talk. Not loud, but kind of hard, like they're used to gettin' their own way. And they dress fancy, but not like real gentlemen. Too fancy, sort of. And—I dunno, miss. I think any one of 'em'd kill you as soon as look at you, and that's the truth." He looked at her anxiously.

Hilda frowned and bit her lip, and suppressed a small yelp as the baby kicked her, hard.

"Miss?"

"It is nothing. A little trouble with my stomach." Too late she remembered that the stomach was not mentioned in polite society, any more than a baby's movements. Perhaps Andy didn't know that either.

"Andy, did anyone know that you were coming here today?"

"No, miss. Leastways, I didn't tell nobody, and this house is on my way home, sorta. And I gotta be gettin' along, miss."

"Yes. There is one more thing I need to know, Andy. No, two. Do you think these men are anarchists?"

Andy shook his head slowly. "I don't rightly know what they might look like, miss, but the pictures I seen of that guy, the one who killed the president, you know?"

Hilda nodded.

"Well, these men don't look nothin' like him. He looked kinda wild-like, you know? These guys look fancy, like I said."

"I understand. But then why did you tell Erik you thought it was anarchists who planned the train wrecks?"

"That wasn't me, miss. Some of the other boys, they got to arguin' about it. The bell captain, he told 'em to shut up, 'cause they were gettin' to talkin' too loud. But I never thought that."

"Could they be union organizers, do you think? The troubles this year in Russia and in Chicago started when the police tried to stop the unions."

"Maybe, I guess. Only I've seen some of them union men,

when they come through town, Mr. Debs and Mr. Gompers and them, and they didn't look like—well, I dunno. And I gotta go, miss, really! Ma'll be worryin' about me."

"Take the cookies with you. And come back tomorrow, if you can. I need you to ask the other boys some questions, and to keep your eyes open."

But, Hilda admitted to herself when he had gone, she knew very little she hadn't known before. And she had, at the moment, no idea what to ask the bellboys to do.

And who were Mr. Debs and Mr. Gompers?

She asked Patrick when they sat down to supper.

"You're slippin', me girl. I thought you read the papers. Pass the potato salad, would you, darlin'?"

"I remember something about someone named Gompers when I went through the papers today, but I did not read very carefully." Hilda passed him the bowl of salad, after taking a second helping for herself.

"Samuel Gompers is only the leadin' union man in the whole country, that's all. He's president of the American Federation of Labor, and he's fought for the rights of the workin' man for years. Last month he went to Chicago to try to make both sides see reason and settle the strike, but it's still goin' on, last I heard."

"They are not still killing people on the streets?" Hilda's tone was horrified, and Patrick hastened to reassure her.

"Not that I've heard, darlin' girl. Why are you all of a sudden so interested in Gompers, and strikes, and all?"

"Patrick! Do you not read the newspapers?" She flung his taunt back at him with a mischievous grin that reminded him of his beloved Hilda, the one who had seemed to be missing for the past several months.

He beamed back at her. "That I do, darlin', but I still don't see what you're gettin' at. My brain never did work as fast as yours."

"*Ja*, I am smart, but you are smart, too. You know it was a strike that began the riots in Russia, and strikes have begun riots in Chicago, and where there are riots other things may happen, things like train wrecks."

He frowned. "You're not sayin' union men—"

"No! I believe in unions. But when there are crowds and riots, things can happen that were never meant to happen. Things get—what do you say when there is no control? Gone from the hand?"

"Out of hand?"

"Yes! That is what I meant. Things get out of hand, and then angry men can get ideas to use the confusion and turn it into madness."

"Hmm. Somethin' in what you say." Patrick thoughtfully cut up his ham.

Hilda smiled again. "Yes. So tell me now about Mr. Debs."

"Now him you should know for sure, me girl. Eugene Debs is—"

"Oh! Eugene Debs. I did not think of him—Andy just said his last name. Of course I know who he is. He wanted to be president!"

"Still wants to, is my guess. He's not made the grade in two elections, so far—barely made waves, in fact. But he's a sticker; he'll try again. And he's a union man, too, and a pretty fiery one. Has a lot to do with the railroads—Hilda! With the railroads!"

Hilda's eyes widened. "But he would not—not a man who could maybe be president—would he?"

"Dunno, darlin' girl. I don't think he'd go so far, but…wait, let me think a minute." Patrick put down his fork. "There was somethin' a long time ago. I was only a boy, meself, and hadn't been in America long enough to hardly know which way was up, but there was a strike or a riot or somethin', havin' to do with the railroads, and Debs was in on it. I'll have to ask me mother, or Uncle Dan. They'll know."

Hilda looked down at her plate and found it empty. "Patrick, I would like some of the slaw, please, and some more ham." He passed her the dishes, and she helped herself. "I am wondering about Uncle Dan," she said when she had swallowed another several mouthfuls.

"What about him?"

"He is…Patrick, do not lose your temper, but he is a rich man with many people working for him. He is a very good man, but is he…does he…what does he think about unions?"

Patrick had stopped eating in surprise. Hilda was not known for hesitancy in speech, or in thought or action, for that matter. "What d'you mean by that?"

"Patrick! I mean what I asked! What does Uncle Dan think about unions?"

That was more like Hilda. Patrick shrugged. "More or less what everybody thinks, I guess. He thinks they can do good where they're needed, and harm when they get too big for their britches."

"Does the store have a union? No," she added as Patrick opened his mouth, "I mean, do the workers at the store belong to a union?"

"No need. Uncle Dan pays fair wages and treats the shop girls right. I guess the delivery-men might belong to the Teamsters. I never asked. Why d'you want to know?"

This time she looked him straight in the eye. "I want to know if he will be fair when you ask him about Mr. Debs and the railroad."

If Patrick's mouth hadn't been full, he might have hit the ceiling. By the time he had swallowed his food, he had also swallowed most of his anger. Here was Hilda, interested at last in something besides herself. She had eaten a large supper. She was acting normal.

And she was over six months pregnant, and should not be upset. "Dan Malloy is always fair," he said briefly.

"Oh! And we must also be fair. I nearly forgot. Tomorrow when you come home, I want you to bring two more electric fans. Eileen needs one in her room, and Mrs. O'Rourke needs one for the kitchen. I want them to be happy and comfortable."

"Don't want to risk a strike in your own home, eh? I'll get 'em. If we have any left, that is. They've been goin' like beer at an Irish picnic, these hot days. Some cherry pie, darlin'?"

5

As it happened, Patrick's mother was the first person Hilda had a chance to ask, the next day, about Eugene Debs and the railroad incident. With Uncle Dan out of town, Patrick had had no chance to question him, and Aunt Molly, when Hilda telephoned her, was busy for several hours with one committee meeting after another. Hilda found herself forced to be patient, not one of her strong points.

Erik showed up before breakfast had been cleared away. "What did he tell you?" he demanded, helping himself to a piece of toast and spreading it lavishly with strawberry jam.

"That is enough, Erik." Hilda moved the jam pot out of his reach. "Did Mama never teach you any manners?"

"Yes, but what did Andy say?"

Hilda sighed. "He could not tell me very much, only that he thinks this is a bad thing. He has heard men talking of it at the hotel, and he did not like the way they looked."

"Ana—anti—?"

"No, not anarchists, at least he doesn't think so. But he really knows very little. He is afraid, even, to be seen talking to me."

"So what are we going to do?"

Oh, dear. Too late, Hilda saw the trap. "*We* are going to do nothing, little one. Mama would skin me alive if I led you into trouble."

Erik hooted. "Where did you learn that one? From Patrick, I bet. And I'm not little. I'm fourteen. And I can take care of myself. So what are we going to do?"

"Nothing, I tell you! You will do nothing. And I do not know what to do until I learn more. Now go. Eileen needs to clear the table, and I must—must—" For the moment she could not come up with an excuse.

"Hah! You don't got nothin' you need to do. You're just tryin' to get rid of me."

"Yes!" Exasperated, Hilda pushed her chair back and stood, with some difficulty. "I must think, and that I cannot do with you bothering me with your terrible English. Go and—and fish, or something."

He went, grumbling, and Hilda sat down to think, a process which turned, inevitably, into a nap.

After lunch, she was reading once more through the stacks of newspapers for any item, however small, about unions and strikes, when Eileen walked into the parlor looking scared. "Mrs. Cavanaugh's come to see you, ma'am."

"Mrs. Cavanaugh? Patrick's *mother*?"

"Yes, ma'am."

"Why?"

"I don't know, ma'am."

The two exchanged glances. Eileen understood as well as Hilda that a visit from her mother-in-law boded no good.

"*Herre Gud!* Do I look as I should, Eileen? My hair—I do not have a good dress on—I was not—"

"You look fine, ma'am, and maybe you shouldn't keep her waitin' in the hall?"

"Oh! No! Please tell her to come in."

Hilda didn't even have time to arrange her skirts before Mrs. Cavanaugh marched into the room.

"Sit down, Hilda. It's foolish you are to get up just for me, the condition you're in."

"Yes, ma'am—Mother Cavanaugh. I mean, no, I will sit. I mean—please to sit down."

Mrs. Cavanaugh sat, ramrod-straight in the most uncomfortable chair in the room. "Are you feeling well?"

"I am well, thank you, but it is very hot. Oh! Would you like some lemonade, or—" Just at the moment, Hilda could not remember what other beverage might be appropriate to offer this woman, who was known to drink alcohol on occasion.

"No, thank you. It's very hot, indeed. You must be uncomfortable."

"I am well, thank you."

They seemed to have come full circle. Hilda sat, mute, trying desperately to think of something to say, and wondering why Mrs. Cavanaugh had come. It was the second time she had been in the house. The first had been Hilda's wedding day.

"Hilda, I—"

"Mother Cavanaugh, may I—"

Hilda choked on the words she had been about to utter. "I am sorry. Go ahead, please."

Mrs. Cavanaugh sat up even straighter. "Hilda, I've learned from Mrs. Malloy that you're gettin' yourself mixed up again in skulduggery. I could hardly believe me ears. She said she *encouraged* you to it! Is this true?"

Hilda licked her dry lips. It was certainly very hot. "Yes, ma'am—Mother. She asked me to learn what I could about the train wrecks, because Mr. Malloy might have been killed if he had been on the train that was wrecked, and she thought I was good at learning things, and I needed something to do, and..." She ran down. Mrs. Cavanaugh looked furious.

"You have something to do! You have my grandchild to protect! In my day, women didn't go gallivantin' around when they were expectin', and I'm amazed Mrs. Malloy would allow it, let alone put you up to it."

Hilda's temper was rising, and with it her courage. "I do not gallivant, Mrs. Cavanaugh. I have not left the house, and I will not. It is not proper, and it might not be good for the baby. But I can talk to people, and I can think, without doing any harm to *our* child." She put the very slightest emphasis on the word. This baby did not belong to its grandmother! "Aunt Molly thought it would be good for me to have something to think about, and she was right." Hilda had sense enough not to mention her own mother's part in the plan. "I feel much better when I cannot yoost—*just* think about how hot it is. And since you are here, Mother Cavanaugh, there is a question I would like to ask you. Patrick says you will know the answer," she added, lest Mrs. Cavanaugh refuse to talk to her.

"Hmph! A question about what?" Hilda thought she could detect a slight thaw in the older woman's attitude.

"It is about Mr. Debs, Eugene Debs. Patrick says that when he was a boy—Patrick, I mean, not Mr. Debs—there was a railroad strike or something like that, and that Mr. Debs was part of it. He could not remember what it was all about, but he said you would know."

"Oh. Well, yes, I do remember that. Hard not to, when it made such an uproar at the time."

She stopped as Eileen, who was getting better and better at anticipating visitors' needs, brought in a tray with glasses and a pitcher of iced tea, the fashionable drink made popular at the World's Fair in St. Louis the year before. Hilda, nearly dead of heat and thirst, made herself offer the first glass to Mrs. Cavanaugh, who accepted with an almost civil nod.

"This is very refreshing, Hilda," the older woman said condescendingly after a few sips.

Hilda smiled. "Thank you. You were telling me about Mr. Debs?"

"Oh, yes. The Great Pullman Strike. A terrible affair that was, all those men killed and hurt."

As Hilda drank her tea and listened, her mother-in-law recounted the story, and a painful story it was.

The Pullman Palace Car Company, having lost income during the Panic of 1893, had drastically cut wages in their factory, but had not reduced rents for the houses in the "company town" of Pullman, Illinois. In the summer of 1894 ("and well I remember, for I was carryin' Brenda at the time") the Pullman workers walked out, and the strike escalated when members of a union headed by Eugene Debs began to boycott all trains pulling Pullman cars. Rail traffic west of Chicago was paralyzed; the Pullman factory production came to a halt.

Patrick's father, alive then, had been a laborer at the Oliver factory in South Bend. Though they made plows and had nothing to do with the railroads, their products were shipped by rail, and the strike hurt them badly. Mr. Cavanaugh, along with the rest of the work force, went on short hours, and the lost money was a hardship to the large family. "Mind you, we had some money put by. Mr. Cavanaugh was never a spendthrift. But there were already eight children to feed, and if it had been winter, I don't know as we'd've had enough to eat."

"But that is dreadful! With you expecting a baby, too. And you said people died?"

"That was when the soldiers came in, shootin' folk left and right. That only made things worse, as anyone with as much sense as a spalpeen could have told 'em. By the time it was all over, the blessed saints only know how much harm'd been done, what with the dead and the maimed, the wages lost, and railroad lines all over the country tore up. And that Eugene Debs, he went to jail for it all."

"But—but he has tried to become president. A man who has been in jail?"

"He wouldn't be the first crooked politician in this country, would he now? Nor he wasn't the only one to blame for the strike, neither. It was all of 'em, seems to me, from the company men right on up to President Cleveland. But that Debs—he's a Socialist, you know. And that's the next thing to an anarchist, and look what they get up to!"

Hilda knew a good deal about that. It had been nearly four years since McKinley's assassination, and Hilda had been deeply enmeshed in an offshoot of that tragedy. She profoundly hoped that anarchists were not behind the present series of calamities, for her acquaintance with their methods still caused her the occasional nightmare.

"It is odd, Mother Cavanaugh," she said thoughtfully. "A union is meant to help the workers, but so often a strike causes terrible things to happen to everyone."

"Ah, well, that's the way of the world, isn't it? When the big bosses want to stomp on the poor folk, there's goin' to be explosions. And you listen to me, girl." Her belligerent manner returned. "There's already been explosions with this railroad business, and I don't want my grandchild blown up in another one. So just you keep your nose out of it!"

Hilda gritted her teeth. "I promise I will not harm myself or the baby. Would you like some more tea?"

❧

Well, that wasn't as bad as it might have been, thought Hilda, waking after a short nap. Her mother-in-law hadn't actually insulted her, and she had provided some useful information. Eugene Debs was a person of great interest. Connected with the railroads, a Socialist... Hilda got up from the couch, straightened her rumpled skirts, and went to the telephone in the hall. Before she picked up the handset, however, she had second thoughts.

She wanted, needed to talk to John Bolton, but a telephone call to Tippecanoe Place, however convenient, was not an appropriate way to reach him. The phone would either be answered by the butler, who would be incensed at being asked to call a servant to the instrument or, worse, answered by Mr. Studebaker himself, or his secretary. No, it wouldn't do. She debated for a moment, then went to the desk in Patrick's den, wrote a note, and rang the bell.

"Eileen, would you ask Mr. O'Rourke to take this note to John Bolton, please?"

"He'll not be pleased at havin' to take the horses out on such a hot day, ma'am," said Eileen. "I could take it meself. I'm not very busy."

There was a note of eagerness in the maid's voice, and Hilda hesitated. John Bolton was a handsome man. He was also a man of doubtful probity where young women were concerned. Hilda, when she worked at Tippecanoe Place, had had to fend off his attentions more than once. But Eileen was scarcely more than a child, and she could surely come to no harm in a brief visit on a summer afternoon. "Very well. Do not hurry. It is too hot. But do not waste time, either, or Mrs. O'Rourke will be angry with both of us!"

"Yes, ma'am!"

The clock had just chimed the half hour when Hilda heard the clatter of hooves on the brick pavement. A moment later, Eileen tapped on the parlor door. "Mr. Bolton, ma'am." Her face was pink and her cap slightly askew. Hilda decided to attribute both to the heat of the day.

"Come in, John. Thank you for coming. Eileen, would you—"

But Eileen had vanished. Probably something cool would be forthcoming soon.

"Sit down, John. It is good to see you again."

If Hilda had expected John to be somewhat abashed in her parlor, when her former milieu had been the servants' hall, she was disappointed. He lounged back in her best chair and gave her an impudent grin, his head tilted to one side.

"Marriage agrees with you, Hilda, my dear. Oh, I beg your pardon—Mrs. Cavanaugh, it is now."

"It is, yes. And I should call you Mr. Bolton."

John grinned even more broadly. "As you wish. Eileen said you wanted to talk to me, and loath though I am to rush you, Mrs. George wants the carriage at five. So…"

"Yes. I need to know what you know about Eugene Debs."

The grin faded. John sat forward. "Why do you want to know about him? He's—he can be an unpredictable man. Sound principles, mind you, but he sometimes goes too far."

"How far? That is what I want to know. Would he wreck a train?"

It is easier to be a lover than a husband...

6

—Honoré de Balzac,
   letter to a friend, 1829

S o THAT's WHAT this is about! I might have known you'd
be poking into that affair. But is it wise for you—that
is, just now?" Even John seemed slightly uncomfortable
discussing her condition.

Hilda felt herself blushing. It was difficult, this transition
from servant to lady. She and John had been friends, easy in one
another's company, though she had occasionally had to scold him
for over-familiarity. Now...

She made a decision. "John, I am the same person I always
was. You are the same person. Except when other people are
around, I am Hilda. You are John. Yes, I am looking into the
train wrecks, because Mama and Aunt Molly asked me to do it,
but I cannot easily leave the house. So I must talk to other people
and learn what I can. So. Do you think Mr. Debs could be organizing the wrecks?"

John sat back again, but his grin was gone. "Hilda, I don't
know. I don't think he'd go so far."

Patrick had said the same thing, Hilda remembered.

"He's on the side of the railroad men, of course. He's head of
the ARU—American Railway Union."

"But in that strike years ago—the Pullman Strike—railroad
men were killed. That does not make sense."

"Debs wasn't in favor of that strike, from what I hear, or at
least not of the boycott that caused most of the trouble. But the
union men organized the boycott anyway, and Debs finally went
along with it. It was when the army came in to break it up that
the killing started.

"Look, Hilda." John was very serious now. "These wrecks are different. They're meant to kill people, and some of the ones who've died are train men, union men. I can't believe Debs would be involved in something like that."

"But he is a Socialist. Do not Socialists want to change the government, and do they not believe that violence is the way to change it?"

"Some of them," admitted John. "But Debs is no anarchist. He just wants a better life for the working man. I still don't think he would agree to wrecking trains."

"But the men in his union—they do not always listen to him. You told me that."

And John had to agree.

Eileen brought in some iced tea, and they spoke of other things. But as he was getting up to leave, Hilda said, "John, talk to people you know. See what they think about the wrecks. What you hear will be rumor, and guesswork, but in all of it there might be some truth."

"I'll do that, Hilda. And I'll give you a report. Maybe it would be better if I sent you a note?"

Regretfully, Hilda agreed. Her social position was already precarious. Too many visits by John Bolton, and her reputation, too, would be in question.

Even if she was getting as big as a house.

❧

Of course when Patrick came home he knew all about John's visit, and he was not pleased.

"What's this I hear about that blasted coachman comin' to call?" were his first words, after he had given Hilda a perfunctory kiss.

"How did you know?"

Hilda knew the moment the words were out of her mouth that they were not what she should have said.

"Tryin' to keep it from me, were you? Now you listen here, me girl—"

"Patrick. You listen to me! Already today your mother has been here to scold me. I do not need a scolding from you, too. John may have some information that will be useful to me. We have agreed that he will not come here again, but—"

"He shouldn't have come in the first place! I don't know what's got into you, Hilda. People think we don't know our place, anyway, me but a fireman and you a maid. If you can't behave like a lady—"

"It is your aunt who asked me to look into the train wrecks! I cannot do that without talking to people."

"Well, they don't have to be people like John Bolton!"

At that Hilda dissolved in tears and went upstairs to bed. Eileen snubbed Patrick all evening, and after he had poked at his dinner and tried to read, he stomped upstairs himself. Hilda, curled up on the far side of the bed, pretended to be asleep when he came into the room.

Muttering in the Gaelic he thought he'd forgotten, he turned out the light and went to bed.

❧

Hilda did not come down to breakfast the next morning. It was Saturday, when Patrick did not always go to work, but with Uncle Dan out of town, someone needed to be there to keep an eye on things. Patrick read his newspaper, drank his coffee, and ate his toast quickly, waited on by a stony-faced Eileen. He had no appetite for a real breakfast. He was already repenting his hasty words to Hilda. They had never before had a serious quarrel. Oh, arguments, disagreements, yes—about almost everything, in fact—but those had been fun. This was different. He had been unfair, and he knew it, but he couldn't make up with her if she was still asleep, could he? For sure, if she was of a mind to be friends again, she could have waked and said something.

He stalked off to the store, thinking a walk would calm him down. It didn't. The heat of the sun only added to the heat of his temper.

Hilda, for her part, heard the door slam behind him. She

was awake, had been for hours. She had waited for Patrick to say something, to stroke her hair, to kiss her cheek—anything to show he wanted to be friends again. But he had left the house without even speaking to her.

Very well, if he wanted to be stubborn, she could be stubborn, too. She did not intend to apologize for what was plainly his fault. She had done nothing wrong. He knew quite well that John Bolton was—well, harmless wasn't quite the word, but Patrick should have more trust in her. He should know she would not permit John to take any liberties.

Hilda rang the bell for Eileen.

"Oh, ma'am, I was that worried you were maybe sick again! And it wouldn't be no wonder, the way Mr. Patrick was treatin' you!"

"I feel well, Eileen, but it is still very hot. I will have a cool bath, and then I will dress to go out."

Eileen's eyes widened. "To go out, ma'am? Are you—I mean, if there is some place I could go for you—"

"I will go out, Eileen, after I have had breakfast. Find me a cool dress. And no corset!" That there were corsets designed for pregnant women, Hilda knew. She considered them even more idiotic than the customary ones.

Eileen opened her mouth to remonstrate, but closed it again. When her mistress looked at her with that icy glare, she knew she had best do as she was told.

It was Saturday, Hilda reminded herself. With any luck she would find her friend Norah at home. Norah, companion of many years when they both lived at Tippecanoe Place and worked for Mrs. Clem Studebaker, had taken a job as a daily maid for Mrs. Hibberd when she married. After time off when her baby was born, she'd gone back to her job, now that the baby was six months old, but she worked only five mornings a week. Sean's new job at Studebaker's paid enough that they could afford to sacrifice part of Norah's pay, and it gave her more time to look after the house and the baby—little Fiona, born in Hilda's house and named, in a roundabout Irish way, after her.

Hilda ate such a large breakfast that Eileen was dubious about fitting her into a summer dress—especially without a corset—but a gusset quickly let in at the waist made it possible, though Hilda sighed at her reflection in the mirror. "If it were not so hot, I could wear a shawl and hide the fatness. I wish we would have cooler weather!"

Eileen wished so, too. Soon Hilda would have nothing to wear to church, even. She, Eileen, would have to ask Mr. Patrick for some muslins and lightweight silks from the store, to make up into loose-fitting dresses.

When she was speaking to Mr. Patrick again, that was.

Mr. O'Rourke was no happier about Hilda going out than Eileen was, and expressed himself with an inaudible rumble of disapproval all the way to Norah's small "company house" near the Studebaker factory. "Shall I wait, madam?" he asked in his chilliest tone.

"No, O'Rourke." He had taught Hilda to address him thus; it still made her uncomfortable. "No, thank you. Let me just make sure Norah is at home, and then you can come back for me in an hour."

Hilda could only imagine what Norah's neighbors would think if a carriage waited outside the house for an hour.

Norah came to the door, the baby in her arms. "Hilda! What's wrong?"

"Nothing is wrong. I came to see you. And Fiona, of course."

"But—oh, well, come in then. But you shouldn't be out, in your state."

"You came to my house, *ran* to my house, in a howling blizzard, the day before Fiona was born." Hilda walked past her into the tiny parlor.

"That was different and you know it. I was in big trouble or I'd never have dared do it. Besides, I'm not a fine lady!"

"Norah, I am sick of being told what I may and may not do.

I will do what I wish, so long as it does not put the baby at risk."
She sat down and raised her arms to Fiona, who held out her
own chubby arms.

Norah handed over the baby with a smile and a shake of her
head. "The same old Hilda, I see. Mind you don't jiggle her too
much—she just ate."

Hilda crooned to the baby in Swedish, holding her up so she
could bounce on Hilda's knees. Fiona chuckled happily, blowing
bubbles. She sat down suddenly and reached for Hilda's earring.

"Oops! Anything shiny, she can't resist. It's very strong she
is; don't let her pull it off. Here." Norah proffered a stuffed bear
almost as big as Fiona, and the baby instantly lost interest in
Hilda.

"That is a pretty toy," said Hilda, putting Fiona on the floor,
the bear clutched in her arms.

"It's a Teddy bear. Mrs. Clem bought it for Fiona."

"Mrs. Clem is a very nice lady. Norah, I need your advice."

"You askin' me for advice? I thought you knew everything.
Fiona, don't bite off Teddy's ear, there's a darlin' girl."

"Always you say that. I do not say I know everything; I say
I am smart. There is much I do not know, but I know where to
find out. Norah, what should I do? Patrick is angry with me, and
he will be more angry when he knows I have come here, but I
have done nothing wrong."

Norah sighed and picked up her daughter, who was beginning to fuss. Rocking the baby, Norah said, "You'd better tell me
all about it."

Briefly, Hilda recounted her search for information about the
train wrecks and possible union involvement. "And I do this only
because Mama and Aunt Molly asked me to. And if I asked John
Bolton to come to the house, it was because I needed to talk to
him, and I could not go to him. You know I would do nothing
wrong. Why does Patrick not understand?"

"He doesn't understand because he's jealous, for a start, and
because this pokin' around you're doin' might get you in bad

trouble. Now don't get your dander up! I know you don't want
to be told what to do, but you did ask me for advice. So my advice
is this: be extra nice to Patrick when he comes home for lunch.
Don't say anything about yesterday, or about trains or unions or
anythin' else that'd set him off. He's as stubborn as you, remember. He won't admit he was wrong if you argue with him, but he
might if you let it go. And don't tell him you came over here!"

"He will know. He knew about John. I do not know how,
but servants know everything and they talk, and Mr. O'Rourke
brought him home from the store yesterday."

"Hmm. Well, so tell him, but say I sent for you, that Fiona
was colicky, or I was sick—no, don't tell him that, he'll be afraid
you'll catch somethin'. Just say I sent for you and you came because you were afraid somethin' was wrong with Fiona."

"Eileen knows you did not send for me."

"You can talk her around. I'm bettin' she's mad at Patrick.
Now, I'm bettin', too, that you didn't come all the way over here
just to talk about a spat with Patrick."

"You are right. You are right almost as often as I am. I want
to know, what does Sean say about unions and strikes?"

"There's no union at Studebaker's, never has been."

"This I know, Norah. But what do the men *think* about
unions?"

"I reckon if they thought much of 'em, they'd organize one.
You know Mr. Clem always treated the men right, and now Colonel George and J.M. do, too. Not that Colonel George has much
to do with runnin' the place, it's mostly J.M. When the factory
has trouble, it's when some other place goes on strike, and Studebaker's can't sell their stuff, or move it, or get supplies. Then the
men lose hours, and wages, and that's not good for anybody. Me,
I'm against unions. They only cause trouble."

Hilda was on the verge of replying that unions had their
good side, when the front door opened and Sean burst in.

"There's been another train wreck! Right down by the plant,
and there's men dead and dyin', and a fire that's fixin' to spread!

I'm goin' back to help, but I wanted you to know. Don't know when I'll be home."

The door banged. Fiona started to wail. Hilda and Norah looked at each other.

"Do any of your neighbors have a telephone? I must go home."

Marriage is like life in this—that it is a field
of battle, and not a bed of roses.

—Robert Louis Stevenson,
   Virginibus Puerisque, 1881

7

THERE WAS NO NEED to telephone for O'Rourke. The carriage was rattling down the street toward Norah's house as Hilda stepped out the door, and—oh, *Herre Gud,* Patrick was in it.

He was nearly speechless with rage and fear. Nearly. Unfortunately, not quite.

"And what d'you think you're doin', sneakin' out like this? And with the wreckers right here, right *here,* not two blocks away, and a fire startin' and maybe goin' to spread to these houses… What were you *thinkin'*?"

"I did not know there would be a train wreck, Patrick. Please help me into the carriage; I cannot get in by myself." Hilda was trying hard to keep hold of her temper. Patrick had a certain amount of good sense on his side, and besides, Hilda was genuinely frightened. She could see the smoke rising near the factory, a black cloud that was growing by the moment. "Let us go home—please, Patrick."

"You're goin' home." He jumped down and gave her a hand up. "I'm goin' to the fire to help."

Only then did Hilda notice that her husband was in his old fire-fighting gear, his helmet under his arm. She started to voice the thought that the carriage should first deliver him to the fire scene and then come back for her, but the look on his face changed her mind. "Yes, Patrick. Be careful."

He turned away without another word and started to run in the direction of the smoke.

By the time Hilda reached home, tears of frustration were

forming in her eyes. If only she could have gone with Patrick, have stayed at the scene of the accident—if accident it was. She might have seen something, someone, heard talk, might have been able to make some sense of what was happening. But no, she had left like a good wife and expectant mother, had gone back to where she and the baby were safe, while Patrick had gone to a place where he was certainly *not* safe. Train men were not the only ones who had been killed in the fires following wrecks.

There should, thought Hilda drearily as she climbed the steps to the porch, also be rules for expectant fathers.

Eileen met her at the door. "Oh, Miss Hilda, ma'am, I was that worried about you! When we heard about the wreck, so close to the factory, we was all afeared the fire might spread to those houses. You'd best come upstairs and have a lie-down. You know you didn't ought to be runnin' around like this, with wrecks and fires and all!"

Hilda allowed herself to be cosseted. She hated to admit it, but she *was* tired. A baby was such a nuisance!

And then she thought of little Fiona, soft and warm and trusting in her arms. Maybe, after all, there was something to be said for babies. At least once they got themselves born.

But what had her exhausting little trip gained her? Nearly nothing. Norah's advice about how to handle Patrick, while sound, had, as things turned out, been useless, though maybe she could use it on another occasion. As for information, she had already known that most Studebaker workers were perfectly content not to be unionized. Her own brother Sven told her that, frequently. A deeply conservative man, and the valued foreman of the paint shop, he had little use for unions, regarding them as disruptive and liable to cause far more harm than good.

Hilda thought about the fire. If it spread to the factory it could destroy wagons and carriages in production. It might even damage or destroy some of the motorcars Studebaker was now selling in increasing numbers. If it got as far as the paint shop— she didn't want to think about that. Surely Sven would not be there. He would be out fighting the fire, for if it reached the paint shop, everything would go up like an explosion. Workers—no, they would get out safely. They had to!

But it could spread to the company houses, the workers' houses. They were nice enough houses, though small, but they were built of wood. They would burn like tinder.

Not like this house. Hilda deliberately made herself relax and think about this good, safe house. This house was built of stone. It would last a long time, a home for her child, and for that child's children, and theirs....

When Patrick came home in the middle of the afternoon, tired, reeking of smoke, and ravenous, he found Hilda sound asleep. The sight of her lying in bed in her shift, her hair curling damply on her forehead, her cheeks flushed, made Patrick forget everything else—his weariness, his hunger, his anger. Heedless of the soot clinging to his garments, he sat on the bed and stroked her forehead. "Darlin' girl," he murmured.

"Mmm." Hilda opened her eyes. "Patrick! You are safe!"

"That I am, darlin'. The fire's not out, quite, but it's under control."

Hilda yawned widely and woke more fully. "And you have brought most of it home with you! Look at what you have done to the sheets!"

"I'll have a bath in a minute, but first..." He leaned over, kissed her cheek, and then touched the sooty mark he had left there. "There. That's to remember me by. Is there anythin' to eat?"

Eileen, who had watched all this from the door, torn between approval of his attitude and dismay over the grime he was leaving everywhere, answered. "On the table, Mr. Patrick, as soon as you've cleaned up."

Hilda, too, was famished, so it was some little time before the two stopped eating long enough for conversation.

"Patrick," said Hilda, "I am sorry I went out this morning without telling you. It was only to see Norah and Fiona, and I did not think you would mind." That was not the whole truth, and she had a feeling Patrick knew it, but he, too, was eager to mend their quarrel.

"I let me temper get the better of me, darlin', but when I heard about the train wreck and the fire, and found out you'd gone to that part of town—well, I got that pothered, and…" He spread his hands in silent apology.

"Yes, the wreck. Patrick, did you see anything, hear anything about how such a thing might have happened? Was it an accident?"

"Don't know. Reckon nobody knows, not yet, at least. One o' the front cars jumped the track, just as it was gettin' close to the factory. Carryin' coal, it was, and should 'a been goin' a lot slower than it was, the way I hear it. Anyway, it tipped over and spilled the coal all over the track, and then o' course the rest of the cars behind it tipped, too, and the weight of it all brought the engine down, and that's what started the fire. The engineer and the fireman were killed, and the brakeman's bad hurt. He was thrown off when the cars jumped the track."

Hilda knew the brakeman walked along the tops of the cars to set the brakes. "But—is there not a law about automatic brakes? I am sure I read something in the newspaper that said the driver, the—the engineer had to be able to stop the train himself."

"There is, but there's what they call a loophole in the law. If a train goes from one state to another, it has to have automatic brakes. But some of these coal trains, they just bring coal up north here from the coal mines down in southern Indiana, and so they can use old trains with the old systems. I talked to a couple of the train men, though, them as was at the other end and wasn't hurt, and they said as how this train did have the new brakes, so somethin' was maybe wrong with 'em, and that's why the brakeman was up top, and why the first car jumped."

"The brakeman would know," said Hilda.

"He would, and so would the engineer. But the one's dead and the other maybe dyin', so how's anyone to tell?"

"And—the fire. Was anyone—did everyone—?" She had

been afraid to ask before, and Patrick was quick to reassure her.

"Sven's all right. He was in there fightin' the fire with the rest of us, and so was Sean. Nobody was bad hurt, savin' a few burns here and there. The factory buildings were never in real danger, though a few windows got smashed. And it never came near the houses."

Hilda's sigh of relief came from so deep inside her, it seemed as if the baby must have sighed, too. Her mind set at rest, she bent it again to questions. "But was there no one there who might have—have caused this to happen? I know that if someone damaged the brakes, or the track, he could have done it hours ago, but I have heard that when someone does a bad thing, commits a crime, he wants to stay and see what happens."

"I know what you're gettin' at, darlin'. But there's no tellin', honest. You've never fought a fire. When there's coal burnin', like today, there's so much smoke, sometimes you can't tell who's next to you, helpin'. And you're hot and scared, and workin' as hard and as fast as you can. You don't have time to notice hardly anythin' but where the flames are, if you can find 'em for the smoke.

"As for damagin' the track, that couldn't hardly have been done much before the train came along. There's trains along that track all day long, and most of the night, too. It must 'a been the brakes. Maybe somethin' could 'a been done to 'em so they'd work okay if the train was just slowin' down a little, but when it was tryin' to stop, they'd give out."

"Could not someone tell by looking at the wrecked cars?"

"Darlin', the shape those cars are in, it's my belief nobody could tell now if they'd been cut apart with an axe."

And with that Hilda was obliged to be content—for the time being.

She slept badly, visions of burning train cars playing behind her eyes. When morning came, very early, she was glad to get out of the rumpled bed and take a cool bath. By the time Patrick came downstairs, she was dressed and breakfasted and ready for church.

For the past several months, with Hilda so uncomfortable, they had abandoned their practice of a family dinner after church. It had been their habit, with Sunday the servants' afternoon out, to alternate between the Johansson and the Cavanaugh homes, facing in either place veiled resentment and chilly courtesy. Hilda had been glad to go to her church while Patrick went to his, and come straight home afterwards. Today, though, she felt better.

"Patrick, let us go to Sven's house after church. Mama and everyone will be there, and there will be plenty of food."

"There always is," Patrick agreed. "Your mama is goin' to want a report, though, and seems to me you've found out precious little."

"That is why I want to go, to talk to people at church, and then to Sven and the others. Mama will think I should know all the answers by now, but she will be pleased that I work at finding out. And someone might know something, a little hint that might lead me to bigger ones. And you, Patrick, you will ask at your church. We work together, *ja*?"

"*Ja,*" he echoed. "But you'll be careful what you ask, darlin'? Somewhere around, there's someone who doesn't mind who he kills."

"And you, too, be careful." She raised herself on tiptoe to kiss his cheek. "Pah! Your hair still smells of smoke."

"Ah. It always does for a while, after a fire."

"I never noticed it before we were married, when you were still a fireman."

"That, darlin' girl," he said, taking her in his arms and kissing her properly, "is because you never let me get close enough so's you could tell."

A few clouds had gathered in the sky, but instead of moderating the heat, they seemed only to intensify the humidity. Hilda felt completely wilted when she stepped out of the carriage at her church. She was early; few people had gathered outside, so Hilda went inside, where it was stifling, even with the windows wide open, but at least she could sit down in the pew her family always used.

They came in just before the first hymn, so Hilda had no chance for more than a greeting. Sven, she noticed, smelled slightly of smoke. Or maybe it was just that the church was near the scene of the fire.

"Sven, Patrick and I would like to come to dinner today—if it is all right with you and Mama," she said as soon as the last prayer was said, the last hymn sung, the final blessing pronounced.

"You have found out something!" said Mama in Swedish.

"No," Hilda replied in the same language. "Anyway, not very much. But it has been a long time since we have had dinner together."

Patrick and the carriage arrived just then. The distance to Sven's small house was not far, but Hilda was not expected to walk even a few blocks, especially not in the heat.

"Today, I think," announced Sven, "we eat outside. A picnic we have!"

"Hooray!" shouted Erik, tossing his hat in the air.

As tables were brought outside, cloths were laid, and all the girls bustled in the kitchen, Hilda had the unusual pleasure of sitting and watching. Mama might be perfectly willing to have Hilda investigate murder and mayhem, but she was not about to have her helping in the kitchen on a hot day!

After Sven and Erik and Patrick had arranged the tables and chairs to their liking, there was little for them to do but watch the womenfolk arrange the meal. Hilda sat down next to her older brother.

"Sven, what happened yesterday? No, I know *what* happened. *Why* did it happen? What do people say?"

"Some say it was no accident. The men at the plant think the brakes must have failed, and if they failed, there might have been a good reason."

"Why do they say that? Do they know who might have done it?"

Sven paused and looked around. Hilda's four sisters were bringing out dish after dish of herring and potatoes and salads. Erik was getting in their way, trying to sample everything. Mama was supervising the whole operation in the kitchen. Nevertheless, Sven lowered his voice to a whisper only Hilda and Patrick could hear.

"Some odd things have been happening in the paint shop. Men we don't know come in and talk about how bad our working conditions are, how we ought to organize. Most of us pay no attention, but they come back and come back, and some of the men, the young ones who know no better, are beginning to listen."

"Who are they?" asked Hilda eagerly.

"I tell you, we don't know. They give names like Schmidt and Sovinski and Svenson, but they are not German or Polish or Swedish, this I know. And worse, Hilda, there have been accidents. Oh, nothing serious," he said when Hilda looked alarmed. "A few gallons of paint disappear and then are found where they don't belong. A cart is left in a dark corner where someone can trip over it, and someone does, and cuts his head. Tools are found in someone's pocket, never the same person twice, never someone who would have any reason to steal them. It is all just—odd. And I do not like it."

As if the storms could give repose…
  —Mikhail Lermontov,
    "A Sail," 1841

8

MAMA WAS STRICT about mealtime conversation, especially on a Sunday. It was to be cheerful and uplifting. So there was no talk about the wreck or the fire until dinner was over and everyone was sitting, stuffed to the eyebrows, in whatever shade they could find. Hilda wanted a nap, but she wanted even more to hear everything Sven could tell her.

"Sven, if it was the brakes, who could have done that? And when?"

"We have thought about that, all of us who work there. It must have been done after the last stop, and that would have been Mishawaka—it was coming from the east."

"At the Woolen Mills, I suppose. But Mishawaka, that is only a few miles away. Why would the train have been going so fast?"

"The men say maybe someone damaged the air hoses while the train was stopped in Mishawaka. That would mean that the train would just go faster and faster, and the engineer wouldn't be able to slow it down at all. Mishawaka lies a little higher than South Bend, you know, so the train would get up speed going downhill, and—"

"But that is a terrible thing! Anyone might have been killed, at a crossing, or around a curve!"

"Mind, Hilda, we do not know that is what happened. But we cannot think how else the train might have derailed. It is fortunate that the fire was not worse, and that more people did not die." He looked at her very seriously, glanced over at Mama, dozing under a nearby tree, and switched from the Swedish he had been speaking to English. "My sister, I know Mama asked you to study these things. But you understand, now, that if evil men did what we think, they have no respect at all for life. They are wicked and malicious. It is better that you leave it alone."

The baby gave Hilda a vigorous kick just then. Hilda sighed and put her hands protectively over her swollen belly. "Everyone says the same thing, everyone except Mama and Aunt Molly. I think maybe they wanted me only not to think so much about myself. I have done that. I am much better, even though it is still so hot I cannot breathe. Maybe I will do what everyone says and not try anymore to find out what has happened with the wrecks. Probably I could do nothing anyway."

ᕦ

Later she thought that she had meant it, at the time. And she might have kept to her do-nothing plan, if it hadn't been for the next thing that happened.

ᕦ

It didn't happen immediately. That hot Sunday was followed by more hot, airless days. Fans waved, dusty trees drooped, day followed oppressive day. Hilda woke, dressed, ate, read the newspaper, napped, and wished the baby would hurry up. Her temper was greatly improved, but she was bored nearly to tears.

Patrick fretted at the lack of business at the store, but Uncle Dan wasn't worried. "It'll pick up as soon as the heat breaks, and it's got to, soon."

A week went by. Tuesday, July 4, dawned hotter than ever, with a gray-green sky that seemed to put a heavy lid on the stifling air. "Glad we're not doin' a picnic today," Patrick commented as he sat at the breakfast table in his shirtsleeves. Even though it was a holiday, both he and Hilda had risen early, unable to sleep any longer, but Patrick hoped for a nap later. "There's goin' to be a storm, or I'm a Chinaman."

The city had planned no Independence Day parade, which was a good thing, because shortly after Hilda and Patrick had finished picking at a cold lunch, the sky was riven by a lightning bolt and a clap of thunder shook the house. "Here it comes!" Patrick cried, and ran to close windows and doors. Hilda insisted on leaving the back porch door open. The linoleum on the kitchen floor would take no harm if water came in through the screen, and she basked in the cool, sweet-smelling air that blew in with the rain.

It poured all afternoon, and both Patrick and Hilda napped, grateful for the respite from the punishing heat. Then in the evening the rain moderated to an on-again, off-again drizzle that made a lovely sound as it pattered on the roof. Everyone in the house, servants included, was yawning by nine o'clock. Eileen unearthed a light blanket from the linen closet and put it on Hilda and Patrick's bed, and they were glad of its warmth as they snuggled in. "At last," said Hilda with a deep sigh, laying her head on Patrick's chest. "Tonight I will sleep."

Her sleep was doomed to be short. Long before there was any morning light in the sky, there came an agitated knocking at their bedroom door, and Eileen, candle in hand, put her head in. "Please, Mr. Patrick, it's sorry I am to wake you, but Mr. Malloy is callin' for you on the telephone. He says there's a fire down at the store, and he needs you!"

Patrick made muffled noises, sighed, and pulled himself out of bed. "You go back to sleep, darlin'. Likely it's nothin' serious, and I'll be home before you even wake up."

She tried to do as he said, but could not. How could she sleep when Patrick might be in danger—and not only Patrick, but his job, their livelihood? She got up, wrapped a warm robe around as much of herself as it would cover, and went down to the kitchen to make coffee. At four in the morning, she was safe from Mrs. O'Rourke's disapproval, and she, Hilda, still made better coffee—strong, proper Swedish coffee.

The rain continued, slow but steady. Hilda pulled her chair close to the stove, which still exuded some warmth, and sipped her coffee, and thought.

This fire had reawakened all her questions, all her fears. True, it had nothing to do with a train wreck—or did it? When so many terrible things happened so close together, could they not be part of a pattern? But try as she would, even after several cups of coffee, Hilda could not make a pattern in her mind that would encompass train wrecks, random fires, and labor unrest. It was, she thought, like one of those new puzzles, jigsaw puzzles, they were called. Hilda had played with one once. There were so many oddly shaped pieces of the picture, and if even one were placed incorrectly, the picture could not be completed—the other pieces would not fit.

None of these pieces seemed to fit. They did not even seem to be from the same puzzle. Locomotives, flames, angry laborers marching, angry soldiers and police firing weapons—the pictures formed and re-formed in her mind's eye and began to blend, a picture in red and black with no shape, no meaning....

"Is there any more of that coffee, darlin'? And what are you doin' in the kitchen? Mrs. O'Rourke'll likely skelp you."

"Patrick!"

She rubbed at her eyes with her knuckles, looking so much like a sleepy child that Patrick's heart ached a little with his love for her. Maybe it wouldn't be such a bad thing, after all, if their baby turned out to be a girl, looking like her mother. There was plenty of time for a son, after all. He kissed her gently. "What are you doin' down here, me girl? You'd no need to get up."

"I could not sleep. You are wet, Patrick, and you smell of smoke. Take off your raincoat and tell me. Was the fire bad? Is the store all right? Is Uncle Dan all right?"

"There was nothin' much to the fire atall." Patrick shrugged out of his raincoat, which was not only wet, but sooty. "It was in the little storeroom at the back. You know, where we keep boxes and wrapping paper and that?"

Hilda nodded. "But there is much there to burn!"

"Sometimes, but not just now. We're gettin' low on boxes and our new order hasn't come in yet. Lucky, that was—the fire might've been much worse with that extra fuel. What was there mostly made a lot of smoke, and the night watchman smelled it and turned in the alarm, though he passed out just after—from the smoke or somethin'. He just managed to get back to his cubbyhole before he fell. He would have been burned up, too, but for that. Anyway, the firemen got there right away, and they had it all under control before I even got there." He stopped abruptly. "Is there coffee, still?"

"It is cold. I will make more. Patrick, there is something you are not telling me. It—it is not Uncle Dan?"

"No, darlin'. Uncle Dan's fine, and the store wasn't hurt atall, barrin' a lot of smoke smell we'll have to wash out of the linens."

"Then what is it?"

Patrick spread his hands in a weary gesture of resignation. "Someone was killed in the fire, Hilda. A man. We don't know who, yet, nor what he was doin' at the store at that time of night. Now I'm goin' up to get a little sleep. I need to get back to the store in an hour or two to start puttin' things to rights."

He knew more by midmorning. Uncle Dan came back to the store as soon as he had finished talking to the police. He sat down wearily in his office to talk to Patrick. "His name was Bill—William—Beeman. His father came to the police station to say he hadn't come home last night, and they had him identify the body. By the belt buckle, a present for his birthday in April. That was all—well." Dan wiped his eyes; the handkerchief came away with soot on it. "He was only a boy, it seems, eighteen years old and just starting his first job, up at the Merchants' National Bank."

Patrick frowned. "But, if he didn't work for us, what was he doin' in our storeroom in the middle of the night?"

"That we don't know. The police did find one thing, though, in the corner of the room: the remains of a Roman candle. They're guessin' that the boy was settin' off fireworks, it bein' the Fourth, and maybe got into the storeroom to shelter from the rain. There's an outside door, y'know."

"It's kept locked, though. And why would he try to set off fireworks in the rain, anyway?"

"I don't know, me boy. I'm past thinkin'. I need to get home and clean up and get to bed for a bit. Can you manage here for an hour or two?"

So Patrick telephoned that he would not be home for lunch, and Hilda, who was longing for news, was forced to wait, though not as long as she had feared. In midafternoon, Eileen showed Aunt Molly into the parlor.

"You're feeling better, my dear," Molly said. Her hat was damp, but not soaking wet; the rain had moderated. "I'm so glad." Her voice was warm, but her attention seemed not to be entirely on Hilda.

"It is cooler. I can sleep." She brushed the topic aside. "Aunt Molly, what happened at the store last night? Patrick has not had time to tell me, only a little."

"Well, it's all a bit strange." Molly related what she knew. "What no one can figure out," she concluded, "is why that boy was where he was. Setting off fireworks, the police say. In the middle of the night? Indoors? What claptrap!"

"That is maybe what someone wants the police to think," said Hilda after a pause for thought. "About the fireworks, I mean. Me, I think—"

"Hilda." Aunt Molly, who was a tiny woman, could be a commanding presence when she chose. "Hilda, I don't want you 'thinking' anything. I know, I know." She raised a hand as Hilda started to speak. "I encouraged you to look into these incidents. I'm sorry now I ever did so. The trouble has come too close to home. If we hadn't had that soaking rain yesterday, the store could have been badly damaged—and both Mr. Malloy and Patrick could have been hurt, fighting the fire, if it had come to that."

"But the fire was not bad, and they were not hurt. Only that poor boy. I think—"

Once again Molly interrupted. "Hilda, please listen to me. At this time in your life, you must not involve yourself in such great danger. My dear, Mr. Malloy and I have no grandchildren, you know. Your baby is a great hope for our family. If only—but you and Patrick are as dear to us as our own children. Please say you will leave it alone."

Hilda looked at the carpet. Molly Malloy could read minds, Hilda was firmly convinced. And she didn't want her mind read just now. "It is confusing," she said slowly. "I do not see how the fire can be connected to the other things that have happened. And I see that there could be peril. Aunt Molly, I promise I will do nothing that could harm my baby."

It was an ambiguous reply, and Molly wasn't fooled for a moment. "Hilda, there are—there has been a—a development. I don't know—no, never mind about that. But can you not trust me when I say that you *must* not pursue this matter further?"

Hilda was saved from having to reply when Eileen appeared in the parlor doorway. "Beggin' your pardon, ma'am, but Mr. and Mrs. O'Neill are here to see you."

"Mr. and Mrs.—oh, Norah and Sean! Why are they here at this time of day, I wonder? Sean should be at work. But show them—oh, Norah, I am glad to see you!"

Norah had never stood on ceremony with her best friend, and she was not about to now, even if Hilda had metamorphosed into a fine lady. She slipped past Eileen, Sean close behind her, and was about to speak when she saw Mrs. Malloy and hesitated. To curtsey, or not? Mrs. Malloy was a lady. But she was also the aunt of Norah's best friend, and this was her friend's house, where she, Norah was not a servant but a guest....

Aunt Molly saw her uncertainty and stood. "I will leave you to your guests, my dear. Mrs. O'Neill, it's good to see you again, and Mr. O'Neill. Little Fiona is doing well, I trust?" For Molly had helped with Fiona's birth and knew all about the difficult circumstances surrounding it.

"She's bloomin', thank you, ma'am. Our neighbor's lookin' after her for a bit."

"And enjoying it, I'm sure. She's a sweet baby. Hilda, we will talk again."

Hilda was sure of that.

When Mrs. Malloy was safely out the door, Norah plumped herself down on a chair, settling her damp skirts, and Sean took the chair beside her. "Hilda, we had to see you, right away. Sean's on the early shift this week, and he heard some things at work this mornin' that you need to know."

Sean cleared his throat. "See, Flynn works with me. Norah's brother, you know?"

Hilda nodded.

"And him and me both used to work for Sam Black, you remember, before Black's went out of business. And there's talk, Flynn says, that Sam's somehow mixed up in all that's happenin', or most of it, anyway."

"I thought," said Hilda, "that Mr. Black moved away, after he lost his house and the bicycle factory."

"Lost everythin' he owned. And he did move away, 'cause he couldn't find any work here. But he's back. Flynn's seen him. And he's lookin' like he's doin' well—fine clothes and all."

Hilda frowned. "But I thought you liked him. Why would you, why does *anyone* think he has done these wicked things?"

"I did like him, when I worked for him. He wasn't a bad boss, as bosses go. Not good at managin' money, was all, and that led to the trouble, and put a lot of us out of work, when the factory went bust. Anyway, nobody's sayin' he *done* 'em. *Mixed up* in 'em, is what they say."

"What does that mean? And who says so?" Hilda was skeptical. Gossip was interesting, but not necessarily reliable. She wanted facts, details.

"But that's the point, see!" Norah broke in, impatient with the slow pace of the narrative. "The man who was braggin' he knew all about it, claimin' it had somethin' to do with banks and Sam Black and I don't know what-all—that fella was Bill Beeman, and he was burned to death last night at Malloy's Dry Goods!"

O tiger's heart wrapp'd in a woman's hide!

—William Shakespeare,
   Henry VI, Part 3

W AS BURNED TO DEATH,'" Hilda repeated. "Then you do not think it was an accident?"

"Do you?" Norah's tone was scornful.

"No, I do not see how it could have been. The rain, the late hour—no, I think someone tried to make it look like an accident. But that person was not very smart or he would have made it more—more true, more—"

"Convincin'?" supplied Sean, with a grin.

"That is the word. It is not at all convincing, the way it was done."

"But we're thinkin'," Sean continued, "what if the plan was different, and the rain spoiled it all? See, it had to be on the Fourth if fireworks was to be blamed. So probably they was goin' to do it outside somewheres, and earlier, while everybody else was settin' off their rockets and such. They didn't know it was goin' to pour down like Niagara Falls. After the weather we've been havin', who would have thought we'd have that sockdolager of a storm?"

"Anybody who's lived around here for a while," retorted Norah. "Heat like that always brings a thunderstorm sooner or later, and this one was overdue."

"But nobody knew it was goin' to happen just when it did," Sean argued. "And by the time the rain started, it was too late to change plans. So they waited for a while for the rain to stop, but it never did, and finally they had to move the whole shebang indoors. And that's kind of an argument for it bein' Sam behind it all, if you think about it. He'd only lived here a few months when his factory failed, and then he left town, and he just came back, from what I hear."

"Hmm," said Hilda. "But why would Mr. Black do such a thing? Or have someone do it?" she added as both Sean and Norah began to protest. "And why would he choose Malloy's as the place to do it? He did not have a quarrel with Uncle Dan, that I have ever heard."

And neither of the O'Neills had an answer to that.

It was still raining when Sean and Norah left, not pouring, but a steady drip, drip that looked like it meant to keep up all day. Hilda fretted. She peered out the parlor window. Between the raindrops that made their way steadily down the glass, she could see the maple tree in the front yard, its branches drooping with the weight of the wet leaves. The grass was turning green again, and from some shelter birds were chirping their approval of the weather.

Hilda did not agree with them. Oh, yes, it was wonderful to have cool air to breathe again, but she wanted to talk to Andy, and how was she to manage it?

She looked at the clock. Patrick would not be home for at least an hour, probably more. The fire had closed the store for the day, but there was no doubt a great deal of cleaning up before they could open up tomorrow.

She made a decision and rang the bell.

"Eileen," she said when the maid appeared, "I am going out. Would you bring me my oldest hat, please? It will not matter if it is ruined by the rain. And ask Mr. O'Rourke to bring the carriage to the door."

Something in Hilda's voice stilled the protest that trembled on Eileen's lips. She made do with a subdued snort, and went to do Hilda's bidding.

Mr. O'Rourke's criticism was also silent. He was in fact aggressively silent, responding to Hilda's attempts at conversation with grunts. She gave up.

When she arrived at the Oliver Hotel, the doorman handed her down from the carriage with barely hidden astonishment.

Very few ladies in her condition arrived at the hotel, and none, in his experience, unaccompanied.

"Good afternoon," she said haughtily. "I wish to speak to Andy—" she searched her mind frantically "—to Andy Mueller, if he is available."

The doorman's expression changed. He studied Hilda's face (his attention having formerly been concentrated on her figure). "You've been here before," he said almost accusingly. "You're that woman who goes around asking questions."

"I am Mrs. Patrick Cavanaugh," she said, her voice icy. "Perhaps you have heard of my uncle, Mr. Daniel Malloy. Show me in, please, and call Andy for me."

Well, of course Daniel Malloy was Patrick's uncle, not hers, but now that Hilda had important relatives, she was not above using them. Especially to put an officious doorman in his place.

She was shown to a corner behind a potted palm, and in due time Andy came to her.

He was worried. "Miss, you didn't ought to have come here. People might see you. And me talking to you."

"Yes, I know, Andy. I came only for a moment. I must talk to you about the fire at Malloy's. Can you come to see me after work? I will give you your supper, and some food to take home to your family," she added hastily.

He stood up straighter. "Dad's workin' these days. We don't need no charity."

Another mistake! Hilda bit her lip. It was so hard, finding her way into her new position in life. "I know that, Andy. But Mrs. O'Rourke makes very good chocolate cake, and I thought the children might like some. And it is better, I think, to talk there. Will you come? I can stop at your house on my way home to tell them you will be late."

"I don't got nothin' to tell, miss."

Hilda took a deep breath. "Andy. A boy died last night, a boy not much older than you. Oh, I know, he thought himself a man, but he was only eighteen. Eighteen years old and murdered. Will you help me?"

Andy looked at the floor. "Yes, miss. I'll come to your house. No need to tell Ma; I'll have my chum Tom let her know. He lives almost next door."

The next obstacle was Patrick. Hilda made it home before he got there, but not by much, and of course Mr. O'Rourke had told him all about Hilda's little excursion. Patrick was tired and discouraged, and not in the best mood to hear that his very pregnant wife had been "out gallivantin'," as he put it.

"You promised," he grumbled. "You said you wouldn't leave the house, and here you've gone to the hotel, of all places!"

Hilda was tired, too, tired of making apologies and excuses. "Yes. I went because I must talk to Andy, and I knew he would not come here unless I asked him myself. He will be here for supper, Patrick." She gulped another breath. "I know I said I would not involve myself in these matters, Patrick, but that was before a boy died. In your store, our store.

"It is not, now, just a train wreck that happened many miles away. Now it is a train wreck here, and a fire here, a fire that killed someone. Now it is a threat to where we live, where you work and where Sven and Sean work—to this whole city. So now I must find out all I can. Maybe I cannot solve the puzzle, all of it, but I must do what I am able." She fixed her eyes on him. "I am sorry if you and your family are unhappy with me. I do not want to make you unhappy. But I must do this."

Her blue eyes glistened with unshed tears. Patrick saw them and sighed. "Darlin' girl, I should have learned long ago not to try to stop you doin' anythin'. Just be careful, will you promise me that? And—" he held up one finger "—don't be goin' behind my back again. Tell me what you're gonna do, before you do it, and if I can help, I will."

That was a promise Hilda could keep. Most of the time.

Mrs. O'Rourke was sour about baking a chocolate cake at the last minute. She had planned tapioca pudding for dessert. Hilda kept her temper with some difficulty. "I could order a cake from Osborn's Bakery, if it is too much trouble for you to make one."

"Hmph! No bakery cake is goin' to be served from *my* kitchen, trouble or not!"

Eileen was sour about serving Andy at the table. With her, Hilda took a different tack. "Eileen, when you worked for Mrs. Schmidt, you did not always have enough to eat. Now you have all you want, yes?"

"Yes, ma'am, but—"

"Andy is a working boy, as you are a working girl. He often does not have enough to eat. He is proud, and will not beg, but when he does me a service, I want to give him something. Thanks to Mr. Patrick, I can do that, now." So far as Hilda knew, Andy and his family seldom went hungry, at least not when his father was working. A strict regard for the truth had never impeded her.

"Yes, ma'am." Eileen was still reluctant, but resigned.

Mrs. O'Rourke outdid herself in the matter of supper. Her honor as a cook had been called into question, so fried chicken followed tomato soup, with baked beans and potato salad and a green salad and homemade pickles and fresh bread and strawberry jam, and then the famous chocolate cake. Andy ate until he could eat no more.

"Gosh, miss," he said when they had adjourned to the parlor and he had regretfully turned down another piece of cake. "Do you have this much food every day?"

"No, Andy, this was in your honor. But we have been eating little when it was so hot, so it is nice to have a good meal. Now. I want you to tell us what you have heard about the fire."

"Well, miss—and sir—there's a lot of talk. You know it was Bill Beeman who died?"

Hilda and Patrick nodded.

"Well, like you said, he wasn't much more than a boy. And he wasn't rich—I mean his family wasn't—so he hung around with some of my chums. He bragged a lot when he got that job with the bank, but he wasn't nothin' but an errand boy. He kept sayin', though, that he was in with the bankers, now, and he could go right to the top."

Patrick nodded sadly. "He might have been right, too. Times are bad, but a hard worker can still climb the ladder."

"That's what he said. But then—well, he never talked to me all that much, but the guys he did talk to said he began sayin' things wasn't all hunky-dory in the bank. Not his bank, he didn't mean, I guess, but the bankin' business. Some funny stuff goin' on, he said."

Hilda leaned forward, or tried to. She sat back with an annoyed glance at her swollen belly, but asked eagerly, "What kind of funny stuff?"

"I never heard that. I guess he didn't say, just hinted, like. But he said he was goin' to get to the bottom of it, and then he'd get a raise, sure. Instead, he got…" Andy's voice trailed off and he dragged a sleeve across his face.

"I have heard," said Hilda, "that he claimed he knew who was behind some of the—troubles."

"He said he did. He said it was that Mr. Black, the one whose factory failed." Andy's voice wasn't friendly. Hilda couldn't remember if his father had lost his job when Black's failed, along with Sean and Flynn and the others, or if Andy was simply bitter on general principles about anyone who cost honest working men their livelihoods.

"Andy, why do you think Bill Beeman was killed?" For that he was killed, Hilda had no doubt.

"Everyone thinks he was killed because he knew too much, and talked too much. And that's why, miss, I don't want to come here no more. It's not that I'm scared, miss, anyway not much, but—well, I don't want anything to happen to you. And besides, my family needs me, see."

Hilda saw. "I understand. But Andy, there is still one thing you can do for me. If you learn something really important, will you tell Erik? He still comes to talk to you, does he not?"

"Yes, miss, almost every day."

"Then no one will think it strange if you talk to him. If it is something important, though, do not let others hear what you say."

"It could still be dangerous, miss."

"Yes, Andy, it could. But there is also danger, to everyone, in doing nothing. We cannot escape danger; we can only do what is right and believe that the *Herre Gud* will protect us."

Andy crossed himself and made off for home, carrying with him half a huge chocolate cake carefully wrapped in a tea towel.

Hilda was quiet for the rest of the evening, so quiet that Patrick was a little worried about her. "Are you not feeling well, darlin'?" he asked finally.

"I am well. I am t'inking."

Only rarely, these days, did Hilda lose control of her digraphs—usually when she was under considerable stress. Patrick looked at her sharply, but she seemed serene. He waited.

"I must plan. Now that I cannot go about the city as I used to, I must think how to find things out while staying at home. I wish I could ask Aunt Molly to talk to people for me, but she came today to ask me to stop my questioning. She was very strange about it. She made hints, but would say nothing definite."

"Uncle Dan's actin' a bit queer, too. Seems like he's thinkin' of somethin' else when you're talkin' to him. But it's only to be expected, what with the fire and all."

"I think it is more than the fire, but I cannot guess what it is. But as long as Aunt Molly is acting peculiar, I must find other people to ask questions for me."

She looked pointedly at Patrick. He sighed loudly. "I've me own business to tend to, y'know. But tell me what you want to find out and I'll do me best."

Thus it was that Patrick went to work the next day armed with questions for Dan Malloy and others at the store. He never got them asked.

How sharper than a serpent's tooth it is
To have a thankless child!

    —William Shakespeare,
      King Lear

ATRICK GOT TO THE STORE early that Thursday morning. All the excitement had put him behind in his work, and he wanted to get caught up. Never did he forget that he owed everything to Daniel Malloy, who had made him a partner when Dan's own son had proved such a disappointment. Dan had great faith in Patrick, and Patrick was determined to justify that faith. He let himself into the store, went upstairs to his office, hung his dripping raincoat on the rack, and got to work.

He was deep in a pile of invoices, checking their copperplate script against receipted order forms, when a tap sounded on his open door. It was still too early for the office help to be at work. He looked up, annoyed at the interruption.

The man at the door was not tall, but he was bulky, in an unhealthy sort of way. Not fat, exactly, but as if once-solid muscle had softened, like a melon gone bad. His face, too, had probably once been ruddy and handsomely chiseled. Now it sagged in pouches and furrows of pasty hue, and it was badly in need of a shave.

"Well, cousin, don't you know me?"

"Clancy!"

He was stunned. He had thought—everyone had thought—that Clancy would never return. There were those in South Bend who knew things about Clancy Malloy that would put him in jail for a long time. The family had given him the choice between prison and exile, and Clancy had wasted no time in leaving town.

And now he was back. And Patrick was sitting at the desk that would have been Clancy's if he'd behaved himself.

"So, boyo." Clancy settled himself comfortably in the one visitor's chair. Patrick's office was utilitarian, no grandiose affair of large windows and fancy carpets and a massive desk. He was the junior partner, true, but he needed to prove himself before he was awarded all the privileges of an executive. Now, perhaps, he never would be able to do so.

"So," repeated Clancy. "Glad to see me, are you?"

"No," said Patrick. "I'm busy."

"Busy doing my job, are you? Oh, not that I mind." Clancy held up a beefy hand. He was, Patrick saw, wearing a heavy gold ring with a large black stone, carved like the beak of an eagle. "I've done very well for myself, cousin. No two-bit dry goods store in a one-horse town for this boyo, not anymore."

Patrick's patience was wearing thin. "Clancy, if you didn't come home to kick me out, what did you come for?"

"Why, to see all me lovin' kin, of course! And to think they didn't even tell you I'd come. Wantin' it to be a nice surprise, I'm sure, a real family reunion." He cocked an ear toward the hallway. "Ah, that's me father comin' or I've lost me ear for a footfall. Good-bye for now, cousin Paddy."

He closed the door behind him. Patrick sat and stared at the door, unable for a moment to think what to do. What did Clancy want? What in the name of all the saints did Clancy want?

Patrick shook his head and smiled grimly. The saints probably had very little to do with Clancy's plans.

Clancy's return was obviously what was bothering Uncle Dan and Aunt Molly. That among other things. What a time Clancy had chosen to come home! Dan Malloy was already up to his ears in difficulties. And Aunt Molly was so upset that she wanted Hilda to give up her quest for the truth about the train wrecks, and the fires—

The fires. Patrick's head began to clear. He pressed a buzzer on his desk.

Uncle Dan's secretary tapped on his door and entered. "Good morning, Mr. Cavanaugh. Miss Morgan isn't here yet, but is there something I can do for you?"

"Mornin', Miss Cassidy. Would you try to get Mrs. Cavanaugh on the telephone for me? It's early, I know, but she isn't sleepin' so well these days."

Miss Cassidy smiled. "Of course, sir. I believe the switchboard is open, so it should take only a moment."

A few moments later the telephone on Patrick's desk rang. He pulled it toward him, picked up the handset, and held it to his ear. "Hilda? Is that you?"

"Yes. What is the matter?"

Her voice sounded anxious and Patrick hastened to reassure her. "Nothin's wrong. I just wanted to know—what was it Aunt Molly said to you yesterday? You said she was actin' funny, not like herself, hintin' things."

"Patrick! Can this not wait? I have not yet had any coffee."

"I need to know now, darlin', whatever you can remember."

Hilda sighed. Patrick could hear it even over the scratchy telephone wire. "She said that something had happened—no, that something had developed. 'There has been a development,' that is it. And she said she would not tell me about it."

"And that's all?"

"She said, over and over again, that I was not to ask any more about the troubles. 'There is great danger,' she said. But she would not explain."

"Well, me dear, I can tell you what the development is. About the danger, the added danger, I mean, I don't know. But as to what Aunt Molly wouldn't tell you—it's not good news, darlin' girl."

"Patrick! What?"

"I'm not even sure I should tell you, not like this, over the telephone. People are maybe listenin'. And I'd rather be with you."

"You are as bad as Aunt Molly! You are teasing me, Patrick."

"I wouldn't tease about somethin' this serious, You're not goin' to like it, Hilda, but—well, Clancy's back."

There was dead silence save for the crackles on the wire.

"Hilda? Hilda, you there?"

"I am here, Patrick. You are right, I do not like it. I remember what Clancy did to me, and to Uncle Dan." Three years before, Clancy had been involved with a group of men who, among other things, had murdered a man, had kidnapped Hilda and left her to die, and had badly mistreated Uncle Dan—his own father. Granted, Clancy had not done the deeds himself, but he had known of them and had abetted the others. Hilda shivered at the memory. "He is not a good person, your cousin Clancy. Why has he come?"

"That's what he's not tellin', or not tellin' me, anyway. He came to see me in my office, just to taunt me, but he wouldn't say what he wanted."

"Whatever it is, it can be nothing good." She paused. "I am afraid, a little, Patrick."

From Hilda, that was a devastating admission. "I'm comin' home, darlin'," said Patrick.

"No, Patrick! Wait! Is Clancy still there, at the store?"

"He was a minute ago. I think he still is, in talkin' with Uncle Dan."

"Then stay and find out what you can about Clancy's purpose. He has a purpose, Patrick. He did not come back here yoost to see his family."

"And well I know that! He's not sentimental, our Clancy, not like most of the Irish. Family means nothin' to him atall. He's out for himself, for money and more money, and if it means he has to do mischief to get it, that doesn't bother him."

"He likes it, I think. Mischief. Menace. He is a gambler, and a bad man. When you know what he wants, come home and tell me. I will feel safer when you are here."

"I'll be there the minute I can. Lock the doors, Hilda."

∼

Meanwhile, Dan Malloy was having a difficult interview with his son.

"I told you not to come to the store, Clancy."

"And where else can I see you? Riggs won't let me in the house, and I can guess by whose orders."

"Yes, my butler is obeying my orders, and they're for your sake as much as mine. Have you forgotten, boy, that you're still in deep trouble in South Bend? That affair of Bishop's murder is still an open case, and it wasn't all that long ago. You left this city in disgrace, with the understanding that you were not to come back. I'm not the only one in town who knows how heavily involved you were."

Clancy's face darkened. "Yes, you and Ma and me lovin' cousin and that meddlesome girlfriend of his! He took on a pile of trouble when he married that one."

Dan ignored the outburst. "We had a bargain, Clancy. I refrained from turning you over to the police, and gave you enough money for a good start elsewhere. You appear to have prospered, and I'm happy for you if it was done honestly, about which I admit I have some doubt. But you haven't kept your part of the bargain. I don't know why you've come home, but you must leave immediately. If the police learn that you're in town, I won't be responsible for their actions."

"I suppose you'd tell 'em. No fatted calf, just a call to the law. Some lovin' family I've got."

"No," said Dan heavily. "No, I'll not tell them. Not unless you get yourself into more trouble. You're still my son. But if you remember the rest of the story you just referred to, that prodigal son returned home in rags, and repentant. I see no sign of repentance in your behavior. Quite the opposite, in fact. You're gloating."

"First time you've been right." Clancy sprawled in his chair. "Damn right I'm gloating. I didn't do anything so awful, and if I did I've paid for it. I nearly starved those first few months, until I landed on my feet."

"I gave you plenty of money. What did—"

"None of your business what I did with it. I'm doing well now. Better than well. I'm doing just fine, thank you very much, and I can't wait to shake the dust of this hick town off my feet. But I came here to do some business, and I'm not leaving till I've done it."

"What business?" Dan's voice was full of foreboding.

"That's no affair of yours, either. I never meddled with your business, and I'll thank you not to meddle with mine. The point is, I'm goin' to be here for a few days. Do you want me to stay at the Oliver, where everyone will know who I am in five minutes, or will you tell that snooty butler to let me in to my own home?"

"It's not your home now," Dan said sharply. "Where did you stay last night?"

Clancy grinned. "Here. Stayed in after the place closed up for the night. There's a nice comfortable couch in the Ladies' Retiring Room. You need a better night watchman, Father dear. He made one round to make sure everyone was out and then curled up to sleep in his own little cubbyhole."

"He was tired. He'd had almost no sleep the night before."

Clancy smiled oddly, and Dan frowned. "Clancy, I'm losing my patience. You've put me in an impossible situation. Have you no sense of responsibility?"

"Why should I feel responsible to you? You threw me out of my home, told me I was no longer welcome under your roof, and put my cousin in the place I should have had. The hell with you! I'm responsible to my boss, and I tell you, he'll not be happy if I don't get my job done."

"And if it's an honest job, I'll eat my hat!" Dan's patience had snapped. He began shouting. "How did I come to have such a son? The only one who survived, and look at you! Oh, I suppose you'll have to come to the house, but we'll need to be discreet about it. You can come home with me, in the carriage, and go in the back way—no!" He stood and slammed his fist on the desk. "No, it won't do. You'd be coming and going as you pleased, and someone would see. I can't have this, Clancy!"

Dan's face had been growing more and more purple. Now he dropped back on his chair and clapped a hand to his chest. "I don't—I think—" His head sagged.

Clancy pulled the office door open and scuttled down the corridor toward the fire escape. He didn't notice Patrick, who had been standing outside the door.

Patrick made no attempt to run after Clancy. He rushed into the office. "Uncle Dan!"

"Get—doctor—heart—"

❧

The doctor got there in minutes, since his office was just across the street. Uncle Dan had lost consciousness by that time, and the doctor looked grave when he had finished examining him. "He is not a young man, but he has great strength. There is some hope for his recovery. He must be taken home at once and given the best of care. With rest and calm and no excitement, he'll survive this. Otherwise..." The doctor spread his hands.

Patrick had telephoned Aunt Molly, so she was ready when Dan arrived home in the care of Doctor McNamara, a nurse, and Patrick. She ignored the mud on their shoes and the water they were dripping on her precious Persian rugs.

"Patrick," she asked in an undertone, "was this—what brought this on?"

"Clancy," he replied. "I'm sorry to have to tell you."

"I thought as much."

She turned away and gave her full attention to getting Dan settled and comfortable. Patrick helped where he could and got out of the way when he saw that he wasn't needed.

He was about to leave the house when Riggs, the butler, approached him. "Excuse me, Mr. Patrick. Your aunt would like you to stay for a moment if you have time."

"Of course, as much time as she wants. This is a terrible thing, Riggs."

"Yes, sir. Mr. Malloy is a very fine gentleman." The old man's face worked a little. He turned away.

"He'll pull through, Riggs. Oh, and your orders about my cousin Clancy?"

"Yes, sir?"

"They stand. If you so much as see his face around here, call the police."

Riggs nodded, looking grim. "Yes, indeed, sir." He, too, had suffered much at the hands of Clancy Malloy.

Aunt Molly came downstairs looking tired, and shockingly to Patrick, old. It had never before been so forcefully brought home to him that his aunt and uncle would age like everyone else, and someday would die.

She sat down in her favorite chair in the drawing room, her tiny feet up on a needlepoint footstool.

Patrick knelt by her side and took her hands in his. They were ice cold, despite the little lace mitts she wore.

"How is he?"

"Comfortable, they say. He looks..." Her mouth quivered and she turned away, like Riggs.

"Aunt Molly, he's strong. He'll pull through this."

Molly waved that away, her mouth firm again. "I think he will. It's not that that's eating away at me. His own son, Patrick! *My* son." She bit her lip so hard it bled a little. She touched her handkerchief to her mouth.

"He's changed since I knew him," said Patrick, trying to find a way to comfort her. "Bad associates..."

"He chose his associates." Molly had herself under full control again. "He has made his bed, and he must lie in it. I won't turn him in to the police—not yet—but I will not, I will *not* allow him to harm his father anymore." She paused. "Patrick, yesterday I went to Hilda and tried to make her promise she would go no further with this investigation. I suppose she told you?"

Patrick nodded.

"And I suppose she told you she made no such promise."

He nodded again.

"I have changed my mind. Yet again. She will think I am as vacillating as a windmill."

"That she will not. She knows you."

"Well, then, tell her from me that I want her, I *need* her to find out anything she can. It will be difficult and very likely dangerous. You, of course, may have something to say about the matter. She's your wife, and it's your child she's carrying."

Patrick shook his head. "I won't tell her what to do. I've

made her promise not to do anything foolish, and to tell me before she does anything at all. Beyond that…"

"Patrick." Aunt Molly looked at him fixedly. "You know the truth, do you not?"

"I—Aunt Molly, what do you mean?"

"Ah, Patrick, don't try to pretend with me. I've been able to see right through you since you were two. You know as well as I do that Clancy is in all this, in it right up to his fool neck." Her voice was steady, but her face wore a mask of deep pain.

...the committee was assured...that Mr. Debs would be here on Thursday night [July 6], and that he would be in the convention on Friday....

—Minutes of the IWW Founding
Convention, 1905

11

PATRICK WENT HOME. There were things to be done at the store, urgent things, but first he had to see Hilda, hold her.

She met him at the door, unlocking it and rushing into his arms. They said nothing for a little time, then he held her away from him. She had been crying; her eyes were red and there were tracks of tears on her cheeks.

"How is he?" she asked.

"You heard, then."

She nodded. "Aunt Molly had Riggs call me. Will he—he will not die?"

Patrick had tried to be cheerful with Riggs and Molly. With Hilda he could only be truthful. "We don't know yet, *acushla*. The doctor says he's comfortable, whatever that means. Honestly, Hilda, if nothin' else awful happens, I think he may be all right. He's strong and he's always kept himself healthy. But just now, there's no tellin'."

"How did this awful thing happen?"

"Riggs didn't tell you that? Well, maybe he didn't know. It was Clancy—you might know. He was in Uncle Dan's office, and I was listenin' in the hall. Clancy was bein' just about as mean as he knows how to be, tellin' his father he had to let him stay at the house—"

"Why? Why would Clancy even want to stay there, after all that happened?"

"I suppose so he doesn't have to pay a hotel bill, for all he's braggin' about bein' rich. I don't know. But he does. But Uncle

Dan said he couldn't, and he'd have to leave or go to jail, and then Clancy got all highfalutin and talked about the prodigal son, and said he wasn't leavin' town till he'd done some business."

"What business does he have here?" Hilda sounded a little panicky.

"He wouldn't say, but he said somethin' about his 'boss,' so I guess he's workin' for somebody."

"He did not say who?"

"No. I guess he might have, maybe, but then Uncle Dan started gettin' really mad and then Clancy hightailed it out of the office and I went in and saw Dan was bad, and—you know the rest."

"Clancy left the office? His father was maybe dying and he *left*?"

"That's Clancy for you. He never did think of anybody but himself. Hilda, if you're goin' to be all right, I've got to get back to the store. What with bein' closed two days in a row, we're goin' to lose a lot of business if I don't get meself busy."

"Yes." Hilda's mind was elsewhere. Patrick dropped a hasty kiss on her nose, patted her tummy, and turned to go.

"Wait. Patrick, you will ask questions at the store, yes? Because someone may know something. We must talk to everyone we can. Or—you must, and everyone else I know. I cannot."

"If I have time, I will, I promise."

"And one more thing. Can you stop at the police station on your way to work, and ask Sergeant Lefkowicz to come and see me?"

Alarmed, he turned back. "You're not goin' to tell him about Clancy? Because Aunt Molly said we weren't to turn him in."

"I would like to tell him, but I will not if you say so. But I am going to tell him everything else. It is time for all this to stop, and for that I need the help of the police."

If the matter had been less serious, Patrick would have smiled at that. The police helping Hilda, indeed! Probably the police would say that it was she who had, on occasion, been of some slight assistance to them.

But now was not the time to share the joke with her. "I'll find Lefkowicz for you," he said briefly, and went back out into the rain.

The sergeant was tired when he showed up at Hilda's door, and more than a little wary. He was just going off duty, and although he had in the past had a good deal to do with Hilda, and liked her, some of those past dealings had gotten him into trouble with his superiors. And all of them, he seemed to remember, had involved his doing quite a lot of extra work. At the end of a day that had begun with a call to a domestic fracas early in the morning and had not improved since, he wasn't sure he wanted to listen to what Hilda had to say. He rang the bell with some trepidation.

No one had thought to tell him about Hilda's condition, so he was covered with confusion when he was shown into her parlor and found her on the couch, her feet up and her mid-section well in evidence.

"Oh—er—how do you do, Miss Hilda—that is—Mrs. Cavanaugh. I hope you are well?" His face, normally pale, was a fiery red.

"I am quite well, thank you, but the doctor has told me to put my feet up every day, now that we are expecting an addition to the family. That is why I asked you to come to me, instead of coming to you. I am sorry if it is not a good time for you."

"Oh, no, ma'am, I don't mind—I mean, a lady couldn't come to the police station."

Hilda had gone to the police station often in the past, but she smiled to herself. Certainly it was no place for a lady, especially not a lady soon to be a mother.

"Good. Sit down, please, and would you like something to drink? Coffee, tea, lemonade?"

What the sergeant really wanted after the day he'd had was something stronger, something to warm his rain-chilled body, but he didn't think it polite to say so. "Whatever you're having, ma'am."

Hilda rang for Eileen and asked for tea for two, and whispered something to her. "Now, then, Sergeant," she said when Eileen had gone to the kitchen, "I asked you to come here to talk about serious things. About train wrecks, and fires, and who is responsible for them. You have helped me so much in the past, and as you see, I cannot go out and find out things for myself."

Lefkowicz blushed again and murmured something inaudible.

Hilda raised her eyes to the ceiling and made an impatient gesture. "Sergeant. I am going to have a baby. It is a normal thing, and nothing to be ashamed of, but society says I may not go out of the house, except to go to church. Also, my family wishes me to be careful, so I have promised. Now, we are friends. So you will please forget about my circumstances, and call me Hilda, and let me tell you what I know so far."

"Yes, ma'am—Hilda." He grinned in spite of himself. "If you don't mind my saying so, I congratulate you."

"I do not mind, but the time for that is when the baby is here."

Eileen brought in the tea, and Hilda poured it. To the sergeant's cup she added a splash from the decanter Eileen had put on the tray. Lefkowicz tasted it cautiously, sighed with approval, and sat back to await Hilda's pleasure.

"Now," she said briskly, "it is about these train wrecks, especially the Twentieth Century one and the one at Studebaker's several days ago. I know that they were not accidents, but what do the police think about them?"

"I'm not supposed to talk," he began, but seeing the menacing look in Hilda's eye, he changed tack. "I'm not *supposed* to talk about it, but I can tell you that we're not happy about either accident—either wreck, that is. Of course, we don't officially have anything to do with investigating the one in Ohio. The only reason we're getting any information about that one is that one of the men who were killed used to live in South Bend, and some of his family live here still. They're putting pressure on us to find out what really happened."

"And what information do you have?"

"Well, you know the switch was left open on purpose. The

newspapers got hold of that, first thing. "

"Yes, yes. And what else?"

"The Pinkertons are looking into just who was on that train. They figure there might have been somebody important that some gang was out to get. And so far they've come up with a pretty complete passenger list, and there were some important people, all right, but no one with real enemies, or not any they've been able to find."

"What about the man from South Bend who died?"

"William Mackey, that was. He was a retired businessman who'd moved to Philadelphia and was going home after a visit to his family that's still here. Not active in business anymore, never was a big name. His family claim he didn't have an enemy in the world."

"They would say that, no matter what," said Hilda skeptically. "When someone dies, no one will ever say anything bad about him."

"You may be right. But in this case, they very much want to figure out who was responsible for his death. I think they would tell, if they knew anything. I've talked to them myself, and I don't think they know any more than they've said."

"Is anyone saying it might have to do with the union?" asked Hilda.

"What union?"

"I do not know! Any union. The railroad workers, perhaps."

"Ah." The sergeant looked closely at Hilda. "You're thinking of Eugene Debs."

"I did not even remember who he was until a few days ago, but he might do such things as this, might he not? Or ask his union workers to do them?"

The sergeant chose his words carefully. "We try to keep an eye on Eugene Debs, you know. Some of his people get carried away, sometimes, but he himself doesn't go in for violence. There's a lot of good in him, you know, and he's a powerful speaker. He'd've made a great preacher. I heard him once, when he was running for president last time, and if he'd said the sun was about to set in the east, I'd've believed him. He's a spellbinder. But I don't think this kind of underhanded villainy is like him. Besides, he's been busy lately, organizing a new union. International Workers of the World, they call it. Their first meeting was in Chicago a week or two ago, and I think it may still be going on."

"In Chicago. That means he was near South Bend."

"Yes. But he was tied up in meetings."

"Not every minute. And there are his followers. But we can prove nothing." Hilda was dissatisfied, but accepted that, for the moment at least, she would have to put that part of the investigation aside. "What, then, has been learned about how the Studebaker wreck happened?"

"Not much. We're on that one, of course—it happened in our territory. But the Pinkertons are helping, because there've been so many wrecks lately. They're looking for a pattern of some kind."

"So am I," said Hilda grimly.

"We have witnesses who say that the train started speeding up as soon as it hit the grade just outside the Woolen Mills, and was going way too fast when it hit the curve coming into South Bend. Then just before it got to Studebaker's, somebody says he saw the brakeman walking the top of the cars, maybe trying to set the brakes by hand. But others didn't see him at all, so we don't know for sure."

"Has someone looked at the air brakes? Patrick knows about these things, and he said if a line was cut, it would mean the train could not be stopped."

"Hilda, there's not enough left of those brake lines to tell anything at all. That was a hot fire, with all the coal to fuel it. Whoever did this was smart. They knew there'd be nothing left to tell the tale."

"And the brakeman is badly hurt, and the engineer and fireman are dead, so no one can tell us." Hilda pounded her fist on the arm of the couch in frustration. "And there is one man who knew about what was happening, and he is dead, too."

"A man who knew?" This was apparently news to Lefkowicz.

"Yes, did no one tell you? The man who was killed at the store—at our store, Sergeant—he told people he knew a lot about the wrecks and the fires. They are killing everyone who might tell anything. They are evil, and we must stop them!"

"Tell me everything you know about Bill Beeman." Lefkowicz was all attention now.

So Hilda told him what little she knew, that Beeman had claimed "funny business" at the bank, that he had claimed Sam Black was connected with it somehow, that Black was back in town. "And he is not the only—" she began, and then made a little sound like a hiccup and closed her mouth.

Lefkowicz waited a moment before asking, "He's not the only what?"

"Nothing. I meant to say, he must not be the only one who knows something. Those who worked with Mr. Beeman at the bank, maybe, could tell you what he was saying."

Lefkowicz was a good policeman. True, his work had mostly to do with wife-beatings, with fights at the local saloon when things got a little rowdy, with raids on the disorderly houses that were the shame of South Bend, and with tracking down the occasional runaway child or delinquent father. But he had learned to tell when people were telling the truth, and he was sure now that Hilda was holding something back.

"Are you sure that's what you were thinking?" He looked her straight in the eye.

"There was another thought, but I have forgotten what it was," she said, returning his look with one just as determined. "And it does not matter. Has anyone talked to the people at the bank, where Mr. Beeman worked?"

"No. We didn't know about his claims. They might be nothing, you know. He was young. Maybe he was just trying to make himself important."

"Perhaps. But Sergeant, we know nothing! You need to talk to Andy Mueller. He is the one who hears all the rumors, all the talk at the hotel. But I do not know how you are to go about it."

"How I go about it? I go up and talk to him, is how I go about it! Or bring him to the station, if he doesn't want to cooperate."

"No! You cannot do that! Andy is afraid, and he has reason. He will not even come here to talk to me anymore. He is afraid that he will be watched, that someone will think he, too, knows too much. Sergeant, people who know too much die!"

"Then what do you suggest?" His voice was just a trifle sarcastic.

"I have thought about this. Why do we not have a meeting of the Boys' Club? A party. A picnic, if the rain ever stops, in Howard Park, and you can attend, and Patrick, and my brother Sven, and all of you can talk to Andy and the other boys and learn all they know. You will not wear your uniform, of course."

"Howard Park? Isn't that sort of public, if you want this all to be hush-hush?"

"No. It is a good place. No one can hide behind a door and listen. We will have it down by the river, far from the rest of the park, so if there is a stranger, he will be noticed."

"It's not a bad idea," Lefkowicz admitted. "But I suggest an improvement. I *will* wear my uniform, and so will other policemen, as many as we can spare that day."

Hilda looked puzzled.

"It would be natural, don't you see? There are still a lot of people who think the Boys' Club caters to a lot of ruffians. So we can spread the word that the police will be there to keep them in line. Then it won't look funny, if anybody does happen to be watching, when we go up and talk to a few of the boys. But the real point is this: if anybody *is* watching, they'll know that the boys have talked to us. Then there wouldn't be any reason to hurt them to keep their mouths shut, see."

Hilda thought about that for a moment, and then gave Lefkowicz a brilliant smile. "That," she said with a brisk little nod, "is a very good idea. Tell me a good day and I will plan the party."

"And what if it rains?"

"If it rains we will move to—to somewhere. The High School, maybe. They have a large meeting room, and they will not be using it in summer." She waved away the difficulty. "And meanwhile you will talk to the people at the bank, all the people you can find who knew Mr. Beeman, and you will report back to me."

Lefkowicz resisted the impulse to salute.

When Patrick came home that night he was too tired to do anything but eat a little supper and fall into bed. He told Hilda, before he sank into sleep, that Uncle Dan was feeling better, resting easily and in no pain, but very weak. The doctor was still worried about him. "I told Aunt Molly to tell him everythin' at the store was under control and business was good. It's true, too, but oh, Hilda, I'm not used to doin' everythin' myself. I'll be glad, the Lord knows, when he can come back. If he can."

"Has he said anything about Clancy?"

"He tried, but Molly shut him up. Said it upset him too much. She had the nurse give him more of the stuff the doctor ordered, to make him sleep. Until he gets well, we won't know anythin' more from that source." He yawned mightily and Hilda let him drift off to sleep.

Our days begin with trouble here
Our life is but a span
And cruel death is always near
So frail a thing is man.

—*New England Primer,* 18th century

12

THE INFORMATION Sergeant Lefkowicz brought her the next day was startling, and disturbing.

"Nobody's talking." He took a long drink from the tall glass of beer Hilda had provided (at Patrick's suggestion). The rain had stopped and the weather had turned warm again, though happily not like the former oppressive heat, and cold beer from the local Muessel Brewery hit the spot. "I talked to everybody at Merchants' Bank from the president on down, and nobody knows anything, nobody suspects anything, everything is lovely. The accidents were just accidents, and how could they have anything to do with the bank?" He took another pull at the beer. "And they're every one of them lying through their teeth."

Hilda accepted that. She, too, was adept at spotting a liar. "So you learned nothing?"

"I learned that they're scared. There's lies and then there's lies, and these were the running-scared kind. But I got the feeling that the bigwigs were scared of me, and the rest were scared of the bosses."

"Then that means," said Hilda, sipping her lemonade and thinking hard, "that there is something the bosses do not want to talk about, and they have told their employees not to talk, either."

"That's the way it looks to me. But as to what it is, this thing they're hiding—" He spread his hands. "There was just one hint, one little ray of hope. The other errand boy, the one who worked with Bill Beeman—well, he didn't say any more than the rest of them. But he gave me a look before he left, like he was wanting to tell me something, but didn't dare say it in front of the others. I hung around for a while, hoping he'd maybe come out and talk to me alone, but I guess he was too scared. It's a pretty good job for a young man just starting out, and he can't afford to lose it."

"That is not all he might lose," said Hilda. "Do you know his name, where he lives?"

Lefkowicz gave her a look of mock anger. "What kind of a cop do you think I am? Of course I know. And yes, I do plan to go see him. Whether he'll tell me anything, I don't know." He finished his beer. "Hilda, I'm getting an odd feeling about all this. Every place I look, every idea I get, it all comes to nothing. It's as if there's nothing to find out, nothing happening, nothing, nothing, nothing! As if all these incidents, the wrecks, the fires, are unconnected, accidental."

Hilda opened her mouth to protest, but Lefkowicz held up his hand. "I know. There isn't a shred of real evidence to prove otherwise, but I'm as sure as you are that these things are not accidents, and that they're linked together."

"There is the open switch for the Twentieth Century Flyer. That is evidence."

"Not really. Everyone says it was done on purpose, but it could have been left open by mistake. We can't *prove* anything, either way."

That was to change. Patrick came home late, but with important news.

He was very tired again. Impatient though Hilda was to hear what had transpired during his day, and tell him what little she had learned from Lefkowicz, she saw that he needed rest. So she chatted about the weather and the baby's somersaults while Patrick downed a large glass of beer. Then she said, "Well?"

Patrick grimaced. "You first. What did Lefkowicz say?"

"He learned nothing, Patrick. No one will talk to him. He thinks they are—wrapping, is that the word?"

"Coverin' up, I expect you mean."

"And he believes that all these things, the fires, the wrecks, are linked somehow, but he says there is no proof that any of them are not simply accidents."

"So it's proof he wants, is it?" He sounded grim.

"Patrick! You know something!"

"I do. It's not good hearin'. Do you want to eat supper first?"

"No," she said decidedly. "If it is not pleasant, it is better to have it said and done with."

He fidgeted in his chair. "Do you suppose there's any more beer?"

Hilda rang for Eileen. "Go on," she said.

"I suppose you're right. Better to get it over." He took a deep breath. "It was just before I came home, when Jacob came to work for the night." Jacob Loeffler had been the night watchman at Malloy's ever since Patrick could remember. He was getting old and gray now, but the work was mostly honorary, and Dan hadn't the heart to pension him off.

"Seein' I was still there," Patrick went on, "he came in to talk to me. I thought he was just checkin' in, like, but there was more to it than that.

"Well, he hemmed and hawed a bit first, asked about Dan. Oh, by the way, Aunt Molly called the store to say he's a bit better, but the doctor's still keepin' him quiet with pills. Anyway, Jacob finally got to the point. Thanks, Eileen."

Another swallow of beer. Hilda thought she would die of impatience if *Patrick* didn't get to the point.

"What he said, Hilda, was that Clancy was there the night of the fire."

"Herre Gud! How does he know?"

"Seems Jacob heard a noise in the middle of the night, from the storeroom. He naps some when he's on duty, but he sleeps like a cat; the littlest thing will wake him. Well, the rain was still comin' down pretty hard, so he thought there might be a leak in the roof or somethin' of that sort, makin' some noise in there. So he went down and smelled smoke. He pulled the alarm then, first thing, before he even opened the door, and it's a good thing he did. Because when he opened it he saw there was someone in there, and the outside door was open. Now that was bad, because with both doors open the fire would spread worse, so he turned to close the door he'd just opened. And then he turned back, and even with all the smoke he saw it was Clancy."

"Oh! What did he do?"

"Nothin' atall. Jacob couldn't think right, he says. Smoke does that to you, makes your brain slow and fuzzy. Besides, he saw Clancy reach in his pocket, and he was scared, because he thought maybe Clancy had a gun. He told me he never did trust him. But all Clancy pulled out of his pocket was a handkerchief, and Jacob was just wonderin' about that when he smelled somethin' powerful sweet, and that was the last he knew until he woke up in his own cubbyhole with a rotten headache and sick as a dog."

"Oh! Clancy gave him—I do not know the word in English."

"Chloroform, that's what he gave him, and it's a wonder it didn't do for an old man like him." Patrick finished his beer and set the glass down with a thump. "It muddled him, though, and he wasn't sure enough about what he remembered to come to me earlier. But now he is sure. So you see, darlin', now we have our proof."

He didn't sound happy about it. Hilda reached out her hand to him. "Have you told the police?" she asked gently.

"Not yet. I have to go tell Aunt Molly first."

"Yes. Oh, Patrick, my dear one, I am so sorry. Your cousin..."

Hilda used few endearments. Patrick understood the depth of her sympathy. "You know, I never liked him much, even when we were boys. But he's family, and Dan and Molly are..."

He couldn't go on.

Hilda slipped quietly out to the kitchen to put back supper. Mrs. O'Rourke wouldn't be pleased about this invasion of her domain, nor about ruining a perfectly good meal, but Mrs. O'Rourke would just have to accept things, for once. This was a crisis.

When she returned, she found Patrick in the hallway, ready to leave. "Patrick, shall I go with you?" she asked anxiously.

He thought a moment. "No, I don't think so. It'll be upsettin', and I don't want you upset." He glanced at her swollen abdomen.

"It will not upset the baby, Patrick! I will go, I think. Aunt Molly is already distressed about Uncle Dan, and worried over what Clancy might do. She is very strong, but this news will trouble her greatly. I would like to be there with you."

Patrick was too troubled himself to argue with her. "I told O'Rourke not to put the carriage away. Watch out for the steps; they're still slippery from the rain."

The Malloy house was in the same block, an easy walk, but not for Hilda, not right now. Patrick bundled her into the carriage and helped her out again when they reached their destination.

Riggs greeted Patrick with what looked to Hilda like relief. "Mr. Patrick, sir! And Mrs. Patrick. Mrs. Malloy will be happy to see you. She's been fretting."

"I'm fearin', Riggs, that I've brought her somethin' more to fret about. She's upstairs, is she?"

Riggs nodded.

"Could you fetch her for us? I'm not wantin' Uncle Dan to hear this, if he's awake."

Riggs paled. "Begging your pardon, sir, but it isn't—it's not Mr. Clancy, sir?"

"I'm afraid it is."

Riggs bowed and trudged up the stairs.

Patrick led Hilda into the parlor. There were tears in her eyes. "Riggs loves Aunt Molly, yes?"

"And do you know anyone who doesn't?"

"It is just that I never used to think butlers were human. Mr. Williams never seemed to be when I worked for him at Tippecanoe Place. But Riggs—he had a son he loved, and that son died. I learned that at Christmastime. And now I know he loves Aunt Molly. I wonder if there is—or was—someone Mr. Williams loves?"

"I reckon," said Patrick. "A person can't hardly get through life without lovin'. His mother, anyway—hush!"

He stood as Aunt Molly came into the room.

Hilda was shocked at her appearance. Always a small woman, she seemed to have shrunk, to have drawn into herself. Her face was taut with worry, her eyes sunken into deep purple shadows. She was, however, faultlessly groomed and as gracious as always. "Please sit down, Patrick. Hilda, I'm happy to see you, child, but should you have made the effort to come?"

"It was not an effort, Aunt Molly. I wanted to come. There is something—Patrick has something to tell you."

Aunt Molly seated herself in her usual place with care, her small hands groping for the arms of the chair before she lowered herself wearily onto the cushioned seat. Her shoulders sagged. Patrick pushed the stool under her feet and stood, as if to await instruction.

"Do sit down, dear. You're making me nervous, hovering like that. Now what is it you need to tell me?" Her sigh was, Hilda thought, unconscious.

The best thing, Patrick decided, was to come right out with it. He kept his voice low, in case Uncle Dan might be awake. "Much as I hate to tell it, Aunt Molly, I've found out that Clancy was at the store the night of the fire."

Molly's hands tightened convulsively on the arms of the chair. "Go on," she said in a voice that threatened to break.

"Jacob saw him, just after he pulled the alarm. That was when Clancy chloroformed Jacob and dragged him back to his cubbyhole."

"At least he did that," Molly whispered. "The poor man might have died."

Another man did die. No one said the words, but they hung in the air.

"You haven't seen him today?"

"No. He would not have been admitted to the house, even if he had dared come."

"Aunt Molly, I must go to the police. I have no choice now."

"Yes." She took a deep breath and drew herself up in the chair, seeking for strength to deal with this latest blow. "I will be grateful if you will tell them everything. I would rather not talk to them just now, unless I must. There is your uncle to think of."

"I'll tell them, Aunt Molly. Don't worry."

And what a meaningless phrase that was, thought Hilda. What could Molly do except worry, with things the way they were? Her husband desperately ill, her only son a criminal?

Hilda looked at her with deep pity, and then saw the answer to her question. Molly slipped from her pocket a beautiful rosary, kissed the cross, and began silently to pray.

To protect the workers... in their health,
their homes, their firesides, their liberties....
The attainment of these is the glorious
mission of the trade unions.

—Samuel Gompers, 1898

13

P ATRICK SAW HILDA home and then went to the police
station with his awful burden of news. Hilda dragged
herself up to their bedroom and lay on the bed, too
weary in body and spirit even to undress.

A tap on the door. Eileen came in, her eyes full of worry. "Is
it ill you are feelin', ma'am? Shall I get the doctor?"

"No, thank you, Eileen. I feel ill, but not anything a doctor
can cure."

Eileen frowned. "Will you be wantin' your supper then,
when Mr. Patrick comes home?"

Hilda sighed. "I do not want to eat, Eileen, but save something
for Patrick. He may be hungry. I do not think so, but he may."

"Oh, ma'am, what is it? What's wrong?" Eileen was wring-
ing her hands. "It isn't somethin' wrong about the babe, is it?"

Hilda sat up and pushed back her hair, which was in limp
disarray. "No, not the baby. There is no reason you should not
know. The whole town will know soon. It is Mr. Clancy. He was
at the store the night of the fire, and he gave chloroform to the
night watchman to get him out of the way."

"Ooh, ma'am! Would he have been startin' the fire, then?
And a man killed in it—such wickedness!"

"We do not know that yet. It may be so. Patrick has gone to
the police. Clancy must be found and arrested. This time there
will be no wrapping—no covering up what he has done."

She allowed Eileen to help her undress and get into her night
things, but she lay on the bed, tired to the bone but unable to
sleep. If only Patrick would come home!

But night had fallen before she heard his key in the lock, and when he came up, he looked even more exhausted than she felt.

"They can't find him," he said, sitting on the bed. "I stayed at the station so as to know they'd got him. But he's nowhere to be found, and the good Lord only knows where he is and what he's up to. They'll keep on lookin', of course, and they'll track him down sooner or later. If he set that fire, it's murder, and this time he won't get off."

He leaned over and put his arms around Hilda, his head buried in her shoulder. "We used to play together. He was a bully, even then, but there were good times, too." His voice caught on the last words.

"Come to bed, dear one. You are tired. It will not be so bad in the morning." But even as she spoke the words, Hilda could not really believe that morning would be any better.

Both found it hard to sleep that night. The patter of rain that had been their lullaby for two nights would have helped, but the night was filled only with the usual night sounds. Hooves clattered on the brick pavement as someone went on a late errand. Far off, the hoot of an owl and the cry of some small animal meant doom in the owl's claws. Once the clamorous bells of the fire wagon brought them both sharply awake out of an uneasy doze.

"Another fire. Patrick, do you think...?"

"No tellin'. Go to sleep, darlin'."

❧

Morning came, as it always does, even after the most restless night. Saturday.

"Must you go to work, Patrick?"

There was a slight wobble in Hilda's voice. She suppressed it instantly, but Patrick heard and understood. "I hate to leave you alone, darlin', but there's double work to be done with Uncle Dan laid up. Triple, for we're still all behind with everythin'. Why don't you stay in bed and try to get a little sleep?"

Hilda had already pulled herself up and managed to get her

feet off the side of the bed. "I cannot sleep. I will nap this afternoon, I hope."

"You'll have some breakfast, then. I know you don't want it. Neither do I, but coffee will wake us up and food will give us a little strength."

For one moment Hilda thought about arguing. She didn't want any breakfast and didn't see why she had to choke down food she wouldn't taste. But then the baby kicked her, hard, several times. "Kristina is hungry, if I am not," she said, and pulled on a robe to go downstairs.

She ate what Patrick put in front of her, and drank several cups of coffee. To her surprise, she did feel better, although the weight of the baby wasn't the only great weight she felt. "They will find him, yes?"

"They will. They were callin' the Pinkertons, Lefkowicz said last night, and callin' patrolmen in for double duty. They'll find him, but I can't say when. Clancy was always good at hidin'. It's goin' to be a warm day, but keep the doors locked, and tell Eileen not to let anybody in—not *anybody*—unless she knows for sure who they are. I'll come home for lunch, no matter what."

"Patrick, you will be careful, too. He—he hates you, I think."

Her voice was small, and Patrick wished he could reassure her, but he was always honest with Hilda, no matter how many cheerful lies he told to other people. "He hates me, right enough. And he's already bein' hunted for murder, and they can't hang a man twice. Much as it hurts me to say it, he'd kill me as soon as look at me, and then claim it wasn't really his fault, the rat! I'll look after my own hide, you can be sure. And you—you look after yours. *Both* of yours."

"I should go and see Aunt Molly."

"No!" He shouted it, and Hilda looked affronted. "Darlin', I didn't mean to yell. But it's just not a good idea for you to leave the house today. I don't know where Clancy is, but he's not far away or I'm a Dutchman. And he doesn't care much for you, either, you know. If he can't find a way to hurt me, myself, he'd know the worst hurt he could do me would be doin' somethin' to you. Please, darlin'! Stay home!"

His heart was in his eyes. Hilda gave him a long look and then nodded. "I will send her a note."

After breakfast, Hilda allowed Eileen to help her dress. She responded listlessly to the little maid's chatter. All the coffee she had drunk had seemed only to tighten her nerves, without clearing her mind. A pattern. There had to be a pattern to everything that was happening. Clancy. Sam Black. Clancy's "boss," whoever he was. Fires. Train wrecks.

What was the thread that bound them together?

"And what I say, ma'am, is there's somethin' behind all this. Stands to reason. We never had this kind of goin's-on in this town before. That Clancy, he's no good, and all the Irish in town always knew it. But he's never been this bad before. Somebody's makin' him do all this, and I won't rest easy in me bed until they've found out what's goin' on."

Something behind it. Some*one* behind it. But who? And why?

The front doorbell rang insistently, and both Hilda and Eileen jumped. Eileen looked at her mistress. "Yes, answer it," Hilda decided. "But remember what Patrick said. Make sure you know who it is before you unlock the door."

It was a delegation, and an unlikely one. Norah, carrying Fiona in her arms, was accompanied not only by Sean, but by Hilda's brother Sven.

"It's time to talk," Norah announced, when they had all settled comfortably in the parlor. "We thought Patrick wouldn't let you come to us, what with all that's been happenin', so we came to you. It's time to talk," she repeated.

Hilda bristled at the idea that Patrick could prevent her doing anything. "I think it is good for me to stay here," she said, with a slight emphasis on the first word. "I am glad you have come. My head, it will not work today. Maybe all of us together can think of something."

"You are certain you want to do this, Hilda? Certain you

want to continue looking into these evil happenings?" Sven spoke gravely.

Hilda sat up as straight as her cumbersome figure would allow. "No, I do not want to do this. I am fearful, and not just for me; there is the baby I must protect. But my family—Patrick's family, but it is mine now—my family is worried and upset and in trouble. I cannot even sleep at night for the worry. Yes, these things are evil, and I am afraid. I, Hilda Johansson, admit to you that I am afraid. Clancy Malloy is a bad man, and I think he is connected with other bad men, and I am afraid of what they might do—to me, to Patrick, to Mr. and Mrs. Malloy. I cannot let them do these things if I can stop them. If *we* can stop them."

Sven bowed his head in acceptance.

"So," said Norah after a pause, "there's some things we know that you ought to know. As long as there was a chance you'd bow out, we didn't want to tell you, but now—well, Sean, you start."

Sean looked uncomfortable. Sven was his boss at the paint shop, after all, as well as Hilda's brother, and what he had to tell wasn't going to please either of them. Norah gave him a little kick. "Go on, then."

"Well, I guess your brother's told you about some of the funny stuff that's been goin' on at the shop. Tools missin' and things moved, and that."

Hilda nodded. "It did not make much sense."

"More than you'd think, when you've heard the whole of it. Y'see, there's things we didn't tell Mr. Johansson at first, because—well, he might think some of us were tryin' to start trouble or somethin'." He swallowed. "The fact is, there's men comin' in all the time, tryin' to get us to organize a union, but on the sly, like."

"He knows about that," said Hilda. "He told me."

"Yes, but what he didn't tell you, 'cause he didn't know, is that these hooligans have been tryin' to bribe us. Everything from money to better jobs to liquor to—well, other things, we've been offered if we'd join up. And some of the men, I have to tell you, Mr. Johansson, some of 'em have taken the bribes."

Sven looked thunderous, but said not a word.

Sean continued. "But the thing is, after they took the money, or whatever, these thugs have said there were some little jobs they had to do in return. And I think—I don't know for certain-sure, but I think—that maybe some of these fires, and other things, too, were done by our own men."

It is wise to be silent when occasion requires....

—Plutarch, *Moralia,* circa A.D. 100

SVEN'S VOICE CAME, dangerously quiet. "And you have not told me any of these things?"

"I tell you I don't know for sure! Am I to be accusin' men when I've no proof, men with wives and children, who'd get fired in the blink of an eye, and who need their jobs bad?" Sean's Irish was up.

But Hilda had a temper, too, and it was rising. "Sean O'Neill, you cannot believe that my brother would be so unfair! He is a just man. He would not dismiss anyone without proof, and if you do not know that, you do not deserve to work for him!"

"Hilda!" The angry cry came from everyone at once. Fiona, awakened by the shouting and sensing discord in the air, as babies often do, began to wail.

Hilda glared at all of them impartially, even Fiona. A babble of voices arose, but Sven's commanding baritone prevailed. "Hilda, that is enough. You need not defend me. I can defend myself when there is need, but here there is no need. Sean, tell me whom you suspect, and I will talk to them myself. I do not need to know now, but when we are alone."

"You think I will tell someone?" Hilda asked crossly.

"I think it is better if you do not know." Sven was, at least outwardly, back to his usual calm self, an attitude that always infuriated Hilda. "I think that if you know who might be involved, you may do something foolish. I do not want to put you in peril. For if I do," he added with a first faint glimmer of humor, "I will suffer yet more Irish wrath at the hands of Patrick—and I am not his foreman."

Hilda opened her mouth to remonstrate, but Norah fore-stalled her. "Hilda, for the love o' Mike, listen to sense! This time you can't be runnin' around askin' questions and pokin' into what everybody's doin'. You say you're smart, and most times I'll be agreein' with you, but now you've got to be listenin' to what other people tell you. Your brother's right. He has to see to this himself. And I'll be trustin'," she added, turning to Sven, "that you'll not get me husband into trouble with these rascals who've maybe got into more trouble than they bargained for!"

"You may trust me for that." Sven nodded. "Now, Hilda, since we must be your eyes and ears for a time, is there more that we can do for you?"

It went against the grain for Hilda to give in without a fight, but she was tired. She would argue later, when she had thought of what devastating things to say. For now— "Yes, there is something. I am surprised you have not thought of it yourselves. The most important thing for now is to find Clancy Malloy. He is a bad and a treacherous man. It hurts me to say so, for he is family, but it is true. The police are looking for him, but they cannot be everywhere at once. Ask everyone. Tell everyone to look for him, but they must not—*must not*— challenge him. They must go to the police at once!"

Hilda wrote her note to Aunt Molly after they left. In her somewhat stilted English, she expressed her sympathy for Molly's worries, both about Clancy and about Uncle Dan, and her hopes for Uncle Dan's full recovery. Re-reading what she had writ-ten, she added: "These things I cannot say as well in English as I could in Swedish, but I know that the *Herre Gud* will look after you. You know I would do anything I could for you, but I cannot do very much. Others are trying to find things out for me. I do not know if you are allowed to pray for a Lutheran, but if you can, say an extra prayer for me and the others who try to find Clancy."

She was dissatisfied with the note and nearly crossed out the last sentence, but in the end she let it stand. Let Molly make of it what she would. If she thought that Hilda was worried and afraid and felt the need of help from the Almighty—well, it was true.

When Patrick came home for lunch he found her fast asleep on the couch, and didn't disturb her. She could eat when she woke, if she was hungry, and meanwhile she was free in sleep, free from all the troubles that beset their family. He had nothing to tell her, in any case. Clancy had not been found.

When she did wake, she was not only hungry but full of a grand idea, so full of it that she telephoned Patrick at the store.

His secretary, Miss Morgan, sounded harassed. "He's very busy, Mrs. Cavanaugh, and not in his office, but I'll try to find him, if you don't mind waiting."

"It is very important, or I would not bother him," replied Hilda, responding to what Miss Morgan had not said.

Patrick sounded harassed, too, and worried. "It's not the baby, is it, darlin'?"

"No, the baby is well, and I am well. But I have had a thought, Patrick. Do the police know who the men were who made Clancy do all the terrible things before—to Uncle Dan and to me?"

"Oh!" The idea was evidently a new one for Patrick, as well. "I don't know that they do. We kept it all as quiet as we could, y'know."

"I think you should tell them. Because Clancy might be hiding with one of them."

"They're important men, Hilda. They'd not take kindly to the police bargin' into their houses and askin' questions."

"Then the police will not barge. They will be very polite and will treat the men well. But they must ask, Patrick."

He groaned. "I expect you're right. But I hope you're wrong, all the same. There'll be an almighty ruckus raised if those men are involved, or if they're not, for that matter. I'll stop at the police station on me way home. You haven't mentioned this to anybody else, have you?"

"No, Patrick. I have sense."

She also, however, had a cook with excellent hearing, who

happened to be near the hall telephone niche at the time Hilda made the phone call. Mrs. O'Rourke told Mr. O'Rourke all about it when he brought in a bucket of gooseberries from the bushes in the back yard. "And she thinks it's those politicians who nearly killed Mr. Malloy last election time, remember?"

"Hmph! Crooks, the whole boilin' of 'em. I wouldn't put it past 'em, and that's a fact. And I'll tell you this, Mrs. O'Rourke. I'll bet you dollars to doughnuts I know which one is lettin' that Clancy hide out with him, so there!"

Mrs. O'Rourke had forgotten, when she placed the morning grocery order, that she was nearly out of flour for her gooseberry pie, so she sent Mr. O'Rourke to Sindlinger's for a twenty-pound bag. His good friend James O'Brien happened to be there picking up a barrel of molasses, so O'Rourke helped him load it in the wagon. "Say, did you know those scoundrels that nearly did in Dan Malloy are at it again? I hear they're hidin' Clancy Malloy, who's wanted by the police. Most likely it's Goodman who's at the bottom of it. He's a villain if there ever was one alive!"

O'Brien ran into Kelly at the tavern on the way home. Kelly told his whole neighborhood, and the story grew with each telling

Patrick came home late, tired and out of sorts. "I don't know if I'm goin' to be able to manage that whole store by myself," he told Hilda as he threw himself down in a chair. "Dan seemed to run it with one hand tied behind his back, but there's too much I don't know. In just two days I've made a right mess of the office, not to mention lots of other things. I may have to go in tomorrow and try to sort out the tangle."

"Tomorrow is Sunday. You will not go to work. Sunday is a day of rest, and it is rest you need. We will not go to eat with the family, but stay at home, only ourselves. Did you go to the police?" she added without so much as a pause for breath.

"I did. They're not wild about the idea of goin' to some o' the biggest men in town and askin' 'em, are they harborin' a criminal. Seein' as it's Uncle Dan involved, they'll do it, but they're not happy."

The police, however unwillingly, conducted for the next two days (Sunday or not) a thorough search of the houses of nearly every Republican politician in town. They found no trace of Clancy Malloy, nor any clue that he had ever been there.

CLAIMS MANY MORE
Torrid Wave Kills in Various Cities

— South Bend *Tribune*
July 19, 1905

W HERE WAS CLANCY MALLOY?
As July crept toward August, and the punishing heat returned, the Cavanaugh, Johansson, and Malloy families thought about little but Clancy. Where was he? Was he alive or dead? Still in South Bend, or about his dubious business elsewhere? Aunt Molly was torn between outrage at what he had done and agonizing sorrow over what her son had become, between a desperate hope that he would be found and a desperate fear of what would happen when he was. To Dan, who was slowly—very slowly—recovering from his heart attack, Molly presented a bright face and a cheerful attitude. To the rest of the world, especially to Hilda, she allowed her true feelings to show.

For her part, Hilda was quite simply furious with Clancy. "There is no end to the trouble he makes!" she stormed to Patrick. "He gave Uncle Dan a heart attack, he is making Aunt Molly sick with worry. He must be found!"

She had what she thought was a bright idea about that. "Sam Black!" she pronounced one morning with satisfaction. "There was much talk that he was the one behind some of these bad things. Perhaps he and Clancy are working together, and Sam knows where Clancy is."

"The police are way ahead of you, darlin'," said Patrick absently, still reading the newspaper. "They've talked to Sam more than once. He claims he doesn't even know who Clancy Malloy is. Look at this, Hilda. The fools are still doin' it."

He handed her the front page of the *Tribune,* with its article about a speeding Santa Fe train breaking all records from Los Angeles to Chicago. "Over sixty-one miles an hour, on the average. It's craziness, that's what it is. They keep it up, there'll be more people killed."

Hilda fanned herself with the paper. "This heat will kill *me* if it does not stop."

"Don't say that!" Patrick said sharply. "It *has* killed people. Look for yourself." He pointed at the paper she was still holding. "LaPorte, Chicago, even right here in South Bend."

But Hilda, listlessly looking at the front page, had her attention caught by the story below the one about the South Bend man's death. "Look at this, Patrick. Train robberies!"

Patrick looked. "It says the stories aren't true."

"The police always say that when they cannot find out who did something. And the railroad men would not want to admit the robberies, or people will be afraid to use their trains to send money. Do you know what I think, Patrick?"

Since she was obviously about to tell him, he simply waited.

"I think that Clancy is behind this! No, listen, Patrick," as he looked skeptical. "Clancy is in hiding. He has to live somehow. I think he has been stealing from the trains to buy food."

"And nobody knows about it?"

Hilda looked scornful. "Of course they know about it! They will not tell, because they are afraid of him, him and his 'boss,' whoever that may be."

The heat was making Patrick's brain slow and his temper grumpy. "And who might 'they' be, for that matter? You're free with your ideas, but short on facts."

Hilda's temper was not at its best, either. "And you, you do not want to believe me because you might have to do something about my ideas." She pushed her plate back. "It is too hot to argue. It is too hot to live. I will go back to bed." And she did, lumbering up the stairs with none of her usual quicksilver grace.

Patrick shook his head. He would be nearly as glad as she when this baby made its appearance in the world.

~

By the end of July Hilda had decided that none of it would ever be over. The heat would continue to torture her, the baby would never be born, Clancy would remain at large, and life would be unendurable. She ate whatever cold food Mrs. O'Rourke could contrive, but in every other respect she had reverted to her behavior of months before.

Meanwhile Patrick was working long hours, trying to keep the store running smoothly in Dan's absence, and running into obstacles every step of the way. Dan had known by instinct, apparently, what people would buy. He knew all the suppliers, he knew when merchandise could be delivered, he knew exactly what markup would be fair to the customers and still make money for the store. Patrick had been learning these things, but he still had a lot to learn, and he made mistakes, it seemed, daily. The staff were hot and weary, the merchandise limp and dusty. And when, at the end of each long, sweltering day, Patrick came home, everyone there was hot and cross, especially Hilda. Patrick, too, had decided that life was, if not entirely, at least very nearly unendurable.

Then August dawned one Tuesday morning, and the longed-for miracle had occurred. The sky was clear, the air was cool, there was a balmy breeze. Hilda accepted with a smile the coffee Eileen brought her. "You look very nice today, Eileen. Is that a new dress?"

Eileen was wearing, under her apron, a flowery print dress from the Sears, Roebuck catalog, the same dress she'd worn off and on since it had come in the mail a month ago. Prints were the latest thing in summer attire for servants, and Eileen thought it pretty, too. "It's freshly ironed, ma'am," she said tactfully. "What shall I bring you for your breakfast?"

"I think I will go down for breakfast today. And Eileen, run me a cool bath, will you, please, and lay out anything I can still wear."

There wasn't much choice. Hilda was bulging. She could wear only the loose skirts that Eileen had run up for her out of thin muslin, and dressing sacques on top. The sacques were pretty, made with embroidery and lace inserts, but they were still lingerie, and Hilda had at first blushed to wear them downstairs. But Patrick hadn't noticed that they were boudoir wear, and they were comfortable—or as comfortable as any clothing was these days. Thanks be to God, at least she could get through the day, now that the weather had changed, without wishing she were back in Sweden in a snowbank.

All the same, she was disconcerted when Eileen announced that Sergeant Lefkowicz had come to see her.

"It'll be all right, ma'am," whispered the little maid. "He's a man, and men never really know about ladies' clothing."

"Sergeant, it is good to see you," Hilda lied. She gestured at the couch she was lying on. "Please forgive me if I do not get up."

Lefkowicz grinned. "My ma told me I shouldn't come, that you wouldn't feel like company just now." Evidently he had got over his embarrassment about her pregnancy.

"It is all right. I feel better now that it is cooler."

"Well, that's why I've come. It's about the picnic, see."

"Picnic?" Hilda asked blankly.

"For the Boys' Club. Remember?"

"Oh! Oh, Sergeant, I forgot. It was my idea, even, and I forgot completely."

"Well, it's been too hot anyway, for the grownups, at least. And of course I know you couldn't come, now. But we've hit a dead end when it comes to finding that Clancy Malloy, and I thought it might be a good idea to talk to the boys, see what they might know."

Hilda forgot her decision a few days ago that life would never again hold any interest. "Yes! That is a very good thought. I do not know why it did not come to me, but oh, the weather has been unbearable!"

"You're right about that. But I was thinking maybe next Saturday—not this week, but the next. Would that give you time to get it all put together?"

Another thing Hilda had forgotten was her offer to organize.

The thought made her want to go back to bed again, but she had made the offer and she could not go back on her word.

"That will be enough time," she said, her fingers crossed behind her back. "I cannot do it all myself, of course, but I think Mrs. Elbel will help, and perhaps Mrs. Studebaker."

"And Mrs. Malloy."

Hilda frowned. "I do not know about Mrs. Malloy. She is—"

"She's worried sick about Clancy," said Lefkowicz bluntly. "And about Mr. Malloy, too, though I hear he's much better. My ma thinks it would do her a world of good to busy herself with something else for a change."

Hilda cocked her head to one side. "Your mother is a wise woman, I think. We will do it!"

"Ma said," Lefkowicz continued, "that you'd better not do any of it yourself. You can phone people and get it done that way. And if you need an extra hand on the day, she says, she'll be glad to bake some cookies and fry some doughnuts and go over to help get all the food set out."

"Not just a wise woman, but a good woman, too!" Hilda smiled. "Tell her thank you, and that would be very nice. And oh, Sergeant, I nearly forgot. Talking of boys made me remember. That other errand boy at the bank, the one who wanted to talk to you maybe. Have you found him?"

"No, and it's not for want of hunting. It seems he's been out of town, looking for another job."

"He left his job at the bank?"

"So I hear tell. Kind of a foolish thing to do, times being the way they are, but that's what his ma says."

"It might not be a foolish thing," said Hilda thoughtfully, "if there are bad things happening in banks. Do not give up, Sergeant. I think he has things to tell us, if we can find him. And now I must go to the telephone."

16

To sleep: perchance to dream: Ay, there's the rub...

—William Shakespeare, *Hamlet*

ER FIRST CALL was to Mrs. Elbel. The two had not gotten along well at first. Hilda had resented what she thought of as a patronizing attitude on the part of the older lady. But Mrs. Elbel had gained considerable respect for Hilda over the way she handled the Boys' Club Christmas party, and had worked with her smoothly ever since.

"Of course I'll be happy to help," she told Hilda promptly. "Some of the ladies are out of town, but I'm sure we can find enough to get the job done. Now let's see. We'll need tables—I can borrow those from the church—"

Together they made a list of duties and assigned each, tentatively, to one of their hoped-for volunteers.

"If you will write the invitation, I will give it to Patrick to have it printed," said Hilda. "Your English is much better than mine."

"Yes, and I'll phone Mrs. Studebaker. Mrs. Clem, that is. I believe Colonel and Mrs. George are in France just now, but Mrs. Clem will be happy to help. At least—" She paused.

Hilda said, "She has not been well, I have heard." There was sorrow in her voice. Mrs. Clem Studebaker, Hilda's mistress for all the years she had worked as housemaid at Tippecanoe Place, was a true lady, kind when Hilda worked for her and kind now that Hilda had a home and a life of her own. But Mrs. Clem missed her dear, departed husband every day of her life, and Hilda had the awful feeling that she was longing to join him.

"She's been a bit frail," Mrs. Elbel admitted. "She's in her sixties, you know, and that operation a while back laid her low. But she'll have her cook prepare most of the food, I imagine, and she always has good ideas. It will do her good to help with this."

That reminded Hilda. "And I will ask Mrs. Malloy to help, also. She, too, has been sad and worried, but she will want to work with us." At least Hilda hoped so. She had not talked to Aunt Molly for several days, and the last time, the older woman had sounded tired and worn, not at all like her usual self.

Hilda did not confide the real purpose of the picnic to Mrs. Elbel, but to Aunt Molly she was entirely candid.

"Aunt Molly, I need your help," she said after Riggs had called his mistress to the telephone, and Hilda had asked after Uncle Dan. "It is about a picnic for the Boys' Club, but it is more than that. Would you come to see me, so I can explain? I would come to you, but—"

"But you're feeling as big as a house, and tired as a washer-woman on a Monday night. Of course I'll come, dear."

The two had not seen each other since soon after Dan's heart attack. Molly's eyes widened when she saw Hilda. "Goodness, child, you *are* as big as a house. The baby's not due for another month, is it?"

"Yes, but I think maybe the doctor is wrong. Kristina, she kicks like a chick trying to get out of its shell!"

"A good, healthy baby, then. Now sit down, dear, and tell me what it is you need of me."

Hilda explained about the picnic. "But Aunt Molly, it is not just to give a treat for the boys. That, too, but we think, Sergeant Lefkowicz and I, that it will be a good chance to talk to them about all the dreadful things that have been happening. Boys know a lot, and see a lot, and they may be able to help us." She took a deep breath. "They might even know where Clancy is."

"I see." Molly was silent for so long that Hilda was afraid she was offended.

"I fear they will not find my son," Molly said finally. "I fear he is dead. I would know, I think, if he were still alive. A mother can sense, sometimes, when her child is in peril. When I think of Clancy, when I pray for him, I get no feeling that he is in jeopardy. I get—nothing."

Hilda was shocked. It was always possible, but— "You may be wrong, Aunt Molly. I remember, when Uncle Dan was missing, you thought he was dead. But he was not."

"He was near death, though. If you hadn't found him when you did—but yes, that time I was wrong. It was, I think perhaps, my mind that kept insisting he might never come back to me. In my heart, I could not believe it. But now—some of my people had the sight, you know. Oh, way back, it was, and the family never talked about it, but every now and then I—know things. And just as I am certain that Mr. Malloy will recover completely from his illness, I am sure, in my heart, that we will never find Clancy."

She sat with head bowed for a moment, then looked up. "But this picnic is a good idea all the same, my dear. Especially if Clancy is never found, we must use every resource we have to get to the truth of the train wrecks, the fires, all the evil around us. I will certainly help all I can, and if we don't learn anything useful, well—" she spread her tiny hands "—the boys will have a good time, and that's worth the trouble."

So they worked out the details, and Aunt Molly went home, leaving Hilda filled with wonder at the strength of this little woman who, believing her son dead, nevertheless went about the business of life with grace and courage.

Hilda's background didn't encourage a belief in clairvoyance. The spirits that live in trees, in woods, in water, yes—perhaps. Hilda wasn't sure she actually believed in the *tomte* and trolls of her Scandinavian folklore, but she didn't like walking near woods, especially at night, and she was careful about streams. Just because one was a good Christian didn't mean one shouldn't be careful.

But she had also learned not to scoff at the beliefs of others. And if Aunt Molly thought, believed, that Clancy was dead, well—she, Hilda, would bear it in mind as a possibility.

Maybe her dreams would be less troubled.

For Hilda had not been sleeping well. She had blamed the heat and her heavy, ungainly body that made comfortable sleep impossible. But when, finally, she fell asleep, she had nightmares that she could never remember in the morning, except the impression of trying to run, run away from some undefined horror—only she could not run, could not walk, could only try to crawl from the Thing that came nearer, nearer.... She would scream and then wake with Patrick's hand on her hair, soothing, calming, easing her back into sleep.

For the next few nights after Molly's visit the dream was different. This time she was chasing the Thing down endless corridors, twisting, writhing tunnels, a labyrinth that led nowhere, and always with mocking laughter in her ears. In the mornings she would remember that laughter and clutch Patrick's arm tightly until its echoes faded from her mind.

The day of the picnic arrived, a beautiful day, warm, with no hint of rain. Hilda's capable crew had made all the arrangements. Mrs. O'Rourke had volunteered to bake enough of her famous chocolate cakes to feed an army; she and Mr. O'Rourke were to drive them to the park in state in the carriage.

As they were carrying the last load out, Hilda made a decision. Patrick was at the store, so she could not consult him. "Mrs. O'Rourke, can you fit me into the carriage? I could hold a few of the cakes on my lap."

Mrs. O'Rourke looked at the bulge where Hilda's lap used to be. "No need for that, madam. There's room enough. But—"

Hilda didn't let her continue. "I will not get out. No one will see me. I want to hear children laughing, to smell the fresh air. I have been in the house too long."

"Yes, madam." Mrs. O'Rourke didn't quite sniff, but her disapproval was evident in every line of her body.

Hilda didn't care. This picnic was her idea and she intended to be there. If anything exciting happened, she wanted to be on the scene. With most of the city's police force there, she and Kristina would be well protected.

All the same, she hoped Patrick wouldn't find out until she was safely back home.

It began well. O'Rourke drove the carriage to a spot where Hilda could see everything without being conspicuous. She had feared hers might be the only carriage, but there were several others, waiting, she assumed, for the fine ladies to be finished with their charitable work. She recognized the Malloy coachman, who had left his driver's seat and was chatting with—oh, *Herre Gud*, with John Bolton! She had never thought Mrs. Studebaker would come in person.

If John saw her, there could be trouble. He would certainly come over to chat, and that would attract attention. She slid down in her seat until she could barely see out, a most uncomfortable position in her present condition. As an afterthought she snatched off her hat, but it was too late.

"Doing an imitation of an ostrich, are you?" It was John's lightly sarcastic voice. "But no, it's their heads they stick in the sand."

"Go away, John," said Hilda through her teeth. "I don't want anyone to know I'm here."

"And why are you here, is what I'd like to know. Or no, let me guess. It's Hilda Pinkerton, hot on the trail of Clancy Malloy."

"What do you know about Clancy Malloy?" In her eagerness to gain whatever information John had, she forgot to keep her voice low.

"Nothing I want to tell the whole world." In a quick movement, John hoisted himself onto the seat beside Hilda.

"John! Get down! If anyone sees you in here with me—"

"If anyone thinks I'd be up to no good with you at this particular time of your life, they've got a filthy mind. Do you want to know about Clancy, or don't you?"

"I want to know, but quickly, John." She looked around nervously. No one seemed to be paying any attention. O'Rourke had gone off with his wife to help arrange the cakes on the serving tables, and the boys, of course, had no eyes for anything but the food.

"I don't know if this is going to make things better for you, or worse, but I have it on good authority that the blot on the Malloy family escutcheon will deface it no more. In short, Clancy has departed for a better world. Or maybe a worse one, come to think of it. I somehow can't see the pearly gates opening wide for such as him."

"Aunt Molly said so." It was the barest whisper.

John looked at her sharply. "His mother knows?"

"No, she—yes, she knows, but not that way. She—oh, John, you would not believe me, anyway. How do you know? What happened?"

"It's only rumor, but a pretty reliable one. If you want to know the whole story, talk to your little friend Andy Mueller. He's the source of the story, as far as I can tell. I expect you'll have to wait a bit, though."

His last remark came over the strident sound of a dinner bell that set up a cheer from something like a hundred young male voices.

"I think I'll join them," said John, stepping down lightly. "Shall I bring you a plate, milady?"

"Do not make fun of me, John Bolton! And I do not want any food, but I would like some lemonade, please—lots of lemonade."

She had to wait until the boys had eaten their fill, and that took some time. All healthy boys have good appetites, but boys who almost never have enough to eat can resemble a plague of locusts. The trestle tables, groaning with food to start, were left with plates of crumbs. Mrs. O'Rourke's eighteen chocolate cakes had vanished down to the last dollop of icing, leaving that good lady both gratified and annoyed. She had planned on taking at least one back home for supper at the Cavanaugh house.

John, having eaten his own lunch, went off in search of Andy and brought him to the carriage, along with Hilda's lemonade.

Andy was alarmed when he saw Hilda.

"Miss! I didn't ought to be seen talking to you."

He would have run away if John had not caught him by the

arm and virtually thrust him into the carriage. He came in behind the boy and sat next to him to make sure he didn't bolt. "There, now, nobody will see you. Tell the lady what you know."

So, with hesitations and a few tears, Andy told his tale.

A boy's will is the wind's will,
And the thoughts of youth are long, long
*   thoughts.*

—Henry Wadsworth Longfellow,
    "My Lost Youth," 1858

17

ND A REMARKABLE TALE it was.

"Promise you won't tell nobody, miss!"

"I cannot promise that, Andy. If you tell me what I think you will, I must tell Mrs. Malloy. You see that."

Reluctantly, Andy saw. "But you mustn't let anybody know it was me who told you. You mustn't!"

"People already know," said Hilda gently. "Mr. Bolton knew it was you from whom the rumor came. If you are afraid, Andy, what you must do after we talk is go and tell your story to Sergeant Lefkowicz. He is here. Many policemen are here, and the reason they are here is to protect you and your friends."

"The police don't care about the likes of us, miss. They're here to see we don't make trouble."

"Not this time. This has been planned, Andy. I knew you could not come to me safely, so I have come to you—with many witnesses. You see, when people know you have told the police what you know, you will be safe. If someone wanted to harm you before you could tell…"

Andy got the point. He wiped his nose on his sleeve. "Yes, miss. Sorry, miss. But I was so scared—I saw it, miss."

Hilda was confused. "You saw what?"

"I saw them kill Clancy Malloy."

For a moment Hilda thought she was going to faint. She turned as white as the fluffy summer clouds floating in the deep blue August sky. John handed her a glass of lemonade.

She waved it aside. "I am all right. It was yoost—*just* that

I was surprised." What a weak word, she thought, but in her astonishment she could not think of the proper English word. "Andy, tell me everything. When did this happen?"

"A long time ago, miss. Almost as soon as they started huntin' for him. And it was my fault!" He swallowed hard. At his age, tears were a grievous sign of weakness. He was nearly a man; he couldn't cry.

Hilda had coped with many a case of Erik's near-tears. She forbore to offer sympathy. "Andy! It is not your fault. I do not suppose you killed him?"

"No, miss, but—"

"Then do not be foolish. Tell me what happened."

"Well, miss, when we all heard about Mr. Malloy bein' so bad, with his heart and all, and it all bein' Clancy's fault—"

"Wait! How did you know it was Clancy?"

"Aw, miss! *You* know. When somethin' happens to a big, important man like Mr. Malloy, the whole town knows. It was Mike, see, the elevator boy at Malloy's, and he told Joe, who was deliverin' from Hibbard's, and then—"

Hilda waved away the rest. "Yes. I had forgotten." She felt a momentary sadness. She was no longer a part of that network of servants and delivery boys who knew everything almost before it happened. "Go on."

"So when I found out how sick he was, I was pretty mad, see, 'cause Mr. Malloy, he's a real nice man. He's an honest politician, even, and there ain't many of that kind around. And Mrs. Malloy, she's real good to us boys—like you, miss—and here she was worryin' herself half-sick over Mr. Malloy, and it was her own son that done it! That Clancy never was no good, miss. Oh!"

His hand flew to his mouth. He began to stutter an apology.

"It is all right, Andy. He is no—he was no relative of mine, thank the *Herre Gud*, and his own family know what he was. Go on."

"Well, I just wanted to give him what he deserved. I'm not so big, miss, but I'm tough, and that Clancy, he'd gone soft. I seen him oncet when he first come back to town, and he didn't look so good, sort of pale and puffy-like. So I reckoned if I could find him, I could give him a good fight. I guess I wasn't thinkin' too clear, miss, just sort of boilin' over with what he done to his pa."

Hilda was too troubled even to notice Andy's grammar, much less correct it. "So you went to look for him," she prompted.

"Not right then. I was still workin', and I figgered it was better to wait until night, anyway. So when I got off work I went home, and then when Ma and Pa and the kids had all gone to bed, I snuck out. There's a good tree by the bedroom window, and I can move real quiet when I want to.

"I had a pretty good idea where he might be, too. 'Cause when there's lots of funny business goin' on, I figger it's maybe mixed up together, you know?"

Hilda nodded.

"So there was this business of Clancy bein' back, and up to no good if he was hidin' out in the store, and there was the fire and all, and the wrecks, and I thought—" he paused for breath "—I thought, if Sam Black was behind some of it, maybe he and Clancy were workin' together, so maybe I'd find Clancy at Sam's."

"I thought the same thing, Andy, later on. So the police went to find out. But he was not there, and Sam said he had not been there."

"He was there, all right, miss. That was where he got killed. I saw it."

His voice was sounding shaky again. Hilda, by this time, had herself well under control. "Tell me," she commanded.

Andy gulped and went on. "See, I knew where Sam lived, because when there was all that talk about him, some of the boys told me. It's on up Colfax a ways, out of the fancy houses like yours and into the little ones, you know? It was real dark, and there's no streetlights when you get that far west, but I found the way easy enough.

"When I got there, there was a light on, an oil lamp, inside the house. So I figgered, a light when it's close to midnight, he's got company, or he's expectin' some. And I reckoned it was Clancy, so I got as close as I could and hid in the bushes and tried to look in the window, but it was too high off the ground for me to see much. I couldn't see anybody inside, but if they'd been around the other side of the room, I couldn't've seen 'em anyway. The window was open, though, 'cause it was a warm night, and I couldn't hear nobody talkin', so I thought maybe I was wrong. Maybe he'd just went to bed and left the lamp burnin', but that's a pretty stupid thing to do. So I was tryin' to figger out what to do next, when somebody came up the front walk.

"Well, I'll tell you, miss, I thought I'd die on the spot, I was so scared. I couldn't see hardly anythin', you know, no moon or nothin', just the light from the lamp. And this guy—"

"You could see that it was a man?" asked Hilda, interrupting.

"I wasn't sure, not then. See, he was walkin' real quiet, or tryin' to, but that front walk is gravel, so he couldn't help makin' some noise, and he sounded kind of heavy. And he couldn't walk on the grass, because there's bushes on each side of the walk. After a minute or two, when he didn't say nothin' or come to get me or anything, I realized he couldn't see me, not even as much as I could see him, which wasn't much, 'cause I was hid in the bushes up close to the house. So I thought he'd ring the doorbell or knock on the door or somethin', but he just stood there, not movin', or anyway I didn't hear the gravel crunch anymore. And I could see a kind of shadow where I reckoned he was, just a little darker than the rest of the dark.

"I couldn't move or he'd hear me. I didn't hardly breathe. And pretty soon I heard some little sounds like he'd got off the walk and up on the porch, to get inside. And that's when..."

Andy stopped.

"Did Mr. Black come out of the house, Andy? Is that what happened?"

"No, miss. It wasn't Sam Black killed him. Someone come up behind him, real fast, crunchin' on the gravel walk. I couldn't tell what was happenin' till I heard a sort of crack, like—like somebody hittin' a baseball a real good one. And then there was this awful thud and a crash, and I heard somebody runnin' away.

And then the door opened, just so wide—" Andy measured a space with thumb and forefinger "—and Sam Black looked out and said—well, whispered, I guess—he said, 'Clancy? That you?' And when he didn't hear nothin' he opened the door wide and the lamplight shone out and he saw…"

"Yes. You can leave out that part. Clancy was dead?"

"He wasn't movin', and his head—I reckon he was dead, miss. And I reckon Sam Black was 'most as scared as I was. He went back in the house, anyways, and I lit out of there fast as I could." Andy's fist clenched, and he gave a little dry sob. "See, miss, I reckon if I hadn't gone there lookin' for Clancy, who-ever it was wouldn't have found him. I led him there, and it's my fault!"

"Now, Andy," said John, who had been silent through the recitation, "that's a mindless sort of thing to say, and not what I'd expect of a bright boy like you. Think, boy! If the man who killed Clancy had followed you, he'd have got there before Clancy, and he'd have known you were there. Do you think he wouldn't have disposed of you first?"

Andy digested that, his fist slowly relaxing. "Then you reck-on I had nothin' to do with it?"

"Plainly the man followed Clancy. If we knew where he picked up his trail, we'd know a lot more."

"Followed him," said Hilda slowly, "or already knew where he was going. It was a good plan, I think. The man killed Clancy in a place where someone else, Sam Black, could be blamed. So it was not likely that Sam would tell the police. He would do just what he did—take the body away, probably to the river, and say he had never seen Clancy. He is smart, whoever did this. Andy, you do not have any idea who it was?"

"No, miss. I was too scared to see hardly anything, and any-way it was too dark."

"Not even his size?" asked John. "Tall, short, thin, fat?"

"I never saw him at all! I didn't even hear him come till the last minute. I just heard that crack, and then Clancy fell, and I heard the man runnin' away."

"Ah! You heard him running? That would give some idea of his size. Did he sound heavy or light?"

Andy thought about that. "Heavy, I guess. He was sort of crashin' through bushes and stuff, and maybe his feet thudded on the ground. But I can't say for sure. I was—"

"You were frightened," said Hilda soothingly, with a warning look at John, "and no wonder. But you do not have to be frightened anymore. I am glad you have told us, Andy. Now go back with your friends, and tell them everything. Be sure to say you do not know who the man was. And tell Sergeant Lefkowicz. You see, Andy, if everyone knows, you are in no danger."

"I guess," he said dubiously, but as he left the carriage, Hilda saw that he was headed in the direction of a group of policemen.

"Why did you send him away so fast?" said John in a grumbling tone of voice. "There were a lot more questions I wanted to ask him."

"That is why. He could not bear any more. He had been very brave, but he could not talk about it any longer. If you, John Bolton, had seen murder done when you were his age, would you not have been frightened and worried, too?"

"I suppose. All the same, it's a crying shame he didn't say anything about all this sooner. If the police had known right away, they might have been able to trace the fellow. 'Crashing through the bushes,' was he? He might have left footprints, broken branches, other signs the police could have followed up. Now it's way too late."

But Hilda was thinking of something else. "John, would you find Mr. O'Rourke for me, please? I must go to Aunt Molly."

Give us grace and strength to forbear and persevere....

—Prayer by Robert Louis Stevenson, d. 1894, inscribed on his memorial in Edinburgh

18

THE VISIT WITH MOLLY was not as painful as Hilda had expected. She told Patrick about it that evening when he had come home from work and heard the news.

"She is the most wonderful woman I have ever known, Patrick. Even my mother is not so strong as she. When I told her, she sat for a little, so still I was afraid maybe she had stopped breathing. Then she looked up at me and thanked me. *Thanked me*, Patrick, for bringing her such news! I did not know what to say. Then she said, 'It is better to know. Remember that, child. It is always better to know than to imagine. Now I must go and tell Mr. Malloy.'"

"I'd've thought he shouldn't get such news while he's still not well," said Patrick.

"I said something like that, and she said, 'He must know, too. Now he has only one son.' I did not know what she meant, Patrick. I thought Clancy's brother died long ago."

"He did." There was a tear in Patrick's eye. He didn't dash it away, but let it trickle down his cheek.

"Patrick, I—I am sorry. I should have told you more carefully. I thought you did not like Clancy."

"No more I did, and though I'm sorry for Aunt Molly and Uncle Dan, I can't say I think Clancy's a great loss to the world. That's not why I'm cryin'."

Hilda looked her puzzlement.

"She meant me, darlin'. She meant I'm their son now—their only son."

After that there was nothing for Hilda to do but join Patrick in tears.

~

Next morning Hilda woke early. She had slept well for a change, and though her body felt slow, ungainly, and sluggish, her mind was racing.

Patrick was still asleep. It was Sunday, after all, and he had been working very hard for weeks. Hilda did not, she told herself, deliberately try to wake him, but she made enough noise getting out of bed and into her dressing gown that he unwillingly opened his eyes.

"Patrick, I have been thinking."

He groaned and closed his eyes.

"No, do not go back to sleep. Listen. How can they have a funeral for Clancy when they do not have his body?"

"Don't know. Now can I go back to sleep?"

"No. I think, what would I do if I had just killed someone? And it is easy. It is night. No one will see me. I will put him in the river."

Patrick yawned mightily. "Good thing you're not a murderer. You'd do it too well. But girl, you never saw Clancy when he came back to town. He'd put on weight. And Sam Black's house is—well, I don't know exactly where, but a good few blocks west of here. How's a man goin' to move that heavy a weight a couple of miles to the river?"

"And that is what I thought next! And I think, I would use a wheelbarrow. He could not go on the streets, not the brick ones, anyway. It would be too noisy. But it would be quiet if he stayed on the grass, or on dirt streets. And it has not rained for nearly a month. Could it not be that, even after all this time, the police could find the tracks of a wheelbarrow?"

"Maybe they could. But what good's that goin' to do? They couldn't prove who owned the blasted thing, and anyway there's no law against trundlin' a barrow, even halfway across town."

"You are not awake yet, Patrick." Hilda sounded pitying.

"That I'm not."

"And you are cross. But when you have had some coffee you will feel better, and you will think better."

So it wasn't until Hilda had rung for Eileen, and the little maid had brought them coffee, that she explained.

"If they can find the tracks of a barrow, or a cart, they will know where the body was taken. And if it was to the river, as I think, they will know where to start looking for it. Because Aunt Molly and Uncle Dan must have the body so that they can bury it and begin to mourn properly."

Patrick took her hand. "I'm sorry I was cross before, darlin'. You're absolutely right, and I'll stop in at the police station before I go to Mass."

Hilda elected to stay home from church. She was very tired after an active and emotionally trying day. Besides, she wanted time to think about the new knowledge Andy had provided.

It was, in a way, good to know for certain what had happened to Clancy. Aunt Molly was right about that. At least he had died quickly, painlessly. And he had, quite certainly, been up to no good.

What *was* he up to? Why had he come back to South Bend? It was a terrible risk. His collaboration in the murder of a prominent politician a few years ago had not been forgotten. The police were not the only ones eager for a little talk with Clancy Malloy. And while Clancy was stupid in some ways, he had always been very careful of his own skin.

What had been worth taking that risk? He was a gambler, of course. He must have been gambling for stakes high enough that the reward seemed worth the risk.

Well, he'd lost the bet this time. Poor Clancy. All his life he'd gambled for more and better, never content with what he had—a loving family, a good home—everything, seemingly, a man could want. And he'd ended with nothing, not even his life.

In the unlikely attitude of pity for Clancy Malloy, Hilda abruptly fell asleep.

Patrick woke her when he came home. He was quite late; it was after one.

"This is not a saint's day or something, is it, Patrick? You were very long at Mass."

"I called in at the police station again on me way home. You were right all down the line, me girl. It was a handcart, not a wheelbarrow, but they traced the tracks from the back of Sam's house to the river bank just above the LaSalle Avenue bridge. They're draggin' the river now, but they reckon they won't have to work long. The river's low and slow, as dry as the weather's been."

"Have you told Aunt Molly?"

"Not yet. Better to wait, I thought, till they've found him."

"Maybe—" Hilda chewed her lip "—maybe it would be good to tell her he may be in the river. He—it—the body will not be—"

Patrick nodded soberly. "It'll not be pretty, over a month in the water, and warm water at that. And fish... Here! I ought not be talkin' this way, and you so near your time!"

"It is all right, Patrick." She laid her hand on his. "I am upset, but not by talk. We speak only of things that are true, even if they are not good. Nothing about this is good."

"No." Patrick sat still, clasping her hand. "No, that's wrong. There's one thing good. Once they find his body and Dan and Molly get him decently buried, Clancy Malloy will never make their life hell for them again."

Hilda shook her head, Patrick thought in protest at his language, but she said, "No, Patrick. He was their son. They will never stop grieving for him. The sorrow will never end. It does not matter that he was not a good son. This I know, Patrick, now that I will soon be a mother. Aunt Molly carried him for nine months. She gave him life, in pain and weariness. He was blood of her blood, bone of her bone. She will never forget, and she will always grieve."

Patrick took her in his arms.

ᔐ

It was, in fact, Monday afternoon before the body of Clancy Malloy was found in the river. It was, as foreseen, badly damaged by water and water creatures. Patrick, called on to identify the horrid thing, averted his eyes from the unrecognizable face. "The clothes look like his," he said, "and for certain that's the ring he had on the last time I saw him. I'd know that stone anywhere. That's Clancy."

So they took him to the undertaker's to be made as presentable as possible before his parents had to see him, and Patrick went to tell Aunt Molly.

He had not seen her in a few days, and he wasn't sure what to expect. But the face she held up for him to kiss was serene, if a little more lined. He didn't like the way she was dressed. She wore black, as she often did, but solid black, unrelieved by the little touches of lace she usually wore. "I'll wear this until after the funeral," she said in response to his look. "It seems only decent. But I'll put my lace back on as soon as I think I won't shock the whole family. Mr. Malloy doesn't like seeing me this way."

"Nor I don't, either, Molly. But you won't have to wear it long. They found him this morning, so you'll be able to plan the funeral soon."

She did not speak. She closed her eyes. A tear rolled down her cheek, and she clutched her handkerchief. Patrick took a breath to speak, but she shook her head. "A moment, please, dear," she whispered.

The single tear was all she allowed herself. She opened her eyes, took a deep breath, and said, "Thank you, my dear, for seeing to this for me."

"I shouldn't have broken it to you that way," said Patrick. "I didn't mean to—"

Molly shushed him with a gesture. "When something unpleasant must be said, it's best to be quick about it and get it over. I'm deeply grateful for all you've done. Now I must tell his father, if you'll excuse me."

Her back ramrod-straight, her head erect, the rest of her tears unshed, she left the room to perform her next duty.

The child is father of the man....

—William Wordsworth,
"My Heart Leaps Up," 1802

THE MANHUNT WENT ON, but the focus had shifted. The police had stormed Sam Black's house as soon as Andy had told his story, but Sam wasn't home, and neither were most of his clothes and personal effects. "Skipped town, by gum!" said Sergeant Lefkowicz, looking as though he would like to have used a stronger expression. "If that young nuisance Mueller had told us what he knew sooner, we'd have caught Black red-handed!"

The sergeant was sitting on Hilda's front porch, the day after Clancy had been found. If there was a breath of air to be caught, Lefkowicz hadn't been able to catch it. At Hilda's invitation, he had unbuttoned his heavy wool uniform jacket and loosened his collar, but sweat still poured down his face. He took another swig of the beer Eileen had brought out.

"But Mr. Black was not red-handed," Hilda pointed out. "He did not kill Clancy. Andy said he came out of the house and found him dead."

"Figure of speech," muttered Lefkowicz. "Black knew a lot about it, even if his hand didn't strike the blow. Who knows but what he lured Malloy to the house so his accomplice could kill him? For sure Black lied to us about knowing where Malloy was, and we need to talk to him!"

"Yes." Hilda fanned herself with a lace fan Patrick had given her. It was pretty, but the effort of moving it only made her hotter. She sipped at her lemonade. "Sergeant, why was Clancy killed?"

"Miss Hilda, I'm a whole lot more interested in who killed him, and I'll bet that Black knows—"

"Because, if we know why he was killed, we will be able to find out who did it. Who wanted him dead?"

"Well," Lefkowicz began, and then hesitated. "Ma'am, seeing he was a relative of yours, I don't want to speak ill of him."

"He was no relative of mine, and I did not like him. I do not think even his family liked him. They loved him, of course, but that is not the same thing."

"No, I suppose it isn't. But you know as well as I do that there are lots of people in this town who didn't like Clancy Malloy, and a good number who had reason to want him kept quiet."

"People do not kill because they do not like a person. Even hating someone does not usually lead to killing him. But to keep someone quiet… Sergeant, you are talking about politics, yes?"

"It was politics first got him into trouble, you remember. Politics and gambling."

Hilda remembered. She had met Clancy at a time when his father, Daniel Malloy, was running for a county office. It was his first foray into office, and his last, as it turned out, but at the time he was eager to win the seat, minor though it was. His rival, Republican John Bishop, was killed during the campaign, which made Dan's victory hollow and tainted, and he had given up the seat shortly after the election.

But of course the worst blow the family had had to bear was Clancy's involvement in Bishop's murder. Apparently he was only a witness who had been kept quiet by a shrewd mix of threats and bribery, having to do with his gambling debts, but in the eyes of the law, and of his family, that amounted to criminal complicity.

And who was the man behind the scenes, the puppeteer who had so successfully pulled Clancy's strings?

"What," asked Hilda, "has become of Mr. Vanderhoof?"

Lefkowicz took a deep breath and put down his empty glass. "Now, Miss Hilda, that's the kind of question you ought not to be asking just now. He's a slippery man, Vanderhoof, and the Pinkertons and the police would like to know what he's been doing these past couple of years. But he's a powerful, influential man, and he's got the reputation of not caring much who he hurts."

"He hurt us. Hurt our family. Stole the money we'd saved to bring Mama and the others to America."

"Yes, and your family wasn't the only one, not by any means. But he's not to be taken lightly, do you understand? You're not to try to find out anything about his affairs. Patrick and I have been friends a long time, but if I let you get mixed up with Vanderhoof, he'd never speak to me again, and that won't be the worst of it, either. I mean it, Miss Hilda. You leave Vanderhoof to us."

It was far too hot to argue, and besides, Hilda badly needed a nap. She shrugged and asked the sergeant if he would like another glass of beer, in that unmistakable tone that indicated his answer should be no.

She was too hot and uncomfortable to sleep for long, though, and when she woke she thought about what Lefkowicz had said. At the very mention of Mr. Vanderhoof, he had become alert and wary. She was reminded of a cat scenting an enemy. His very hackles had seemed to rise, his figurative tail to bristle.

She had never had any intention of trying to trace Mr. Vanderhoof's movements, or find out what his activities were these days. Now, though...

There is a very old story about the woman who, having to leave her children alone for a time, gave them detailed instructions about what they were and were not to do in her absence. "And don't put beans in your ears!" Until she said it, such an idea had never occurred to the children, but of course when she came home every last one of them had to have the beans painfully removed.

Surely it wouldn't do any harm if Hilda were just to put out a few feelers. Sven, she felt sure, would be glad to look into the matter for her. He still felt keenly the loss of the four hundred dollars that Mr. Vanderhoof had taken from them. Even though the Malloys had kindly paid the transportation for the rest of the Johansson family to come to America, the idea of being taken in still rankled. Yes, Sven would be happy to learn what he could.

She wouldn't tell Patrick, though. He was all too apt, these days, to lay down the law about her activities. Besides, he often talked to Sergeant Lefkowicz, and she didn't want the policeman to know, either. Tomorrow, she would send for Erik and have him take a message to Sven. In that roundabout way, even the servants wouldn't know what she was doing.

She would have done well to remember what she so often said to others, that the servants know everything.

That settled, she turned over, placed herself in the direct stream of air from the electric fan, and fell asleep.

Patrick was late coming home from the store. "I had to stop and see Aunt Molly," he explained when he had settled in the parlor with a glass of beer. "I've made most of the funeral arrangements, but I had to ask her about a couple of things, and she's fair distracted, what with Uncle Dan to think of, and Cousin Mary comin' in from Chicago on the evenin' train."

The funeral was to be on Thursday. Hilda would not go to St. Patrick's, of course, but she did plan to attend the graveside ceremony. "For that is not in a Catholic church, and I can wear a shawl to cover up, even if I nearly faint with the heat."

"I don't like the idea of you faintin', darlin'. Could you not stay in the carriage, close by? That would show respect, but you wouldn't have to stand in the heat. Or you could stay home. Aunt Molly said you weren't to feel you had to come. She understands, havin' had three herself."

"And now she has only one daughter," said Hilda. "Life is sad, Patrick."

"That it can be," he acknowledged, and finished his beer.

༄

Hilda sent for Erik the next day, as planned, and he arrived in a combative mood. "And what's gonna happen to Andy?" he demanded as soon as he saw Hilda on the porch.

"What do you mean, happen to him? Do you think the police will do something to him? Do not be foolish." She was feeling as tired and hot and miserable as she ever had in her life, and was very cross. "That is not why I asked you to come here. I want—"

Erik wasn't having a good day, either. A neighborhood dog had chewed the strap on his brand-new roller skate, a fact he hadn't noticed until the strap broke. He was skating down a hill at the time, and had skinned both knees and one elbow, and torn his pants. Mama would have plenty to say about that when she came home from work. And *he* was hot, too. "You didn't ask me to come," he interrupted. "You dragged me away, and I was just about to go swimmin'. And I don't care what you want. Andy's scared stiff the crooks are gonna come and get him, and what are you doin' about it?"

It was like a blow to Hilda's solar plexus. She leaned forward on the porch swing so suddenly it nearly threw her off.

"I did not think about that. Oh, Erik, you are right! I must— I do not know what I must do."

She sat back—sagged back—and looked so near tears that Erik was disarmed.

"Well, you don't need to cry about it," he said, his voice dropping into the low, man's register that was becoming his normal speech. "Andy's okay, prob'ly, as long as he's at the hotel. It's comin' and goin' that scares him, 'specially comin' home at night. It's gonna start gettin' dark earlier pretty soon, y'know, and he has to work late sometimes."

Hilda nodded. "Yes. But what—I thought he would be safe if he told what he knew in front of everyone."

"He thinks they'll try to get him, though, just to teach him not to be a snitch."

"Is this something he has heard anyone say, or is it just a feeling?"

"He says—" Erik's voice broke into its higher register again "—he says he hears people whisper things behind his back, but when he looks to see who's talkin', there's never anybody there."

"What kind of things?" Hilda's mouth was dry.

"He didn't say. Just—mean things."

Hilda looked at her little brother, her tears near the surface again. He was lying, and he knew she knew he was lying, but he wasn't going to repeat to his sister the words, the cruel, menacing words that Andy had heard flung at him by unknown voices.

Erik was becoming a man.

"What do you think we should do, my brother?" she asked him, and they both understood. She had called him "little one" for the last time.

"I had an idea," he said, digging his toe against the wooden floor of the porch and shedding about five years of his new-found adulthood. "I don't know if you'll like it."

"Yes?"

"I thought maybe Patrick could give him a job at the store, and maybe walk him back and forth every day. He doesn't live so far from here."

Hilda considered that. "Patrick needs more help, I know, now that Uncle Dan is ill. Do you think Andy would like working at the store?"

"He's been wantin' to get a better job," said Erik eagerly. "He's been sayin' there's no chance to make anything of himself as long as he's just a bellhop. He'd work real hard, I know he would."

Hilda wanted to hug him, but she knew he didn't like it anymore. Even if she could have reached him, she thought ruefully, looking at her prominent bulge. "I will talk to Patrick as soon as he comes home. But for today, I will have Mr. O'Rourke meet Andy when he gets off work, and take him home."

"Not in the carriage!" said Erik in alarm. "Because the crooks would know—"

"No, not in the carriage," Hilda agreed. "He will walk to the hotel, and Andy will tell him where he lives."

"I'll go tell Andy!" said Erik, ready to dash away.

"Wait! Erik, wait. I nearly forgot why I 'dragged you away' from your swimming. I want to you ask Sven to come and see me. No," she added, seeing the question trembling on his lips, "do not ask me why I do not go to him. This is something secret, Erik, and you must not tell anyone about it. Not even Andy. Will you promise?"

"Promise," he said, in his new adult voice, and crossed his heart. "I gotta hurry, though, 'cause I gotta go find Sven for you, and then stop at the hotel before I go to work at the stable."

"No time to swim today," said Hilda. "I am sorry. Maybe to-morrow."

But Erik was already out of earshot.

Courage is resistance to fear, mastery of fear —
not absence of fear.

   —Mark Twain, *Pudd'nhead Wilson's*
     New Calendar, 1897

20

S VEN WAS ALSO HOT and tired when he came to see Hilda, but Sven almost never lost his temper. He was the epitome of the calm, stolid Swede, the sort that others thought of as "dumb." They could not have been more wrong.

He sat down heavily on one of the wicker porch chairs, so heavily that the chair creaked, and said, in Swedish, "You wanted to see me, my sister?"

"Yes, and I am sorry to keep you from your supper on such a day." She poured some of the fresh lemonade Eileen had brought out, with a passing thought to the number of lemons they must be going through. Time was when a lemon, or an orange, was a rare treat. Lemonade was one little luxury for which she was deeply grateful.

"Yes, it has been a long day. The paint shop is very hot and close on such a day. There are fans, but the smell of paint is hard to bear." He sipped at his drink, then held the cold glass to his temple.

"You have a headache. I will give you some powders, and then you must go home to rest. But first, there is a thing I would like you to do for me."

Sven looked wary. Many of the people in Hilda's life were wary when she asked them to do things for her. "Yes," she said to his unspoken criticism, "it is maybe a fearsome thing, but not I think so fearsome for you as for me. He does not know you."

"Who does not know me, Hilda?"

"Mr. Vanderhoof. Always we dealt with his agent, Mr.

Andrews, about getting Mama and the children here. Mr. Vanderhoof knows me, or he knows who I am, because of what happened later, but he does not know you."

Sven's jaw worked. His cold blue eyes seemed to grow even colder. "And what is it you want me to do about Mr. Vanderhoof?"

Hilda lowered her voice. Across the street a sweating boy was mowing the lawn. The cicadas were buzzing loudly. She would not be overheard. "I want to know what Mr. Vanderhoof has done, where he has been, since he left South Bend. It was said that he left the country. I do not know if that is true, or just a story that was told to protect him." She moved closer to Sven and spoke even more quietly. "He is an evil man, Sven, and I think maybe he still has colleagues here, political friends, who would do anything he asked of them. I think—I do not know, but I think—maybe he has been setting these fires, and killing people, and even wrecking the trains, for some reason of his own. Oh, he did not do these things himself, but I think maybe he has had other men do them."

Sven heaved a great sigh. He was extremely tired, and his head ached badly. "My sister, you say these things, but you have no proof. Yes, Mr. Vanderhoof is a bad man. He is a thief, and he has killed one man, at least. No, not by his own hand, but by his bidding. But why would he do these things you now say he has done?"

"I do not know, Sven. I know only that he helped Clancy to turn bad. He used him. Then Clancy returned to South Bend, and now Clancy is dead—murdered. I think there is a connection. I do not know what it is. Will you help me to find out?"

Sven rose, ponderously. "I must go, Hilda. I will think on it. I do not like to accuse a man—even a bad man—with no evidence."

"That is why we must find the evidence, my brother. Wait. I will give you something for your headache."

He took the medicine, thanked her gravely, and trudged home, refusing Hilda's offer of the carriage. She had not gotten the pledge of help that she had hoped for, but she knew it was no use trying to coax or plead. Sven would do what he thought was right, and anything more that Hilda could say would have as much chance of moving him as of moving one of the old elms that lined the street.

And if she felt any slight qualms about breaking her implied promise to Sergeant Lefkowicz, or putting Sven in possible danger, she pushed them to the back of her mind, hoping they would be less troublesome there.

When Patrick came home a few minutes later, it was with Andy Mueller in tow. Andy was carrying a box so big he was almost invisible behind it.

Hilda was not best pleased. "Patrick," she whispered, "what if someone is following him?"

"That's fine, lad," said Patrick loudly. "Just set it down in the hall, and then go and have yourself a wash. The scullery's just off the kitchen. Then maybe Mrs. O'Rourke will give you a little somethin' to eat."

When he had gone inside, panting a little under his burden, Patrick motioned to Hilda and they both went in to the parlor.

"Hush, now, before you say a word," said Patrick, going to the sideboard to pour himself a whiskey. This was so unlike him that Hilda stared open-mouthed and obeyed his command.

He took a swig, sighed, and looked at Hilda. "All right, darlin', you want to know what's goin' on."

"Yes!" Her tongue unleashed, she let it run freely. "He was not to be seen with you, not yet. If anyone saw him with you, it could be very bad. I had a plan, but it—"

"Things don't always work out accordin' to plan." Patrick took another pull at his stiffener. "The boy's a bit muddled, but if I understand what he was tellin' me, Erik went to the hotel and told him there was maybe a chance of him comin' to work for me."

"Yes, he was to say that, and to say that until I had a chance to talk to you about it, Mr. O'Rourke would come to the hotel and walk him home. After he went to work for you, then maybe he

could come home with you. I did not think about how he would
get home from here. I am so tired, Patrick."

"I know you are, darlin' girl. So are we all, in this awful heat.
Anyway, I guess maybe Andy didn't hear another word Erik said
after 'work at Malloy's.' Anyway, he came straight to me, in the
middle of the afternoon. And he said he was followed."

Hilda's hand went to her mouth.

"Yes. Now what was I to do? Tell me that. The boy was
scared nearly out of his wits. So I brought him home, hopin' maybe that big box would hide him from anybody who wanted to
know where he was or what he was doin'. It wasn't a wonderful
idea, but it was the best I could come up with at the time."

"Who followed him?"

"He didn't know. I don't know, meself, if it's true or if he was
just so scared he imagined it. He reads those dime novels, doesn't
he?"

"Yes, but—"

"And Sherlock Holmes and that sort o' thing?"

"But he is not—"

"All I'm sayin', darlin', is it could be so, or it could be somethin' he's made up out o' shadows."

"You will not let me finish. I think it is true. But even if it is
not, he thinks it is true, and he is very frightened. Patrick, I think
we must let him stay with us for a little while."

"What about his family?"

"We will have to let them know. I can send Mr. O'Rourke."

"And what is he goin' to tell 'em? That their boy's been
nosin' around for you and got himself in trouble with some
nasty sorts? That he's seein' things that aren't there? Or what?"
There was a hard note in his voice that Hilda had seldom heard
before.

She said nothing for a moment. Then she swallowed and
said, "You are right, Patrick. I have been foolish in some ways,
and I have put the boy in danger. But now we—you and I, Patrick—must think of the best way to protect him. I think it is to
keep him here with us. We can tell his mother that I need some

extra work done at the house. But do you think that is what we should do?"

Patrick's anger melted. "Yes, darlin' girl, I do. I'm sorry if I sounded—well, I didn't mean to be scoldin'. You're doin' the best you can, I reckon. Let's get Andy in here and talk to him about it."

They found Andy in the kitchen, eating cookies and drinking milk and talking to Mrs. O'Rourke as if they were old friends. Hilda was astonished.

"Sure, and it's good to have a boy around," said the curmudgeonly cook. "I miss my own, now they're grown and gone. Did you want somethin', madam?"

"Yes," said Patrick, since Hilda seemed once more to be struck dumb. "If you're done with your snack, Andy, we're wantin' to talk to you. He'll be back, Mrs. O'Rourke."

Andy looked apprehensive as he followed them back to the parlor.

"It is nothing bad, Andy," said Hilda. "Sit down. We have a plan—an idea—a—"

Patrick came to her rescue. "A business proposition to put to you, me boy. Now, we've agreed you're to work for me at the store from now on."

"Yessir?" Andy had clearly not realized that the deal had been sealed.

"Yes. I can pay you a bit more than you were gettin' at the hotel, to start, but you won't be gettin' tips. So's you won't come out on the short end o' the deal, we thought—Mrs. Cavanaugh and I—that you might like to work for us here at the house for a little while, too."

Hilda, without missing a beat, took up the improvised narrative. "You would help Mr. O'Rourke with the outside work, and maybe some work inside as well. I am—now that I am near my time, I can do little, cannot even carry anything very heavy. I would be very happy to have your help, Andy. But it would mean that you would have to live here for a time. Would that be hard for your family?"

"I'd be here all the time? And go back and forth to work with Mr. Patrick?"

Hilda and Patrick exchanged glances. This boy was no fool. "Yes, Andy," said Hilda gently. "You would be with one of us all of the time."

"I'll have to tell Ma."

"It'll be all right with her, then? She won't be missin' your help around the house?"

"The others'll pitch in. It's summer, so none of 'em's goin' to school. It'll be okay. But I gotta tell her. Already she'll be worried 'cause I'm late."

Patrick grinned at him. "Suppose I go with you, and we can get your clothes and bring them back. And meanwhile Eileen'll fix up a room for you."

Hilda stood, with difficulty, and put her arm around Andy's shoulders. "Tell your mother you will be perfectly safe with us," she whispered, and got a smile in return.

Evil is easy, and has infinite forms.

—Blaise Pascal, *Pensées,* 1670

S O THAT WAS ONE problem solved, thought Hilda as she gave instructions to Eileen. Temporarily, at least, Andy would be under supervision all day long, with no chance for anyone to harm him.

"Will he sleep in the carriage house with the O'Rourkes, ma'am? There's an extra room there."

"No, Eileen. I want him to sleep in the house. The small room on the end will do for now." The place for him, really, was on the third floor where Eileen slept, but Hilda had once been fourteen herself. Better to have the two of them on different floors.

Eileen was no fool, either. If the boy was to be a sort of footman, his place was in the carriage house. If he was to have a bedroom in the house…

"You want to keep an eye on him, don't you, ma'am?"

"Yes, I do, but not because I do not trust him."

"No, ma'am. I know. He's in trouble, isn't he?"

"He—could be. Eileen, do not ask him about it. It is—complicated."

"Yes, ma'am." Eileen went to the linen closet, her face soberly obedient, but her mind racing. Miss Hilda was up to something. Eileen wasn't sure she approved—with the baby so near, and all—but it was exciting, all the same. And even if she wasn't to talk about it, nobody could keep her from listening and speculating.

Hilda was very quiet at supper. She ate, but as if it were a duty. Patrick, tired, hungry, and preoccupied, ate with steady concentration. Eileen, serving at table, was uneasy. High spirits and confidence, that she expected from her mistress. Of late, tantrums and tears were the norm—but that was just the baby. This mood was new, in Eileen's experience, and what with everything else that was going on, she was sure it boded no good.

Mrs. O'Rourke had made a peach cobbler. It was one of Hilda's favorite desserts, but she took only a small helping, and picked at that. Patrick finally noticed.

"Kevin?" he asked.

Hilda didn't rise to the bait. She simply shook her head. "The baby is fine. I am fine."

"What, then?"

"I think. I am thinking," she corrected. "There is much to think about." She took a deep breath, as deep as she could, with the baby taking up so much space. "Patrick, Aunt Molly was right when she told me to give it up. Andy was right when he said it was dangerous. You were right. Everyone was right. But I cannot stop now. I have done too much. In Swedish we have an expression about stirring mud."

Patrick nodded. "In English, too. Stirrin' up mud, we say."

"Yes. I have stirred up mud. I have put other people besides Andy in danger. But your cousin is dead, Patrick. He was not a good man, and we did not like him, but he was your cousin. We cannot let the man who killed him go free."

"But, Hilda, darlin'!" He fought to keep down his rising panic. "If it's as scary as all that—and mind, I've said so all along—what can you do, girl? With the baby due any time now, and all."

"I can think, Patrick. I can still think. And other people can ask questions for me. What else can I do? Sven will ask questions for me. He did not promise, but he will. I know him."

"And how are you goin' to know what questions to ask? Seems to me you're still just stirrin' up mud." He was trying, he was trying very hard, not to let his temper get the better of him.

"No. Sven will ask about Mr. Vanderhoof."

"Vanderhoof! Why him? He's been gone for years, now."

"It is because of Clancy, Patrick. I do not think Clancy was wicked, only weak. It was Mr. Vanderhoof who made Clancy do wicked things when they both lived here. Then they both left South Bend. Who is to say they did not meet again? Who is to say Mr. Vanderhoof did not come back when Clancy did?"

Patrick frowned. "You've not got any evidence of that. And Vanderhoof's a big man, me girl, and he has a lot of influence. If he *is* mixed up in all this, you'd best leave it alone."

"That is what Sergeant Lefkowicz said. But I cannot leave it alone. I told you. I have begun; now I must continue. I have asked Sven to talk to people, to try to learn what Mr. Vanderhoof did and where he went after he left South Bend." She took another deep breath. "I did not plan to tell you about this, Patrick. But if—if something should happen—I wanted you to know that I think these evil things are all a part of the same plot, and I think Mr. Vanderhoof—"

"What do you mean, if somethin' should happen?" Patrick had stood up, and his voice was rising.

Hilda did not flinch. "If I should have the baby before I can find out about all these terrible things, of course."

She was an experienced and competent liar.

❧

She sought out Andy before she went to bed. He was settling in to his new room, carefully putting away his few belongings, making his bed with the clean linens Eileen had provided for him. "Are you all right, Andy? Is your mother happy with this arrangement?"

Andy sighed. "Ma knew I'd be havin' to get a better job soon, anyway, and it might mean leavin' home. She told me to find out when I can have a day off to go and see her. It's not me that's askin', miss," he added hurriedly. "I don't want you to think I'm wantin' time off when I just got here. But Ma, she's missin' me already."

"You are very good to your mother, Andy. Of course she wants to see you as often as she can. But I think, for a little while, it would be better if you stay here all the time. Because—"

"Yes, miss. Because there's somebody out there wants to hurt me." He tried hard to keep his voice from quivering, but he was only fourteen. He turned his head away.

Hilda sat down on the bed. "Andy, I want you to think very carefully. Can you remember anything about that night at Mr. Black's house, anything that would tell us about the man who killed Clancy? I know it is not something you want to remember, but it could be very important. You see," she said, patting the bed beside her so Andy would also sit, "you see, Andy, I think all of these bad things are connected."

"Even the train wrecks, miss?"

"Yes, even the train wrecks. And that means this is a big thing, a terrible thing. So finding the man who killed Clancy might mean finding the men who are planning wrecks and fires that might kill many more people."

Andy's face became unreadable, blank. "Yes, miss," he said. "But I don't remember nothin'."

Hilda had seen that expression before, on Erik's face when he had made up his mind not to do as he was told. She took his hand, but it lay passive under hers. "Please try to remember. Please try."

"Yes, miss. I think I'd better go to bed, miss. I gotta get up early to go to the store with Mr. Patrick."

The Hilda of several months ago might have pursued the matter. The Hilda who was soon to give birth was too tired, too hot, too—too everything. She patted the unresponsive hand and stood. "Yes, Andy. Sleep. We will talk again."

Hilda didn't get to sleep until nearly dawn. She tried to find a comfortable position for sleep, and could not. She threw off the sheet and lay sweating with the fan turned directly on her. Then she started to shiver, and pulled the sheet up again, and began once more to try to figure out what to do about the intrigue in which she found herself entangled. When she finally did sleep, her dreams were troubled, and she woke to find herself as entangled in the sheet as in her problems.

She also found herself alone. Patrick had given up in the middle of the night after being elbowed aside for the tenth time, and had sought rest in the spare room. Hilda lay for a few minutes trying to get back to sleep, but it was no use. Her back ached, she was hot and miserable, but there were duties to be done. As long as she couldn't sleep anyway, she might as well get up and do them. This afternoon was the time appointed for the funeral of Clancy Malloy, an ordeal she dreaded, but she had to face it. She sat up far enough to reach the bell, and rang for Eileen.

Eileen was serving breakfast, with the help of Andy. She didn't really need help serving one person, but Andy had risen early, eager to begin his new duties, and Patrick had decided it wouldn't hurt him to be trained to wait at table. Eileen was enjoying bossing Andy, who put up with it stoically, but when Hilda's bell rang, Patrick looked at Eileen and said, "You'd better go. Andy can finish here. I'm nearly done, anyway, and we need to be off."

He delayed long enough, however, to make sure nothing was wrong upstairs. He was not in the best of moods. In addition to his own apprehension about the funeral, he was irritable from the heat. Most of all, he was worried and irritated about Hilda's continued insistence on pursuing this course of action. But Hilda was his wife and the child she carried in such discomfort was his child, and under his irritation he loved them both. He paced in the hall until Eileen reassured him that Hilda merely wanted help getting out of bed and washing, and that no crisis was yet at hand. Then he and Andy set off for the store in the carriage. Patrick preferred to walk unless the weather was impossible, but now that he was temporarily in charge, Aunt Molly had tactfully suggested that the carriage was more dignified. "Uncle Dan walks to the store a lot of the time," he had said. "Mr. Malloy," replied Aunt Molly, "has no need to demonstrate his position."

Dan Malloy, as Patrick very well knew, was a lively Irishman to whom decorum had not always been a primary concern, especially when he was involved in politics. But he wasn't in politics anymore, nor was he lively right now. This was not a time to argue the point. Patrick conceded, and used the carriage.

There was another good reason for the carriage now, of course. Andy was better protected in a carriage than out on the street.

The streets were quiet as they clopped along. Although it was still early, with few people yet stirring, the heat and humidity were already nearly unbearable. "I've never known a summer like this one," said Patrick, wiping his brow. He carried a spare collar in a small bag Eileen had given him. The one he had put on when he dressed would be wilted before the morning was half over.

"Yessir, it's been a hot one, all right. Wish somebody'd work out a way to keep a place cool in the summer the way you can keep it warm in the winter. If you're rich, you can, anyways."

"Seems to me I've heard somebody's workin' on it. Not sure it'd be healthy, though, steppin' from an ice box of a house to a steam bath outside. Andy, what do you know about Clancy's murder?"

The boy's mouth had been open for a further comment on the weather. He shut it firmly and looked at his hands.

"Ah. Then you do know somethin' and just don't want to tell."

Andy remained stubbornly silent.

"Want me to tell you why you've shut up like a clam all of a sudden, me boy?"

Andy lifted his eyes and instantly lowered them again.

"I reckon," said Patrick deliberately, "it's because you're scared silly. Scared for your skin."

"No! It's not for me! I'm—" He stopped.

"I know, Andy. I had to make you say it. It's not your own skin you're worried about. You're no coward. Whose, then? Your family? Your friends?"

"No! I mean, yes, everybody—but mostly you and Miss Hilda. Mrs. Cavanaugh."

"'Miss Hilda' is fine. And I'm Mr. Patrick, except at the store—I have to be Mr. Cavanaugh there. Now, why are you so 'specially afraid for the two of us?"

"I've heard those men talk, sir! I've seen 'em. You don't know what they're like! Most people are just—ordinary, y'know? I see all kinds of people at the hotel, the rich ones who come to stay or to eat, and the poor ones who wait on 'em. And some are nice and some aren't, and some are smart and some aren't, but they're mostly just ordinary people, not saints, not devils. But these men—they're bad. I don't mean they're not nice. They're not, but it's worse than that. They're mean, and they like it. You can tell by the way they talk. And I saw one of 'em once—" He swallowed and went on. "He was walkin' away from the hotel, and there was a kitten on the sidewalk. Lots o' stray cats hang around the hotel—the cook gives 'em scraps and they get kinda tame. So this one—it was real cute, and real friendly, and this man was walkin' slow, talkin' to somebody else, so the kitten came over to get petted, or maybe to get a hand-out, and he—he kicked it. Not just pushed it out of the way, I don't mean, but kicked it, hard, so hard it went flyin' up against the wall and—" Andy swallowed again, two or three times. When he went on his voice was rough. "And he never even went over to see if it was bad hurt. He laughed and said somethin' to the other man, and just walked on." After he got his voice under control, Andy said, "I took it home and buried it."

Patrick felt a little sick. He liked cats.

Mr. O'Rourke pulled the carriage up to the back entrance of Malloy's.

"Andy, we have to stop talkin' about this now. But before we go in, tell me: who was this man?"

"I don't know, sir, and that's the truth, cross my heart. But he's one of the ones who was talkin' about the railroad men, and like I told Miss Hilda, I think he's in on—on whatever it is, and now do you understand why I don't want Miss Hilda to have nothin' to do with this?"

Patrick nodded and took Andy in to introduce him to the head floorwalker, the man who would be his boss.

Every political good carried to the extreme must be productive of evil.

—Mary Wollstonecraft,
The French Revolution, 1794

HILDA HAD BARELY finished her cool sponge bath and dressed in her coolest clothes, when Eileen announced a caller. "It's your brother, ma'am."

"Erik? So early?"

"Your brother Sven, ma'am." She pronounced it more like *Swen.* An Irish tongue can find Swedish names difficult.

Hilda didn't hurry downstairs. Hurrying was not easy for her these days, and it was too hot. But she didn't waste time. It was too soon for Sven to have found out anything about Vanderhoof, but...

"My sister." He greeted her formally, taking both her hands and kissing her on the cheek. He looked cool and rested. Hilda wondered resentfully how he did it.

"There is coffee, I think," she said. "Me, I do not want any. It is too hot."

"I have had my breakfast," he said, "and I must get to work. But I wanted to tell you something." He looked around. Eileen was in the upstairs hallway, near the stairs. She was not obviously listening, but... "It is private, Hilda."

"Then come into the parlor and sit down." She closed the pocket doors behind them. It made the room even stuffier, but Hilda was so uncomfortable, she thought a little more discomfort didn't matter much. "What is it?"

"I have remembered something." He had switched to Swedish. "You asked me to find out what I could about Mr. Vanderhoof, what he did after he left South Bend in disgrace."

"But he was not in disgrace! That is what made me so angry.

One of the things. He caused a man to be killed, and he ruined Clancy, and nothing happened to him at all."

"Please, Hilda, do not interrupt. I have little time. I thought, last night, about what you had asked, and decided that you had good reason to want to know. So I thought about who might be able to tell me about him, and I remembered some things that people were saying just after he left the city."

Hilda opened her mouth, thought better of it, and closed it again.

"I do not know if this is true, but it was being said then that Mr. Vanderhoof left the city, and the country, but that he came back very soon to New York. That is where he lived before he came here. And it was said that he became active in New York politics. Not, people said, the honest circles of New York politics."

Hilda's eyes widened. "Tammany Hall?" she whispered.

"That is what men at the factory were saying. Again I say, I do not know if it was true."

"But you will try to find out?"

"I will try. My sister, you will be careful?"

"I will take care." She put her hands protectively on her belly. "Of both of us."

Tammany Hall! Hilda felt cold. She saw Sven out and then went to the dining room and asked for coffee. "Lots of coffee, please, Eileen. And bacon and eggs. And toast." She needed comfort. Tammany Hall!

It was a name to produce anxiety and disgust. The notoriously corrupt political machine had run New York for decades, and it was whispered that there was almost nothing they would not do to keep their grip on their power and influence. It was lucrative power, public money being siphoned into private pockets in amounts that staggered the imagination.

But there was the other side of Tammany Hall, too, the benevolent side. Tammany politicians had gained much of their popularity by helping New York's poor. They aided the immigrants to find housing and work, and guided them to citizenship. True, they did it (quite openly) to secure their votes, but they did it. The politicians gave the poor feasts on holidays and provided free entertainment and saw to it that the children had shoes. And if their charity came out of pockets that had been lined with graft and corruption, those at the receiving end couldn't afford to care much. They shrugged and assumed those being robbed in this redistribution of wealth could afford it.

As Hilda's panicked reaction faded and she thought about Sven's information a bit more carefully, she was puzzled. Mr. Vanderhoof was a politician, certainly, but he was a Republican. Tammany Hall was aggressively Democratic. Mr. Vanderhoof had nothing but contempt for immigrants, as Hilda and her family had discovered when he defrauded them.

Why would he involved with Tammany Hall? *How* would he have gained entrance into those tightly controlled circles? Hilda was no expert on politics, but back when she had read the newspapers every day, she had learned a lot about the ways that dishonest politicians could manipulate affairs. Even discounting half of what was said in the South Bend *Tribune*, as Republican a paper as ever rolled off a press, she was sure that New York politicians, if crooked, were not stupid. They were extremely careful about who was admitted into their confidence.

Mr. Vanderhoof and Tammany. "No," said Hilda aloud.

"Ma'am?" said Eileen, startled. "Is somethin' wrong, ma'am?"

"Only in my head. I cannot understand… I think I must talk to Aunt Molly."

"You'll see her this afternoon, ma'am. At the funeral."

Hilda had already pushed her chair back and stood, to go to the telephone in the hall. She sat back down. "Oh. I forgot for a moment. I do not like funerals."

"Nobody does, ma'am."

Hilda thought about it. "But I cannot go to the church, of course, and then at the cemetery there will be no chance to talk. It is not the time, anyway. Aunt Molly will be upset, and there will be many people. No one liked Clancy very much, but everyone likes Uncle Dan and Aunt Molly."

"Will there not be a gatherin' at the house afterwards, then?" asked Eileen. She had little experience of funerals, but she knew about Irish wakes.

"Not this time, I think. It will be a sad, quiet time, with Uncle Dan ill. Cousin Mary will be there to help comfort Aunt Molly, but I do not think she will want anyone else."

The telephone rang, and Eileen, looking troubled, trotted off to answer it. She was back in a moment.

"It's Mrs. Malloy, ma'am. She said to tell you nothin's wrong, but she needs to speak to you."

Nothing's wrong! Hilda could almost laugh. Almost every possible thing was wrong. But Molly presumably meant that Uncle Dan had not taken a turn for the worse. Hilda lumbered to the phone on the wall, leaned toward it, and picked up the ear piece. "Aunt Molly?"

"Hilda, my dear, I know it's terribly early, but I wanted to ask you and Patrick to come back to the house with us after—after it's all over." Her voice shook for only a moment. "It will only be the family, but if you're feeling up to it, I'd like you to come."

Hilda hesitated. She needed to talk to Molly, but would there be any opportunity? And few ordeals could be worse than meeting members of an extended, and extensive, Irish family, especially in her condition. But—"I will come, Aunt Molly. And Patrick will come, of course. I will not look very nice."

"None of us will care how you look, child. It's your company we want, not your dress."

Hilda made some reply, rang off, and hung the ear piece on the hook. She had wanted to ask Molly if there might be an opportunity to speak, alone, but she had not thought it appropriate.

Who else, then? Who else could give her the information she needed? Who else could give her an idea that might start her brain working?

If she was looking into politics, she needed to talk to a politician. Uncle Dan was the only one she knew, and he was out of the question, at least for now.

Patrick knew the mayor, but she did not, and even if she had, there were enough rumors about corruption in South Bend politics that she wasn't about to talk to someone she didn't "know and trust" as Aunt Molly had said.

She knew and trusted her Pastor Borg, but he was, as Gudrun frequently said, "as innocent as a babe unborn." He knew all about evil from reading about it in the Bible, but she seriously doubted if he had even as much personal experience with it as Hilda had, herself.

Father Faherty, at St. Patrick's? Hilda knew him, and trusted him, but though he might be slightly more worldly than her own pastor, the same objection held. She needed someone who had intimate acquaintance with wrongdoing, someone incorruptible who yet knew about corruption—

Someone like an honest policeman.

How could she get in touch with Sergeant Lefkowicz?

A telephone call to the police station was out of the question. Not all the police in town were honest, and Hilda didn't know for sure which were which.

It was risky to send a message by Mr. O'Rourke. He knew too many people. Word might get around.

She certainly couldn't send Eileen. The police station was no place for a young girl.

She could send John Bolton. He came to mind when she had thought of Eileen and the possible hazards to her virtue at the police station. John might be of slightly dubious morality, but his honesty had never been in question, nor his loyalty to Hilda.

She went to the telephone. The butler at Tippecanoe Place would be displeased, but the time to worry about such small concerns was past.

"Hello, is this Mr. Williams? This is Hilda Johansson. Hilda Cavanaugh, I mean. Yes, I am fine, thank you. Mr. Williams, I need to speak to John. Have they put the telephone in the carriage house yet? Oh, that is a pity. Yes, I know it must make much extra work for you. There is no hurry, but when you can, would you ask him to phone me? I cannot go out just now, you will understand. Thank you."

Hilda knew perfectly well that in her position as a lady of her own household, she should address the Tippecanoe Place butler as "Williams," but she found it hard to do. She no longer felt subservient to him, but old habits die hard. Besides, he was more apt to do as she asked if she spoke to him respectfully.

Sure enough, it was only a few minutes before the phone rang. Hilda picked it up, and when she heard John's voice at the other end, said, "Excuse me for one minute, please." She went to the kitchen door and peeked in. Mrs. O'Rourke, her husband, and Eileen were all sitting at the table having some iced tea and cookies. Good. She went back to the phone.

"John, can anyone hear you?" she asked, keeping her voice low.

"Williams is around, trying to eavesdrop. He wants to find out why you called me."

"Then say nothing but yes and no, and make up some story for him later."

"Yes, I can do that."

He certainly could, thought Hilda. John was almost as accomplished a liar as Hilda herself. "I want you to do something for me. Does anyone in the family need the carriage this morning?"

"Not for a while."

"Probably it is too hot for anyone to want to go out. Good. Then I would like you to go down to the police station and find Sergeant Lefkowicz, and ask him to come to see me. You can use the carriage or walk, I do not care—but it is very hot to walk, I think."

"You're right about that, for sure."

"It must be this morning, because the funeral is this afternoon." She didn't need to say whose funeral. Everyone in town know that. "Can you do that for me? And perhaps, if the family does not need you, you could come with him?" For she had just remembered that John had some acquaintance with shady dealings, and might also be of some help.

"Yes, I can do that."

"Good. I will have something cold for you both when you come."

Well, that was done. When John said he would do something, he did it. Now all she had to do was try to figure out an approach to the sergeant.

The last time they had spoken, he had told her in no uncertain terms to leave Vanderhoof alone. He had acted strange at the very mention of the name.

That meant he knew something, or suspected something. If they could work together, as they had in the past, perhaps they could learn more. Enough, maybe, to bring Vanderhoof to justice. Enough, maybe, to end the streak of horrible train wrecks and fires, to stop the deaths—if he was, indeed, the mastermind behind all the tragedies.

But it meant working together, of that she was sure. And the sergeant wanted Hilda out of the picture.

How could she convince him otherwise? What evidence did she have that would be of value in the investigation? What sources of information could she bring to the matter? In short, could she really help?

In the past, her assistance had been mostly with the servants, those invisible beings who came and went in the homes of the rich, did their jobs, spoke little to their employers, and knew virtually everything that went on in those households. Hilda had been one of them, had gossiped with them, had garnered information that the police could never have extracted.

Her situation was different now. She was exiled from her former world by virtue of her marriage to a well-to-do merchant, however "nouveau" Patrick's "riche" position might be. But because she was nouveau riche, she was also exiled from the society of most of the wealthy women in town. She knew well that they had their gossip circles, their sources of information they would never pass on to the police, but she was not yet a part of their world. Perhaps, since she was an immigrant, she never would be.

But Kristina will be, she told herself fiercely. The baby

kicked, and Hilda patted her belly. "You will live in a fine house," she whispered, "and go to good schools, and you will be on their committees and go to their parties and marry one of their sons. If you want to," she added, for the program she had just outlined sounded, actually, a bit dull for a daughter of Hilda Johansson.

However. Back to her problem. How was she to persuade Sergeant Lefkowicz that she was a valuable asset to his investigation? With no entrée into the servant world—and then she stopped and smacked herself on the head.

She had forgotten. She still had contact with servants. There was Norah, who worked for Mrs. Hibberd. There was her own family. Elsa worked at Tippecanoe Place, doing the job Hilda used to do, and Freya was just down the street at Mrs. Cushing's. Gudrun had worked for the Birdsells for years.

And there was, oh yes, best of all, there was John Bolton. Trusted coachman at Tippecanoe Place, trusted friend to Hilda. Well, trusted, anyway, in everything that didn't have to do with the fair sex.

With a pleased expression on her face, Hilda rang for Mrs. O'Rourke, to ask if there was any strawberry ice cream left.

Can I see another's grief
And not seek for kind relief?

—William Blake,
  "On Another's Sorrow," 1789

23

WHEN JOHN ARRIVED, however, he came alone. Hilda was a little worried about receiving him. Patrick wouldn't be best pleased. Eileen showed him in, and Hilda met him in the hall. "Where is Sergeant Lefkowicz?" she asked anxiously.

"John, it's so good of you to come. Let me take your hat," he said, one eyebrow raised.

"Yes, yes, it is good of you, but where is the sergeant?"

"Strange as it may seem, he has one or two other things to do besides waiting for you to send for him. He was out. They said he might be back in an hour or two. Or he might not, if the man he was after wasn't waiting with his hands stretched out for the handcuffs.... Do sit down, John." Head tilted to one side, he looked from Hilda to the parlor.

Hilda capitulated. "Oh, very well, you may come in, but just for a minute. Patrick would not like it."

"So Patrick's telling you what to do these days, eh?" John said when he had seated himself comfortably. "I never thought I'd see the day."

"Patrick looks after me. He cares about my reputation," said Hilda primly. "He does not tell me what to do."

"Well, forgive me for referring to a delicate subject, but just what sort of hanky-panky does he think you're apt to get up to in your—er—at this stage of your life?"

Hilda set her lips, and then relaxed and laughed. This was John, and there was no changing him. "He does not think I would do anything wrong, not really, not ever. He is just jealous, because he knows we are friends. It is all right. I do not mind. He will not be angry when I explain."

"So you've got him twisted 'round your little finger, have you?"

Hilda was not familiar with the idiom, but its meaning was plain enough. She smiled. "Yes. I am good at twisting."

John roared with laughter. "And modest, too. Now are you going to tell me what's so all-fired important that you have to talk to the police about it, and you don't want Patrick to know?"

"It is not that I wish to keep a secret from Patrick. It is to protect him, John. To protect us all." She became serious again.

She told him her theory about Vanderhoof and his possible connection with all that had happened in the past few months. "And the sergeant does not want me to talk to anyone about Mr. Vanderhoof. He says it is not safe. Everyone says this, and maybe they are right. Probably they are right. But I am tired of being told I must sit back and do nothing. This is my family involved, John. Clancy was Patrick's cousin, and even if no one in the family liked him, he was still family."

"And besides that, you're bored silly trying to do nothing but sit around and wait for that baby to be born."

"You are right, John."

"I'm always right. Just like you. But what, my fine lady, makes you think you can figure out what the police and the Pinkertons and the railroad detectives and all haven't? Time was when you'd sneak out and go around snooping, and then you'd put two and two together, and *poof!* Mystery solved! But your sneaking days are over for a while. You have to sweet-talk me into running your errands for you, even."

"But I can still think, John! I must have other people learn things for me, but I can still add up the things I learn. And that is why I need your help for more than errands."

John gave her a sharp look. Then he looked at the clock on the mantel. "I've got to be getting back. Mrs. Clem and Mrs. George both have luncheons to go to, in different directions. But I have ten minutes. Tell me what you want me to do."

"I want you to find out what the servants say about Mr. Vanderhoof. Do you know anyone who used to work for him, when he lived in South Bend?"

"That I do, and I could tell you in one word what they thought of him, except it's a word I wouldn't repeat to a lady."

Hilda's twinkle returned for a moment. "I could guess, I think."

"Then your English is better than it should be—or maybe it's worse. But you want me to find out what's being said about him now."

"Yes, because the servants will know what their ladies and gentlemen are saying. I want to know where he has been since he left here. I want to know what he has been doing. I want to know how much money he has, and how he got it, and—"

"Here, now! You think servants will know all that?"

"I know they will, or most of it. Or they will know what people say, and if we put together enough of what people say, we can come near to the truth. *Ja*?"

"*Ja*. By the way, that's a very fetching thing you're wearing. What d'you call it?"

Hilda had until that moment forgotten that she was clad in what was, essentially, underwear. "It is the new style," she said, head high. "Now go, John. Patrick will be home for lunch soon, I think. You will bring Sergeant Lefkowicz when he is able to come?"

"I'll do my best. I've a job to do, you know, employers to report to. I'm not a lady of leisure, like you."

"But you are a man, with more freedom than I ever had as a servant. More freedom, in some ways, than I have now, even when I am not—even before. But John, remember I told you that there are risks. We are being watched, I think, Patrick and I and our family and friends. I have taken Andy into my house, because men are following him. You will be careful?"

"Now, you know me, Hilda. As many lives as a cat, and very fond of my own skin, thank you. I'll be back as soon as I can, and I'll get Lefkowicz to you one way or another."

"But this morning," she reminded him. "Or late this after-noon. There is the funeral."

"You're going? I'd have thought..."

"Aunt Molly wants me." It was sufficient reason.

Hilda dithered through the rest of the morning, while Eileen sewed, frantically converting two of Hilda's old maid's uniforms into one mourning costume for a very pregnant lady. It wasn't very stylish or attractive, but at least it covered her decently. Her makeshift dress would have done, if she had stayed in the back-ground as planned. As she was going to be seen, she had to be clad in decent black.

Patrick came home for an early lunch. He had left Andy at the store. "For neither of us will be here this afternoon, and he'll be safer there. The store's closed for the funeral, of course, out of respect, but there's plenty of work to do. It's better than him hangin' around here at loose ends." After picking at a little food, Patrick hurried away to the Malloys' house to accompany them to St. Patrick's.

Hilda ate a little, too. She had no appetite, but she knew she must eat. She was growing more and more nervous about the gathering at the Malloys', and snapped at Eileen when the poor little maid stuck her with a pin she had forgotten to remove from a sleeve. Eileen didn't take offence. She understood her mistress very well.

After an eternity of waiting, Patrick was back with the car-riage. He helped Hilda in, and they joined the waiting procession to City Cemetery.

Hilda had never been in the Catholic section before and felt a little uneasy about it, but it was not after all a church. O'Rourke pulled the carriage as close as possible to the grave.

"You'll be all right, darlin'? You'll not be too hot?" said Pat-rick as he stepped down.

Hilda felt exactly like a turkey, slowly roasting in the oven of her voluminous black garments. "I am fine, Patrick," she lied. "Go to your family."

The graveside service was in Latin, of course, but it followed the pattern of the familiar Swedish service, so Hilda could more or less understand what was happening. She bowed her head in her own prayers as the family scattered earth on the coffin. Her prayers were for Uncle Dan and Aunt Molly, not for Clancy. He had chosen his own way, and that way had led to this: murdered in the prime of life. His fate now was up to God, and Hilda hoped God would be merciful, for Clancy was certainly in need of mercy.

By the time the brief service was over, Hilda was genuinely about to faint. She was grateful for the tiny breeze stirred by the movement of the carriage through the streets, but of course O'Rourke kept the horses to a slow, decorous pace. Hilda would have welcomed a brisk trot.

Riggs had gone with the family to the cemetery, but had hurried home to see to final preparations of the funeral meal. He answered the door for Patrick and Hilda. "A sad day, Mr. Patrick," he said solemnly.

There was a time when Hilda would have felt like retorting that the day Clancy Malloy was out of the picture was a day for rejoicing. She knew better now. "But now perhaps Aunt Molly and Uncle Dan can begin to remember the good times," she said gently, remembering that Riggs, too, had lost a son.

"That's very true, Miss Hilda," he said, his voice trembling a little. "Very true." The doorbell rang again. "The family is in the drawing room, if you will excuse me."

Patrick took Hilda's arm in a firm grip and turned her toward the drawing room.

A table was spread with cold delicacies. Hilda had eaten little, but she was too hot and miserable to be hungry. Patrick found a seat for her and presently Aunt Molly, who had been chatting to a cousin, came to her.

"Please don't try to stand up, dear. I can see that you're uncomfortable, but—" she lowered her voice "—you need not have worried about your dress. You look quite nice."

Hilda wished she could say the same for Molly. Stark black did not suit her, even though the dress was beautifully made in the latest fashion, and fitted her slender figure to perfection. And Molly's face was strained and drawn. "Aunt Molly, is Uncle Dan all right? I don't see him."

"No, the doctor made him go right back to bed as soon as we came back from the cemetery. He shouldn't have gone to the grave, but—" Molly made a resigned gesture.

"I think maybe that later, when he is not so upset, the service will be a comfort to him. It is—it makes an end."

Molly kissed Hilda on the cheek. "You are a dear child, and I'm so grateful you're here. Now I'm going to have Agnes bring you some ice cream and some iced tea, and when all these people have gone, we can talk."

"Oh, yes, I wanted to talk to you! But this is maybe not a good time for you. You are tired, and sad, and I do not want to bother you. Maybe tomorrow?"

Molly smiled a little. "If you want to talk about what I think you want to talk about, there aren't all that many tomorrows left before you'll be fully occupied with other concerns. I'll be back as soon as I can."

Hilda sighed, but inaudibly. All she really wanted in this world was to take off her clothes, sponge herself with cool water, and lie in front of an electric fan. All these things being impossible, she accepted the tray of cold food Agnes brought her and tried to wait patiently.

Cousin Mary came over and introduced herself, and they spoke for a few minutes about burials and births (Hilda's imminent delivery being obvious), and then Mary drifted away and Hilda was left alone to wait some more.

All trials come to an end eventually. After what seemed to Hilda like hours of discomfort, broken twice by entirely necessary trips to the lavatory, the guests finally departed, leaving Hilda and Patrick alone with Aunt Molly and Cousin Mary, who kissed Molly and begged to be excused. "Mama, I'm sorry, but I can't stay awake another minute. Hilda, it was a great pleasure meeting you at last, and I wish you well in your confinement. I'm sure you'll be well looked after. Patrick, if I don't see you again before I have to go home, thank you for all you're doing for Mama and Papa." And then Patrick decided to go upstairs and see if Uncle Dan was sleeping or ready for talk, and it was just Hilda and Molly, each of them with a tall, frosty glass of iced tea.

"Are you sure you are not too tired?" asked Hilda. She herself was so weary she could have slept on the floor.

"I am, and so are you, but here we are, and we might as well talk. What do you need to know?"

"Well—I hope it will not make you angry, but there are things I do not understand."

Molly nodded, and waited.

"It is about politics, you see, and I do not know a great deal about that."

"Politics!" Molly's eyes opened a little wider. "You surprise me. Why this sudden interest in politics?"

Hilda leaned forward as much as she was able. "Aunt Molly, I think that, somehow, politics is below all the bad things that have happened."

It took Molly a moment to translate that. "At the bottom of everything, do you mean?"

"Yes, that is it. Always I make mistakes in English."

"Pooh! Your English is excellent, my dear. It's only some of the idioms that give you grief. But I don't understand. What do fires and train wrecks have to do with politics?"

"That is what I do not know. But Sven told me something today, something so odd that I do not understand it at all. I have asked him to try to learn about Mr. Vanderhoof, where he went and what he did after he left South Bend three years ago." She explained her interest in Vanderhoof, mentioning Clancy as little as possible. "And Sven has had no chance to talk to anyone yet, but he told me that he remembered people saying, when Mr. Vanderhoof had been gone only a little while, that he had gone to

New York. And that—this is what I do not understand—that he had become involved with Tammany Hall."

Molly's eyebrows rose. "Tammany Hall! My dear, you can't have heard him properly."

"That is what he said. I could hardly believe it."

"I don't believe it," said Molly flatly. "Vanderhoof's as crooked a politician as ever rigged an election, but he's a Republican. And he's Dutch, or his ancestors were. Who said he joined up with Tammany?"

"I do not know, but I will ask Sven when I see him again. But Aunt Molly, you knew Mr. Vanderhoof. I never even saw him, even though our money went to him—our money that he stole. I know he is a bad man, but I would like to know more about him."

"Well." Molly took a sip of iced tea and sat back. They were in the parlor, since Hilda had decided she was no longer fit to be seen on the front porch, and the room was stifling despite the open windows. "He came to South Bend only a few years ago, from New York. It does make some sense that he might have gone back there, though I understood he was leaving the country after that terrible affair here."

"But he could have come back."

"He certainly could. He had a good deal of money, and we used to wonder, Mr. Malloy and I, where he got it all. He didn't make it in his harness business, we were sure of that. Oh, I think he had some investments here and there, and there were rumors about graft—you know what that is?"

Hilda nodded. "I know a little. It means a politician taking money that belongs to the people and using it for himself."

"More or less. Vanderhoof never held elected office in South Bend, but he was on various committees, and he had influence. If he helped someone get elected, he'd get a nice little present, Mr. Malloy thought. And he certainly did help men get elected, by fair means or foul, but nothing was ever proved against him. He's a clever man."

"He is a wicked man," said Hilda hotly. "He had Mr. Bishop killed. He had those miners killed—"

"That was never proved either, Hilda. The mine explosion was an accident, according to the owners."

"That is the trouble. He does these evil things, and then nothing happens to him. And we know he was the one who—" She stopped abruptly. *Who corrupted Clancy*, she had been about to say, but she could not. Not to Clancy's mother, not with Clancy just a few hours in his grave.

Aunt Molly pressed her lips together and looked down, but said nothing.

"What I cannot understand," pursued Hilda, "what I cannot make sense of, is how all these things could be tied together. Train wrecks, fires, murders—what could be the reason for all these terrible events? If it is Mr. Vanderhoof who is below—who is at the bottom of everything, or even if it is someone else, *why?* What could anyone gain from such things?"

"Oh, child, there's always something to be gained from evil. Sadly, that's the way the world is. If you know anything at all about Tammany Hall, and you talk as though you do, you should know that. Those men—Boss Tweed years ago, and Mr. Murphy and Big Tim Sullivan and the rest now—they do what they do for two reasons: they want money and they want power. That, in the end, is what all dishonest politicians want. That was what Vanderhoof wanted when he—when he trapped Clancy in his snare. And if he has come back, that is what he wants now."

Hilda shook her head in bewilderment. "I know those things, Aunt Molly. I know that men do evil to get what they want. I hear about it in church every Sunday, how the wicked flourish like the green bay tree. What I do not know is how a train wreck could give Mr. Vanderhoof—or someone else—what he wants."

"That," said Aunt Molly, standing, "I can't tell you. Saints be praised, Mr. Malloy's an honest man, and out of politics for good now. You put that brain of yours to work, child, and see if you can come up with an answer. But don't go around asking questions about Tammany Hall to anyone you don't know and trust. This is a fearsome business."

"I know it is, Aunt Molly. I think I should not have started to ask questions, but now that I have started, I cannot stop. I am not sure Patrick understands that, but you do."

"Yes, my dear, I do. May the saints be with you."

She kissed Hilda and went upstairs.

Union gives strength.

—Aesop, "The Bundle of Sticks,"
circa 500 B.C.

24

ILDA HAD HAD no chance to talk to Patrick about John Bolton calling earlier, but she was quick to tell him as soon as they were home. They had both reached that stage of mental exhaustion that prevented rest, and she was afraid to delay lest he hear about it from someone else. "I gave him a message for some of the other servants," she said. O'Rourke had brought Andy home, and he was having a snack in the kitchen, so Hilda kept her voice low. "I asked him to learn what he could of Mr. Vanderhoof's activities."

She braced herself for the inevitable frown of disapproval.

"I know you think you have to do this, Hilda." His use of her name instead of an endearment warned her that this was serious. "And I've decided I'm not goin' to stand in your way. You may be right that goin' ahead with it isn't as bad as—well, you ought to know what Andy told me this mornin'."

He related the story of the kitten.

"But—but that is so—a kitten! A soft, trusting little thing that never did him any harm. Patrick, that is—" She was near tears.

"I know. It doesn't seem as bad as killin' people in train wrecks and fires and all, but in a way—well, I thought you should know what kind of devil you're up against, whether it's Vanderhoof or somebody else. And you just might be onto somethin', thinkin' he's running the show. I heard somethin' else this mornin' that'll interest you."

Hilda's eyes widened. "Tell me."

"It was just one of the customers talkin'. We were busy today, with school startin' again soon, and lots of mothers had their kids with 'em, so it was pretty noisy down on the floor. But there were some men over in the corner lookin' at collars and ties, and I heard one of 'em say, 'Well, if old Cornelius says it'll be good for business, that's good enough for me. He's a pretty sharp man.'"

"I do not understand. Who is 'old Cornelius'?"

"It's a kind of nickname for Vanderhoof. I don't know that I ever heard his real name, but people around here got to callin' him Cornelius—like Cornelius Vanderbilt, you know."

"No."

"The railroad man?"

"No." Hilda's impatience was growing.

"Oh. Well, he was one of the richest men in the country. In the world, I guess. He made his pile building railroads. Died about—I dunno, maybe thirty or forty years ago. Anyway, he was Dutch, and Vanderhoof is Dutch, and the name's similar, so…"

"But Patrick, what do you think that man meant? The one at the store? And who was he?"

"I didn't get close enough to see his face, and I didn't recognize his voice. I only heard that one remark about 'old Cornelius' bein' sharp, and then one of the other men—there were three or four of 'em—he said, 'Sharp enough to cut himself, I reckon.' And then Miss Morgan came down to tell me I was wanted on the phone, and by the time I could get back down to the floor, the men were gone."

"But you are sure they were talking about Mr. Vanderhoof?"

"Darlin', I'm not sure of anythin'. But whoever it was they meant, they were talkin' like they'd heard from him not so long ago."

"And that would maybe mean he is in town."

"Maybe."

Hilda chewed on that for a little while and then changed the subject. "And how is Andy getting along? He works well?"

"He works hard, and he learns fast. I put him to work under Jenkins, who had him restockin' the shelves. I told you we were busy, so the goods were half flyin' out the door. It didn't take that lad but an hour or so, Jenkins said, before he knew where 'most everythin' was in the back room, and then he was everywhere at once, seein' where a department was about to run out of somethin' and then runnin' to get it, and never gettin' in the way while he was at it, either. He's as good as two or three of the kind of boys we've had before."

Hilda saw that the kitchen door was ajar. Patrick followed her glance, and saw the door close gently. "Won't hurt him to know we think a lot of him," Patrick said just above a whisper. "That boy's seen some hard times. I'd like to give him a hand up—like Dan gave me."

"Then we must keep him safe," said Hilda in the same low tone.

Patrick went back to the store after he had rested for a little.

"But I will keep Andy here with me for the rest of the day," said Hilda. "I do not like him going back and forth any more often than he must."

Patrick kissed her and rushed off.

෴

Sergeant Lefkowicz came to see Hilda late that afternoon. John was not with him. Hilda regretted that. She thought that John, who could "charm a bird out of a tree," as the Tippecanoe Place cook used to say, would be a powerful ally in an argument with the sergeant. However, John was apparently needed elsewhere, so Hilda must make do. She showed him into the parlor and explained that Patrick had gone back to the store for an hour or so.

"Miss Hilda, I can't stay long. The chief is up in arms about some of the roughnecks hanging around the train depot, and he wants me there to see about them."

"Good. That is good. I need to know about the train station, and the trains, and the men who work on them. But also, Sergeant, I need to know about politics."

"Politics?" He looked blank. "There's no election this year, you know. Not much going on in politics right now."

"That is not what I mean. I do not care about elections. No, I do care, and I want some day to be able to vote, but that is not what I need to know now. You will not like this, Sergeant, but you will please to sit down and have some lemonade and listen. Or there is beer…"

"Not when I'm on duty, Miss Hilda. I like beer, but seems like it goes right to my head when it's so hot. And sometimes it makes me even hotter. And like I said, I can't stay but a minute."

"Yes. I will be quick." She rang the bell for Eileen and settled back into her chair. "Sergeant, you have told me not to try to find out anything about Mr. Vanderhoof, but I must. Patrick knows I am doing this," she added in a hurry. "And he knows why. The first reason is that my family has been hurt, very badly. Patrick's family is mine now, and Clancy was not a good man, but he was Patrick's cousin. I cannot let him be killed and do nothing. The second reason is that I think it is safer now to continue my search than to end it. I think I must find the men who are doing these things before they find me—and stop me."

"And isn't that just what I said? That it's not safe for you? That's why I won't—"

Hilda held up a hand. "Wait, Sergeant. I have not yet said all I want to say. If you still say no when I have finished, then I will do what I have to do without you, but it will be better if we work together. Because you see, I still have ways of finding out things that you do not. I still have the servants."

"But I thought—I mean, now you're not—"

"Yes. That is what I thought, too, until my head got straight. Now I am a lady with servants of my own. But there is still my family, and there are still my friends, my good friends. My sisters, and Norah Murphy—Norah O'Neill, I mean—and John Bolton, they will all talk to me. And others talk to them. They will not talk to policemen, Sergeant, you know that. If we work together, you with your sources of information and I with mine, we can learn much."

Sergeant Lefkowicz was silent, thinking hard. Then he said, "Miss Hilda, I hear what you're saying, and you have a point. But I don't think you understand what you're up against here. This is not a local crime, a local criminal. We've dealt with that kind before, you and I. This is bigger. Powerful people are mixed up in it. We're little people, both of us. What can we do against a plot that maybe implicates men all over the country?"

"I have thought this, too, Sergeant," said Hilda. "I am one woman, a woman near her time. I cannot even leave the house now. You are one man, and even though you have authority—as I do not—it is limited. It may be that what you say is true, that we can do nothing. But do we not have to try? Can we sit and hide in our houses and offices and be comfortable while boys like Andy walk in fear, and men like Daniel Malloy are worried into illness, and railroad workers and young bank clerks are killed, burnt to death? If there is anything, anything at all we can do, must we not try to do it?"

Hilda's voice had grown loud with passion. Eileen, a tray with a pitcher and glasses in her hands, stood frozen in the hall just outside the parlor door.

Hilda spoke again, in a lower tone. "Sergeant, you know something about Mr. Vanderhoof that you have not told me. I would like to know what it is."

Sergeant Lefkowicz cleared his throat. "I have to go, Miss Hilda, or the chief'll have my head. But I'll be back. I'll tell you what little I know, and I'll find out all I can for you."

"And I will do the same for you." Hilda gave him her hand, and he took it. A bargain sealed.

Eileen moved to let him pass, the tray still in her hands, and tears in her eyes. When he had gone, she pulled herself together and walked into the parlor.

"Cook had to make fresh lemonade, and I was too late. I'm sorry, ma'am. But, oh, ma'am! That was the bravest thing I ever heard anybody say! And I'll do what I can, too, ma'am. The delivery boys and that, they talk to me. I'll ask them what they know about the fires and the wrecks. Nobody pays attention to us kids."

Hilda had almost forgotten how young Eileen was. A servant from the age of twelve, she was only fourteen now, though some of her experiences had aged her beyond her years. Fourteen. Just

Andy's age, and Erik's. Hilda felt a pang. "Eileen, I will worry about you. You will not say anything foolish?"

Eileen looked her straight in the eye. "Ma'am, you don't like it when people tell you to be careful. You're smart enough to make your own decisions, if you'll forgive me bein' so bold as to say it. So am I smart enough. And all this that's happenin' is bad enough that a little risk is worth takin'. If you don't mind my sayin' so."

Hilda took a deep breath. "Eileen, you are so much like me you could almost be my sister."

"Me, ma'am?" Eileen looked astonished.

"You. Oh, we are different—you are Irish and I am Swedish, you are Catholic and I am Protestant, you are still a working girl and I have been lucky and no longer have to work—but we are both brave, we are both stubborn, we are both smart—and we are both some of the little people."

She gestured to the chair next to hers. "Eileen, put your tray down and sit for a moment. I want to tell you a story." Eileen sat, and Hilda went on. "This is a very old story that our papa told us children once, about a lion and a mouse. The lion had once saved the life of the mouse. Then the lion was caught in a trap, or tied up, or something. I forget that part. But because the lion had once helped the mouse, the mouse was not afraid to help the lion. It found some other mice who also were not afraid, and they nibbled and nibbled at the ropes until the lion was free.

"We are mice, Eileen, and this lion has never helped us, so we do not want to free this lion but to tie him up. But I think maybe, like those mice, we can do big things if we all work together. Go and do what you need to do, with my blessing, but remember that if you are hurt, I will never forgive myself."

Eileen whisked away, glowing with importance. Hilda sat and sipped lemonade and sighed.

This passive role of waiting for information to arrive was not to her taste. She much preferred to go out and gather the information for herself, but since she could not, she must wait. And while she was waiting, she would think about what to do next.

And while she was thinking, she might as well be comfortable. She went upstairs to take off her funeral garb and put on cooler clothes.

When Patrick came home for supper he found her sound asleep on the settee. He pulled up a chair beside her. He was very hot and tired. "Had a good nap, darlin'?"

She opened her eyes. "Oh, Patrick, I did not mean to sleep, but I was very tired. And I had dreadful dreams. About lions and mice, and fires…"

"It's too hot, me girl, that's what's the matter with you. Me, I'm wrung out. But the paper says it'll be cooler tomorrow. There was a big storm in Chicago last night, so maybe we'll have one tonight. It sure feels like it." He ran his handkerchief across his forehead.

"Take off your coat and your collar, Patrick. We have no guests. For once you can eat supper in your shirtsleeves. Look at how I am dressed!"

"You've got a better excuse," he retorted, but he went upstairs and did as she suggested. That, and a cool wash, restored him to some degree. He came down and requested a glass of beer.

"Sergeant Lefkowicz says beer makes him hotter," Hilda said as she rang for Eileen.

"When did you see him?" Patrick was too tired to argue about her entertaining yet another man, and alone.

"This afternoon. He is going to help us, Patrick! We are all going to work together, like the mice, and maybe we will trap the lion."

Of course Patrick had to have that explained to him, and when Hilda had done so, he threw back his head and laughed. (Eileen had brought his beer by that time.) "Mice, is it? To bring down a lion. Well, they call Tammany Hall the Tiger, so maybe the other side is a lion, at that."

"The other side?" Hilda was suddenly alert. "What do you mean?"

"I heard some more talk this afternoon. Now that you've got

me listenin' for it, people say more than you'd think they would, if they were smart."

"Many men are not smart," said Hilda complacently. "Tell me."

"Hah! These weren't men! In fact one of 'em was Mrs. What's-er-name—wife of that new banker—I'll think of it in a minute—"

"Wife of a banker? Then she might know something about what had been happening at the banks."

"Hewlitt, that's the name. He's got that new bank on the corner of Lafayette and Jefferson, Midwest State Bank. Anyway, his wife was buyin' dress goods, fancy silks and satins, and lace, and so on. Looked like she was goin' to have a big party. And there were other ladies with her, and I heard one of them say somethin' about Tammany Hall, so you can bet I perked up my ears pretty good. And then Mrs. Hewlitt, she said, 'Well,' she said, 'it's about time we had a few men on *our* side. I'm sick and tired of hearing about the plight of the poor. They have nobody but themselves to blame.' Or somethin' like that. I was losin' me temper by that time, and maybe I don't remember it just the way she said it."

If Patrick's temper had been roused, Hilda's was at the boiling point instantly. "The poor! What does she know about the poor, a banker's wife! What does she know about how hard it is to find work that pays enough to feed your family, and then it is maybe so dangerous it might kill you—"

"That's what riled me up, too," said Patrick, calm now that he was rested and refreshed. "That's why I had to leave before I started throwin' things, and I didn't hear the rest of what she said."

"You should have thrown things," Hilda said, still hot. "You should have told her that she knows nothing, nothing—"

"And then I'd have lost her and her friends as customers, and Uncle Dan would have somethin' to say about that. Too much of that kind o' performance and I'd be out lookin' for one o' those jobs meself, darlin', and then where would you and Kevin be?"

"Oh." Hilda was deflated. "I forgot that you are important now and cannot always say what you think."

"That's not bein' important, darlin' girl. It's just bein' sensible. If you or I, either of us, said what we think all the time, we'd make enemies of the whole town."

Hilda sighed. "I said what I thought when I was a servant."

"Not to that butler, you didn't. Not to Mrs. George. Mrs. Clem I'll grant you, but then you never got mad at her. You've had to learn to hold your tongue, just like everybody else, and just like I had to with that woman. But I wish I'd held my temper, too, and maybe I'd've heard somethin' useful."

"What did she mean, do you think, about someone on our side?"

"On the side of the rich, I reckon. Like Tammany's been on the side of the poor, or at least pretended to be. Not that it stopped them from linin' their own pockets, nor it won't stop these others from linin' theirs."

Hilda nodded sadly. "And we still do not have a hint of who 'these others' might be."

The desire of power in excess caused the angels to fall.

—Francis Bacon, *Essays,* 1625

T HE THUNDERSTORM ARRIVED, as promised, in the middle of the night. It woke everyone in the house, but after the lightning had become distant flashes and the thunder had died to a rumble, they all fell into the best sleep they had known in weeks. Hilda woke early, refreshed and feeling almost comfortable.

"What are you goin' to do today, darlin'?" asked Patrick as he heaved himself out of bed with a mighty yawn.

Hilda stretched. "Nothing, I suppose. What can I do? I cannot go out, even though it is such a beautiful day."

"You could go for a carriage ride." Patrick was still extremely proud of having his own carriage and coachman. "The streets are paved between here and Howard Park, so you wouldn't get jounced around too much, and it'd do you good to get some fresh air."

Hilda sat up. "That is an idea. That is a good idea, Patrick! No one would see me in the carriage, or anyway they would not see the way I was dressed. I will do that, as soon as Mr. O'Rourke comes back from taking you and Andy to the store."

Forever afterward, Hilda would swear that a simple ride to the park and back was all she intended to do that morning.

She took her time dressing. She had a choice between her mourning garb and her dressing gown-cum-dress. The makeshift won out, since it was far looser and more comfortable. Eileen had somehow found the time to wash and iron it, so it was fresh. And the morning was cool enough that a concealing shawl was welcome. She felt almost respectable-looking when she sallied forth. Respectable, and lighthearted. Today she was going to put her terrible problems away from her for a little. Today was a time for enjoying life.

Everyone was in a better mood after the storm. Mr. O'Rourke whistled as he helped Hilda into the carriage. Even the horses seemed happy, their gait brisk, their steps high. People were out on the streets again, children playing, women shopping, men gathering in little knots to talk business or, Hilda thought, to gossip. Men gossiped just as much as women, in her opinion.

What, she wondered, were they gossiping about?

And with that vagrant thought, her troubles were back with her, crowding in, drowning out the glorious sunshine and crisp breeze, the shouts of the children and the fresh scents of damp earth and wet grass and flowers revived after their long thirst.

What were the men saying, these businessmen standing together in their tight groups of three and four, or leaning against the rails of the Jefferson Street Bridge, or sitting on a park bench? Were they talking about the weather, or the price of coal, or their investments, or which tailor made the best suits for the least money?

Or were they, as they leaned closer and lowered their voices and glanced aside to see who might be listening, were they talking about fires and train wrecks and the men who caused them?

Mr. O'Rourke was turning the carriage into the Howard Park drive when Hilda leaned forward. "I have changed my mind, O'Rourke," she said, using the name he preferred, though it always made her cringe with its implication of condescension. "I would like to visit Mrs. Malloy."

The coachman nodded, happy enough to make a detour on such a day. There was a great deal of work awaiting him at the house, and the longer he stayed away, the less of it he would have to do today. Not that he approved of ladies in Mrs. Cavanaugh's condition going out gallivanting. If Mrs. O'Rourke had ever tried something like that when she was expecting, he'd have put a stop to it. But it was no business of his what his flighty mistress chose to do. And if she stayed long enough, he could have a nice chat with Donald, the Malloys' coachman, a good enough fellow even if he was English.

It was too early for a call, of course. And far too soon after the funeral. These Swedes didn't seem to know the rules. Though you'd think a housemaid would remember that sort of thing, even if she was a "lady" now. Grumbling cheerfully to himself, O'Rourke drove the carriage back across the bridge and guided the horses left to get to Colfax Avenue.

Hilda was quite well aware of the rules, but her need to talk was urgent. Molly herself had said that Hilda had not many more days to pursue her inquiries. Hilda wanted to talk about her problem. She wanted, really, to talk to Sven, but that was impossible at this time of day. It would not have troubled her greatly that it might be unwise to bother her brother at work on a busy day. She could justify that, citing the importance of her quest. But go to the factory, to the paint shop, in her condition and her state of near-undress? Never. So it was to Aunt Molly that she went to unburden herself. If that good lady did not wish to see a visitor, Hilda would understand, but she hoped that her visit would be welcomed.

Molly was only mildly surprised to see Hilda. She had accepted her new niece's unconventional behavior long ago, and realized that the improved weather would make Hilda restless and eager to get out.

"Hilda, my dear, I'm so happy to see you today. So many of our family and friends seem to feel we want to be left in isolation, when it's truly the last thing I need. Would you like a cup of coffee?"

Hilda managed not to make a face. She had tasted coffee in the Malloy household before. "No, thank you, Aunt Molly. I have had my coffee this morning."

"Tea, then. I think the weather's cool enough to have it hot, don't you?"

"Yes. It is wonderful. I slept last night, when the storm was over, and then this morning Patrick thought I would maybe like a carriage ride."

"And you decided you'd like to come and talk to me about train wrecks, or politics, or some other pleasant subject. Well, sit down, child, and tell me what's on your mind."

The cooler air had cleared Hilda's mind, exactly as if the breeze had blown through it. Hilda went straight to the point. "Do you know Mrs. Hewlitt? Her husband owns the new bank. I cannot remember the name of it."

"The Midwest State Bank. Yes, I know her slightly."

"Well enough to invite her to tea, or something like that?"

"No. But I can make some sort of excuse. Is that what you want me to do?"

"Yes. Patrick heard her talking to some other ladies yesterday." Hilda repeated what she could remember of the conversation. "And I think she is a stupid, stupid woman, but she maybe knows something we need to know."

Molly considered. "I have spoken with her too little to know whether she is stupid, or simply ignorant. Stupid is far worse. The ignorant can be taught. There is some hope for them. The stupid can do a great deal of harm, because they're so certain they're right. But what do you think she meant by 'our side'?"

"That is what I hope you can find out. I think she meant those who are working against the poor and the immigrants, but I do not know who they are. Men in big business, perhaps, men who do not want the poor to become rich?"

"That's stupidity, for certain. If a man has a factory, and makes—oh, bicycles—it's only people who have money who can buy his product. So when the poor get rich, he makes more money. You'd think even a fool could see that."

"Ah, but the poor work in his factory. And if they are to get rich, he must pay them more, and that will cost him some of his profits. So he would like to keep them low-paid and poor."

"You say you know nothing about politics, child, but you seem to have a grasp of economics. Oh, here is our tea. Thank you, Agnes."

"No," said Hilda when she had sipped a little tea. "I only know what it is like to be poor, and to feel helpless. A laborer is so helpless, Aunt Molly. He works so hard every day—he or she, so many women are laborers, too. My mother is a laborer, my sisters—all my family except me, and I was. We work hard, and we are allowed to say almost nothing, and if we are ill, or we get old, there is no work and no money—it is not fair that the people who do all the work earn almost no money, and the rich men who own the factories and the big houses just make more, and more, and more!"

"Now, my dear, simmer down. You're preaching to the converted, you know."

"To the—oh. Because you think the same."

"That's right. Mr. Malloy and I have always believed in treating our employees fairly. That's why no one at the store has ever tried to organize a union."

"A union! Yes, I sound like a union organizer, do I not? Oh, and that reminds me. There has never been a union at Studebaker's, either, but Sven says men have come round to try to start one. He has seen them and heard them, in the paint shop."

"I shouldn't imagine they got very far. Studebaker's, too, has always been fair to the workers, or so I've heard."

"Yes, and Sven said some of the men got very angry, but some listened because the union men made promises. Money, and liquor, and other things." Hilda was reasonably sure she knew what—or who—the other things were, but even to Aunt Molly she wasn't prepared to discuss them.

"I see. This I did not know, but I did know that Mr. Malloy had heard hints of the same sort of thing at other factories in town. Tell me, did any of the men take the bribes, do you know?"

"The man who told Sven about it—it was Sean O'Neill, Norah's husband—he said that some did, and that then they had to do some things in return for the union men. Small things, but not nice. Stealing tools and setting fires."

"Fires." Molly's voice was very thoughtful.

"Yes." Hilda, too, was thinking. "I almost forgot, because we were busy—" She stopped. They had been busy trying to find Clancy Malloy, and then planning his funeral, and she didn't want to remind his mother about that. "There were other things to think about. But now—no, Aunt Molly, it makes no sense. Nothing makes sense. That has been the trouble all along. Why would union men want workers to steal things and make trouble?"

"Oh, child, unions have used techniques like that for years. Make trouble for the bosses, make it seem as if they've no choice but to let the union in. But it isn't honest, and it isn't even smart, because it usually backfires. If the workers are decent men they get sick of the damage, discredit the unions, and throw out the union organizers. And if the workers are rabble—and sometimes they are, Hilda, don't look at me like that—then the bosses just fire them all and hire a new crew. There are always plenty of laborers."

"Yes," said Hilda bitterly. "Always men and women who need work so badly they will bear almost anything to get it."

"And even if the bosses give in and allow the unions to organize their factories or businesses, the tactics of force leave them— the bosses, I mean—resentful and ready to lash back when they get the chance."

"But do you mean that unions are bad? Because they do give the little people some power, a way to earn more money and work in better conditions and—"

"Gracious, child, I never said they were bad! They can make a factory or a mine or a railroad stronger and better, with more capable workers. That's the other side. There's always another side, my dear. When the workers earn more and don't hate to go to work every day, then the bosses can find better workers, men and women who get the job done better and faster, and everybody's better off.

"What I meant to say was that it depends on the way the unions come in, and the way they bargain, and the way the workers act. If everyone involved has a little common sense and gives a little thought to the Golden Rule, a union can be a great blessing. When greed and self-interest are the motivation, on one side or both, then that's a recipe for disaster."

"Like a mine explosion."

"Exactly. You're still thinking about Vanderhoof."

"Yes. And Aunt Molly, I must tell you." She repeated Andy's story about the kitten.

When she had finished the horrid little tale, she saw on Molly's face an expression she had never seen there before, even when the worst parts of Clancy's saga had driven her to near-despair. It was as if her face had turned to granite, or marble, white and hard, with chips of blue ice for eyes. And when she spoke, her voice had turned to ice, also.

"Pure evil," she said, and Hilda shivered. "Cruelty to a child or a helpless animal is pure evil. He must be stopped. Vanderhoof or another, he must be hunted down and he must be stopped."

The lines are fallen unto me in pleasant
places; yea, I have a goodly heritage.

—Psalms 16:6

26

THE MOMENT PASSED. Molly's face fell back into its
usual pleasant contours. Hilda dared breathe again.

"So," said Molly. "We need to devise a way that
I can find out what Bertha Hewlitt is talking about."

"And soon," said Hilda, "because…" She patted the bulge
under her shawl.

"Yes, of course. Well, let's see. We can hardly use the Boys'
Club as an excuse again so soon. There are no holidays coming
up…"

"Labor Day," said Hilda doubtfully.

"Ah, yes, that would appeal mightily to Mrs. Hewlitt and
her friends, wouldn't it? No, I think it will have to be something
quite simple. A tea, as you suggested, or—I know! I'll invite her
to become a member of the Progress Club!"

That, Hilda knew, was a social and philanthropic organiza-
tion whose membership included the very cream of South Bend
Society. Mrs. Birdsell had been an officer, and one of the Studebaker wives, Hilda forgot which one. "That is a *very* good idea,
Aunt Molly. She will be flattered!"

"Yes, well, I'm not so sure that the rest of the club will actually want her, and they have to vote. But I'll have her here for tea,
and invite a few of the members to meet her, and it will be nice
and cozy and friendly, and we'll get some useful gossip out of her
or I'm not an Irishwoman!"

Hilda almost giggled, in spite of all her worries. It would be
hard to imagine anyone more thoroughly Irish than Molly Malloy.

"And now, my dear, I think Mr. Malloy would like to see you. Yesterday was a bit hard on him, and he's had no pretty women to look at in weeks."

"But I am not pretty! I am big!"

"You're a tall, slender woman who's going to have a very large baby very soon. That doesn't mean you're not pretty. Of course, if you're self-conscious, I could give you one of Cook's aprons to cover up everything but your face. I think she weighs nearly three hundred pounds."

Hilda did giggle at that, and slowly, carefully, climbed the stairs in Aunt Molly's wake.

She found Uncle Dan sitting up in a chair, his face pink, his blue eyes alert. "And if you're not a sight for sore eyes, girl! Mrs. Malloy'll tell you my wanderin' eye's had precious little to wander to lately."

"You are a wicked man, to say such things before Aunt Molly. Besides, she is beautiful."

"And that she is, and the joy of my life, like the very sweetest peach. But a man can't always be eatin' peaches. Now and then he wants some good honest apples. And the Lord knows that nurse is pure prunes. So you just sit yourself down right here and tell me what's goin' on in the world out there."

Hilda looked questioningly at Molly. Dan caught the look.

"And don't think you need to feed me pabulum! I'm no baby. You're up to somethin', as usual, and I want to know what it is."

Molly gave a tiny nod. Hilda took a deep breath, and said, "I am trying to find Mr. Vanderhoof."

That, she thought, was a safer answer than saying she was trying to track down Clancy's killer. Besides, it had the merit of being the truth. If she found the one, she was convinced, she would find the other. She watched Dan closely for his reaction. If he lost his temper—or if he was too surprised and shocked—

He took it quite calmly. "So you think he's behind what's been goin' on, do you?"

Hilda sighed with relief. "You think it might be true?"

"Wouldn't surprise me a bit. I never had a lick o' use for that fellow, even before he and his toughs killed Bishop and kidnapped me. All right, Mrs. Malloy, don't fuss. I'm not goin' to blow up."

Hilda had not thought that Aunt Molly was about to fuss. She had not seen her so much as lift an eyebrow, but Dan could read her mind. Molly smiled and sat back a little on her chair.

"He's back in town, is he, the da—er—dratted scoundrel?"

"I do not know. I think he is, or his—his—"

"Confederates?" suggested Molly at the same time that Dan said, "Stooges?"

Hilda had never heard either word, that she remembered, but she liked the sound of *stooges*. "Men who do his bidding?"

"Smart girl!" said Dan, delighted. "Didn't I tell you this was a smart girl, Mrs. Malloy, when young Patrick first started gettin' interested in her?"

"You did, Mr. Malloy." He had also said a number of less flattering things related to her nationality and religion and station in life. Molly, too, had been extremely dubious about this girl as a wife for her favorite nephew. The thought now made her squirm inside with embarrassment.

"His stooges, yes," Dan went on thoughtfully. "They're the sort who wouldn't blink an eye at settin' a fire here or there, or tamperin' with the brakes on a train." He fell suddenly silent then, and Hilda knew he was thinking about Clancy.

She glanced at Molly, and saw that it was time to change the subject before Dan became upset. "There is a woman who may know something about it," she said quickly. She repeated the story about Mrs. Hewlitt, leaving out the more outrageous parts. "And Aunt Molly has an idea for finding out more. She is going to invite her to join the Progress Club."

Dan snorted. "I've seen her in the store a time or two. Can't say I took to her much, but to each her own. If you want to take up with her, Mrs. Malloy, it's fine with me."

Hilda was about to chide him, to explain that it was all in a good cause, when she saw the twinkle in his eye and the look that passed between them. Will it be that way with Patrick and me, she wondered, when we have been married for so long? Will we know what the other is thinking, know when it is a joke? "It was Patrick who heard Mrs. Hewlitt talking at the store," she said proudly, "and told me about it." And the baby seemed to jump for joy at the look of satisfaction on Daniel Malloy's face.

"So the boy's gettin' along all right, is he?"

"Of course he is!" said Hilda indignantly. "He works very hard, from early in the morning until late at night, and on Saturdays even, and...oh. You were teasing me. You knew he was doing well."

"I have me spies, y'know," said Dan with a grin. "I knew the boy'd be fine. He's made of the right stuff. And that's why," he went on, the grin fading, "that's one reason why," he amended, "I've made him my heir. Made a new will last week, and after my darlin' girl here, it all goes to Patrick."

The lump in her throat kept Hilda from saying anything at all.

∽

Later, back downstairs, when Hilda had dried her tears and regained her composure, she was able to say part of what troubled her. "But, Aunt Molly, why did he make his will? I do not like this. I thought he was getting better."

"As indeed he is," Molly assured her. "He made his first will years ago, child, when the business first started to do well and we began to have a little put by. He changed it every time we had another child. And now we have but one son, so he changed it again."

She was very matter-of-fact, but Hilda had to be very stern with herself to keep back more tears. "Patrick is your nephew," she managed to say. "I do not understand."

"We've long thought of him as a son, my dear. You know that. Now, if Patrick and his mother agree, we will adopt him legally. It makes no difference to the way we feel about him, you understand, but it saves certain complications. However, if Patrick and his family feel at all uncomfortable about the idea—or if you do, child—we will simply leave the arrangement as it is. Either way, Patrick is Mr. Malloy's heir." She smiled at the confusion she read in Hilda's face. "You will have to get used to being a wealthy woman, Hilda. Mr. Malloy has a great deal more money than you might think."

"But I do not want his money!" said Hilda passionately. "There is your daughter. And I do not want him to die!"

"We all die sooner or later, Hilda. The doctor is very pleased with Mr. Malloy's progress, and says now that he may live for years, with care, and I'm sure I hope so. But one day he will die, and so will I. Our daughter will not need our money; she is very well off, you know. Her husband is a banker in Chicago. Of course, Mr. Malloy has made some provision for her, so she won't feel neglected. But by the time we're gone, you will have a fine family. And they will all need shoes—you cannot imagine how many shoes growing children can go through, Hilda—and clothing, and food, and toys, and books, and education—oh, there is no end to it. You will find it comforting not to have to worry about where all those things are coming from."

"I know about shoes," she said, gulping back a sob. "I have four younger siblings. We all had to wear hand-me-down shoes in Sweden, and by the time they came to Erik they were almost all holes. He had to wear girls' shoes. He hated it, but there was no money for anything else. Sometimes, if we were very lucky, someone would give shoes to the church and the pastor would bring them to us." She gulped again. "The very first pair of new shoes I ever had was when I went to work for Mrs. Clem, and she gave me money for a new pair of boots. They pinched at first, but I was so proud of them!"

"How old were you then, child?"

"Sixteen. We came to America a few months before my sixteenth birthday, and I was very lucky to get such a good job. I was just a daily at first, but Mrs. Clem liked me and thought I did a good job, and when the head housemaid left, she gave the job to me." She sighed. "I wish my sisters did not have to work so hard. I feel ashamed sometimes when I think of how easy my life is now, and how hard theirs is still. They work for nice ladies, but they work hard."

"One day you will be able to help them."

"I could help them now, but they are proud. They will not take my help, except I try to give them nice presents for Christmas and birthdays."

"We will think of some way, some things you can do that they won't resent." Molly's voice became brisk. "Meanwhile, though, I must organize a tea party, and you had better go home and take a rest. This has been quite a morning for you."

"Oh! What time is it?" She fumbled for the watch she usually wore pinned to her dress, and then remembered she wasn't actually wearing a dress.

"It's nearly noon. Patrick will be wanting the carriage to come home from the store with Andy. Scoot, now, my dear, and I'll let you know about the tea party as soon as it's settled."

Hilda scooted.

A power has risen up in the government greater than the people themselves, consisting of many and various and powerful interests, combined into one mass, and held together by the cohesive power of the vast surplus in the banks.

—John C. Calhoun, 1836

27

I WENT TO SEE Aunt Molly this morning," Hilda announced when Patrick sat down for lunch.

"Oh? How's she bearin' up?"

"As you would expect. She is a strong lady. I saw Uncle Dan, too." She watched Patrick closely, but his face reflected no unexpected emotions. She went on. "He is feeling very much better. How did he seem to you, yesterday?"

"Better than I expected. Grievin', o'course, but otherwise seemin' pretty healthy."

"What did you talk about?"

Patrick looked surprised. Hilda didn't usually question him this closely. "This 'n' that. How the store was doin'. He asked me to keep an eye on Aunt Molly, see she didn't worry too much about him or break her heart over Clancy."

"He did not say anything about his will?"

"His *will*! Why would he talk to me about his will? I told you, he's looking healthy."

Hilda took a deep breath. "Because today he told me that he has made a new will, leaving everything to you."

It was unfortunate that Patrick had just taken a bite of his sandwich. He choked and started to cough violently. Bits of bread and cold roast beef flew across the table before he could get his napkin to his mouth. His face grew red. Tears streamed down his cheeks.

When the paroxysm had passed and he had taken a few sips of water, he croaked, "What did you say?"

"What you thought I said. No, do not drink more water, you might choke again! Uncle Dan has made you his heir. After Aunt Molly, of course, and with something—I do not know how much—left to Cousin Mary. And Patrick—he wants to adopt you, make you his real son. He did not say I might not tell you. I think maybe he wanted me to tell you, so he would not have to, not the first time."

Patrick was silent. Mechanically he began to pick up the bits of food he had scattered across the tablecloth. He sipped a little more water and cleared his throat. "Why?" he finally asked.

"Because he loves you. They both love you. And because there is no one else. Clancy is dead. Their first son—"

"Sean."

"—Sean is dead. Mary has no need of money, and could not carry on the store, living in Chicago. He wants you to have it, Patrick."

"I don't want it. I mean—of course I want to carry on the store for him, if that's what he wants. I'd do anythin' for him. Look what he's done for me—for us. But all his money, every-thin'—it's too much. Besides, I don't want to even think of him dyin', him and Molly."

"That is what *I* said. And Aunt Molly said everyone must die, one day, and that our children would need shoes and edu-cation and—I forget what else, but she meant that the money would make it easier for us to give them everything they need."

Patrick's face was getting red again. "I can provide for my children," he said almost belligerently. "And anyway there's only the one so far, and not even him quite yet."

"But she will be here soon, and there will probably be more. I have thought about this, Patrick. I have thought of nothing else, ever since Uncle Dan told me. I think it will make him very un-happy if you refuse to accept this. And anyway, he is as stubborn as you. You cannot make him change his will. If you argue with him, it will only make him sad and angry, and he should not be upset until he is well."

"But—it's embarrassin'! What am I to say to him when I see him next?"

" 'Thank you'?"

After lunch Hilda rested for an hour. She was growing more and more tired and her body more and more ungainly. At least the unbearable heat had eased, but she still found it almost impossible to get comfortable. Soon, she thought. Soon it will be over. And then she thought about what lay between now and the end of her ordeal. And decided not to think about it. "Be gentle with me, Kristina," she whispered. "Be a good girl and kind to your mother."

Eileen came in just then and pretended she had not heard. "If you're ready to get up, ma'am, there's that policeman come to call again. I told him you were restin', but he says it's important, so I said I'd see."

"Oh! Yes, I want to see him. Give him something to drink— tea, I think, since it is a cool day—and I will be right down."

Eileen helped her mistress out of bed, smoothed her dress and clucked over her hair, and went off to do her bidding.

Sergeant Lefkowicz was just going off duty, having worked the early shift. He was tired, but he had plenty of time to devote to telling his story, and a long and gripping story it was.

"First of all, Miss Hilda, I found the boy."

"What boy?"

"The other errand boy at the bank, you remember, the one I thought knew something he wasn't saying. Bob Krueger, his name is. A German boy. He's come home, and his ma let me know."

"Oh! And you have talked to him?"

"Yes, yesterday after supper. I'm doing this on my own time, you know, it not being exactly a police case." He sipped from his teacup and picked up one of the molasses cookies Eileen had brought.

Hilda shook her head. "Fires and train wrecks and murders,

and it is not a police case. I sometimes think I am not the one who is crazy."

The sergeant tactfully did not respond to that. "Well," he went on, "he was pretty scared at first. I thought it was just me bein' a policeman, and Polish, and all. The Poles and the Germans in town don't always get along, you know."

"I know. I think it is a great pity that all of us immigrants do not band together. We fight prejudice all the time. We should not be prejudiced against each other. But go on."

"Well, I talked to him for a while, tried to get him to see I wasn't going to hurt him, I just wanted to talk to him. And it turns out he wasn't looking for another job after all. He just left town for a few days because he thought it was safer. It's not me he's scared of."

Hilda waited.

"I was right that he wanted to talk to me when I went to the bank that day, but he didn't dare in front of his boss. And then, after I left, the boss gave him a talking-to. I guess he—the boss, I mean—had seen the look on Bob's face, too. Anyway, the boy was told he'd better mind his own business and not go talking to policemen. The boss said banking was a confidential business and Bob had better learn that if he ever wanted to be more than an office boy. Oh, there was a lot more to it, but the upshot was, Bob understood he'd better not say anything if he didn't want to get booted out."

"But what was there to say? Why was his boss so worried?" Hilda waved her hands in frustration. Was this going to turn into another dead end?

"What Bob told me was that something funny was going on. He didn't know what, but he had carried messages to a lot of other banks in town, and there had been meetings."

"Meetings about what?"

"He didn't know. They were held in a room with very solid doors. But he knew who was in the meetings, because he had to show them upstairs. And they were other bankers, including James Andrews."

Hilda drew in her breath in a sharp gasp. "Andrews! But he was the one—"

"The one you dealt with about getting your family here. Vanderhoof's henchman. Yes. And another man in the room at the bank was John Goodman."

"I do not know that name."

"Prominent Republican in town. He was one of Vanderhoof's men, too. Now I don't know about you, Miss Hilda, but when I hear of a meeting with two of Vanderhoof's—"

"Stooges," supplied Hilda.

Lefkowicz grinned. "All right, his stooges. When I find the two of them in a room with a lot of other influential people, I begin to smell a rat."

"And the name of the rat is Vanderhoof."

"We can't prove that, you know. But I agree with you. So the question is, what are they up to?"

"Does—what is his name, the errand boy?"

"Bob Krueger."

"Yes. Does he know any more?"

"No, he just has a feeling that it's something bad. He says his own bank seems okay, but some of the other bankers are acting strange. They're being too nice to him, he says. Making jokes, smiling at him and shaking his hand, even giving him tips sometimes for ordinary things, things he does as part of his job. He says it's as if they want him to think they're good people."

"But they are not."

"We can't prove that, either, Miss Hilda. What I've asked Bob to do is to try to get his job back. He's going to claim a sick grandmother took him away for a couple of weeks. If he can't get his job at Merchant's back, then he'll try other banks. He'll keep his eyes and ears open, and come to me if he gets any clue to what's going on."

"That will not do, not for him, Sergeant! Bill Beeman was killed because he knew too much, and even Andy Mueller is being followed. Or he was, before we took him in."

"Yes, Bob knows he's in peril. He's willing to take the risk."

"But could we not protect him somehow?"

"How? As I said, this isn't a police case. Even if it were, we haven't got enough men on the force to use them for protection services."

"But is that not what the police are for? To protect?"

"Part of what we're for. Mostly, Miss Hilda, we put drunks and pros—and loose women in jail, break up fights, find lost kids and dogs, and march in the town parades. As you know perfectly well."

She sighed. She knew that the police force was not all it should be. "Then I have an idea. We—I—can hire a Pinkerton's detective to keep watch over Bob. I can afford to do that. I think I can. How much would it cost?" she asked, belatedly cautious.

"Not all that much. Yes, I expect you could afford it. But I'm not sure you want to do that."

"But why not? I know they are not as good as they claim to be, not as detectives. They have not yet found out who caused that train wreck in Ohio, and that happened two months ago. But this is not asking them to be detectives, only to be guards."

Instead of replying, Lefkowicz picked up another cookie, but didn't eat it. He put it down again. "Miss Hilda, how do you feel about unions? Are you for or against?"

*Labor is the superior of capital, and
deserves much the higher consideration.*

—Abraham Lincoln,
    State of the Union Address, 1861

HILDA WAS STARTLED. "Unions?"

"Yes, we talked about them once, a little. You were asking me about Eugene Debs."

"Oh. I remember. But what do they have to do with the Pinkertons?"

"Please, Miss Hilda, tell me what you think of them. Are you in favor of unions, or opposed to them?"

"I am in favor of most of them," she said with some impatience. "They give some power to the little people, the laborers. I know they can turn bad, but I think that is when the leaders become greedy and forget the people who depend on them, or when the managers become greedy and think they can take away what the unions have won."

"Yes, that's what I thought you'd say. And that's why you might do well to stay away from the Pinkertons, because they have been active in strike-breaking and union-busting."

"The *Pinkertons?* But they are on the good side, the side of law and justice—"

"They aren't police, Miss Hilda. They're hired workers, and they're on the side of whoever hires them. When factory owners or railroad men hire them to help break strikes, they're right there holding back the strikers while the scabs go in, and if fights break out, it's the strikers who get the worst of it."

Hilda heaved a huge sigh. "I am sorry you told me. I always thought of the Pinkertons as honorable men."

"I'm not saying they're not. I'm just saying they're—do you know the word mercenaries?"

Hilda shook her head.

"Mercenaries are soldiers hired to fight on whatever side will pay them the most. They do an honest job and get paid for it, but they're doing it for money, not for their principles. That's what the Pinkertons do. It's just that sometimes the jobs they're hired for get ugly."

Hilda's mind was working. "I do not think that is honorable, even if it is honest. There is a difference, I think. My English is not the best, but honorable means good, worthy of trust, does it not? And honest just means not lying or cheating. Honorable is better."

"Right all down the line, ma'am. And that's why you may not want to deal with the Pinkertons."

"But—if they are honest, and I hire them, then they must do as I say, yes?"

"Until somebody else pays them more money to do the opposite."

"Oh! They would do that?"

"I'm not saying they would, not most of them, though there are some bad apples in every barrel, you know. More likely they just wouldn't take on the job at all, not if there was any chance of a strike-breaking job coming up. They pay better."

Something in the sergeant's voice alerted Hilda. "And do you think there is chance of a strike-breaking job for them? Here, in South Bend?"

"There's talk. It's real quiet, but there's talk. A whisper here and there that the unions've got too big for their britches, that they're planning strikes, that they've got to be stopped."

Voices echoed in Hilda's mind. "…about time we had a few men on our side…if old Cornelius says it's good for business…"

"Sergeant Lefkowicz, who is starting these whispers?" She was certain of the answer before he spoke.

"Who else? Rumor says it's our old friend Vanderhoof."

"Then those meetings, at the bank… Sergeant, was the new banker one of the ones who attended? Mr. Hewlitt?"

"I don't know, but I can ask Bob."

They were back where they had started. "But how can we keep Bob safe?"

"We can't."

She looked at him, shocked.

"Look here, Miss Hilda. You told me yesterday we all needed to do what we could to solve these crimes, to find whoever was doing these things and bring him to justice. Or something like that. Now I'm telling you that we can't do that and keep everybody safe. There is risk, a lot of risk, and if Bob Krueger is willing to take it—and he is, since I talked to him—then we have to let him be as brave and determined as you."

"I am not brave," said Hilda in a small voice. "I talk well, but I do not have to face the bad men myself. I sit in my house and talk and talk and send others into danger. That is not being brave. It is being—arrogant, I think."

"Miss Hilda. Your head is in a muddle. Just now, you can't go out and—and fight dragons. You've got your baby to think of. But you've fought them in the past, and won. You've been brave over and over again. Now all you can do is think and plan and put ideas together. You're—you're the general now, but you have to let your troops go into battle. Battles have been lost, Miss Hilda, because generals were afraid to let their men go out and fight."

"A good general fights with his men," she said, still subdued. "Is it fair to send the troops out and stay behind in safety?"

"It may not be fair, but sometimes it's necessary." The clock on the mantel chimed four. Lefkowicz stifled a yawn. "I have to go, Miss Hilda, or I'll fall asleep right here. I'll stop by tomorrow if I can and let you know what I've found out. Don't lose heart. The soldiers in the field need you."

Hilda sat in thought for a long time after he left.

She had gone into this thing mostly to occupy her mind, because her mother and Aunt Molly wanted her to, and—she admitted it to herself—because Patrick didn't want her to. Stubborn and contrary, she had refused to give it up even after repeated warnings. She had, at the beginning, not the slightest idea that she could actually solve a series of horrendous crimes.

And then the crimes had moved close to home. The Studebaker train crash, the fire at the store—these had led to her deeper involvement. Then Clancy was murdered, and the string of calamities became intensely personal.

Yes. Clancy was murdered. Bill Beeman had been murdered. Why?

Bill had known, or guessed, too much. That was easy enough to deduce. He was bothered and worried about what he knew, but a little boastful, too. The wrong people had heard, or had heard about, what he was saying, and he had to be silenced.

But Clancy? Clancy was Vanderhoof's man. Hilda could never prove that, but she was sure in her own mind, and even Aunt Molly had said so. He had been Vanderhoof's stooge three years ago, had helped him cover up a murder then. Clancy had gone to New York; Vanderhoof had gone to New York and become involved, somehow, in the dubious politics of Tammany Hall.

Hilda thought about that. It was the most unlikely piece of the whole puzzle, the one that didn't fit, couldn't be forced into place. Vanderhoof was an outspoken Republican.

He was also a liar and a crook.

Suppose he had pretended to join up with Tammany just to learn their methods. Suppose he intended to bring those methods back to South Bend, so he could practice his graft on an even bigger and better scale.

Then what was Clancy's role?

The store. It had to do with Malloy's Dry Goods.

Hilda's tea was stone cold. She took a sip of it, not even noticing.

Of course it was the store! How could she have been so blind? It was no coincidence that Bill Beeman had been burned to death there. Clancy had meant, perhaps, to burn the store down. That could have served both his and Vanderhoof's purposes. Vanderhoof would have been avenged for his failure at Dan Malloy's hands to secure the council seat for the Republicans, and for the discovery at Patrick's and Hilda's hands of his nefarious activities. Clancy, who hated his father and his cousin, who hated most of his family, in fact, would have brought about their disgrace, at best, and possibly their ruin. If Vanderhoof put the word out, through his other stooges, that Dan Malloy was a careless man whose night watchman allowed the store to burn down about his ears, and furthermore allowed a man inside who had no business there, a man who died in the fire, how high would Dan Malloy's reputation stand? There might also be hints that the business wasn't doing all that well, anyway, that maybe the accident was no accident but an attempt to defraud the insurance company— oh, Hilda could think of a dozen ways in which Malloy's reputation could have been ruined.

But it hadn't happened that way. The watchman had turned in the alarm in time, and the fire had done only a little damage.

Was that why Clancy had been killed? Because he failed at the job? Or was there something else? And what could the fire, and Clancy's death, have to do with unions?

Hilda's head was swimming. She gave it up and went upstairs for another nap before Patrick and Andy came home.

⁓

Patrick was tired and had no fresh news. Nor did Andy, when Hilda called him in from clipping the hedge after supper.

"No, miss," he said when he had regaled himself with some peach ice cream. "I don't get the chance to hear stuff at the store like at the hotel. There's not people comin' and goin' all the time, see? And people talk louder at the hotel, too. I dunno why, but it's sorta quiet in the store, and then it's mostly ladies shopping. They giggle a lot and act kind of silly, a lot of them, but they don't say much that's interestin'."

"I know, Andy. Are you sorry you left the hotel?"

"No, ma'am!" he said with emphasis. "I was goin' nowhere there. And it wasn't safe, not anymore. I used to like it, but seems like the town has changed lately. There's more nasty things goin' on and more nasty people around, and I'm a lot better off where I am. Mr. Patrick says I'm comin' along good."

"Coming along well, Andy. That is good. And you are safe.

That is the most important thing. I am sorry you cannot go home to see your family, but…"

"It don't matter, miss. They're okay. And my little brother come to see me today. He ain't never been—"

"He hasn't ever been."

"—hasn't never been to Malloy's before. My ma can't afford to buy stuff there. But he come just to see where I work now, and Mr. Patrick let me give him a little wooden wagon. It's just a tiny one, meant for real little kids, and my brother's nine. But he was so tickled! You should've seen his face. He looked like it was his birthday and Christmas all rolled into one."

Hilda wished Andy weren't too big to hug.

After Andy had gone off to his room to read a Rover Boys book that Patrick had found for him, Hilda was thinking about going up to bed herself when the doorbell rang. It wasn't late, really, but late for callers. Patrick went to the door himself. These days he was being extra careful.

It was Sven. He came into the parlor, full of apologies.

"I am sorry, my sister. I stayed late at the factory, after my work was done, to talk to some of the men. Then Gudrun…"

"Gudrun scolded you because dinner was spoiled. Was it really?"

Sven smiled his slow, broad smile. "Not really. It was cold herring, mostly. But you know Gudrun."

Hilda nodded, with a little sigh. "She is a good cook, and she is annoyed when people do not come to her meals on time. But you did not come to complain to me about Gudrun."

"No. I told you I talked to the men. And I have learned some important things."

Hilda forgot her weariness. She turned to Patrick. "Do you mind if we speak Swedish? It is easier for us, if something is complicated. I will tell you everything later, I promise."

"Don't mind me," said Patrick with a wave of his hand. "I'm goin' to my den, anyway."

So Sven set out his tale in a mixture of Swedish and English, and quite a tale it was.

"You know I told you of the rumor that Vanderhoof was involved with Tammany Hall?"

"Yes, and I could make no sense of it."

"You were right. It was not sensible, and it is not true. I got to the truth of it today, I think. Two of the men in the paint shop have family in New York, whom they write to regularly. Back when Mr. Bishop was killed, and it was suspected that Mr. Vanderhoof was somehow involved, my men wrote to their relatives about it. These relatives have done well in New York and know many important people, including some politicians, so when Mr. Vanderhoof came back to New York and the news was spread, the relatives wrote to my men about *that*. And the story they told was that Mr. Vanderhoof was said to be spying on Tammany Hall politicians, trying to find out their plans and learning their methods."

"Ah!" said Hilda. "I thought as much. He wants to practice graft here, so he was learning the best way to do it, learning from the experts."

"That is a part of it, but not all. The New York people say it is rumored that he was also studying the ways Tammany organizes people, the common people, the laborers."

"But Tammany has nothing to do with unions, or not that I have ever heard."

"No, not unions. But they are very good at organizing people into voting blocs, groups of people who will always vote their way, blindly. The New York people think that Vanderhoof was learning how to organize effectively. There were no rumors about his plans, precisely—about whom he planned to organize, and for what purpose—but the feeling was that he was up to no good."

"I believe it!" said Hilda with a shudder.

"So," continued Sven, "they were very glad to see the back of him. But they warned their relatives—the men in my shop—to watch out for him."

Hilda sat back, disappointed. "That is interesting, but it does not take us forward. We know only what we knew before, that

Vanderhoof is a wicked man, that he plans something bad—but we knew or suspected that already."

"Wait. There is more. I spoke, also, with Sean O'Neill and some of the men who have been approached by the union organizers."

"They have got over being afraid you would fire them, then?"

"Not entirely, but they trusted me enough to tell me some very odd things. Some of them have had dealings before with union men, and they said these men operated in a way very unlike any they had ever experienced before. For one thing, since there has never been any labor problem at Studebaker's, there was no reason why they—the organizers—could not have called an open meeting, for anyone to attend who was interested in a union. But they chose to do it in secret, instead, approaching one man at a time."

Hilda frowned.

"Then, instead of trying to woo my men with promises of higher wages, shorter hours—all the things a union tries to accomplish—they offered money up front, right then. That also seemed peculiar, and to the men who did not succumb, quite irregular if not illegal. Then, too, the organizers never made mention of any specific union. They were vague and simply said that if the men made enough trouble for the company, the company would be forced to consider their demands."

"What demands?"

"Exactly."

Hilda thought about that for a while. "They are not union organizers at all," she said at last, slowly. "They pretend to be, but all they really want is to cause trouble. Why?"

"Perhaps to make Studebaker's less profitable?"

Hilda thought about that one, too. "The only people who would benefit from bringing Studebaker's down are their competitors. Vanderhoof had a harness business in town, and Studebaker's makes harness for their carriages."

"Not so much anymore. We make some, but mostly we buy it from other suppliers. Like Vanderhoof, at least before he left town. Without him, his business isn't doing so well these days."

"Then that is not the reason. Maybe—maybe it has nothing to do with Studebaker's. Sven, do you know if these organizers—these pretend-organizers—have been to other big factories? To Oliver's, maybe, or Birdsell's?"

"I do not know, but I can find out. What is in your mind, my sister?"

"I am not sure. It is cloudy. I am sure only that Vanderhoof is behind everything, and he must be stopped."

"Yes," said Sven, and took his leave.

When Hilda related the conversation to Patrick, he could make little of it. "Why would someone pretend to be a union man, only to make trouble? That's what gives unions a bad name, the trouble-makin'."

"That is what Aunt Molly said. She is the wisest person I know, Patrick. I love her very much. I think I maybe married you to have her for my aunt."

"Then I owe her even more than I thought I did. Come to bed, *acushla*."

For her own breakfast she'll project
a scheme,
Nor take her tea without a stratagem.

—Edward Young,
Love of Fame, circa 1725

HILDA SLEPT RESTLESSLY and awoke early. Patrick was still in bed. It was Saturday, and though he had to go to the store, he had decided he could leave it till a little later than usual.

Hilda needed something to do. She remembered the first few months of her marriage, when she thought she would go mad with boredom. Neither a servant nor yet a lady, she had not found a pattern for her days. That had changed when Norah's husband, Sean, had been charged with a serious crime, and Hilda had to untangle a web of lies and deception to clear him.

Things were different now. She had a great deal she wanted to be doing. The trouble was, she couldn't do any of it. Standing at the open window in her voluminous nightgown, she looked down at her swollen body. She couldn't see her feet, but she knew they were swollen, too. Her back ached. Oh, how she wished this baby would make its appearance soon.

But then she would be confined to bed for quite some time. And meanwhile, that monster Vanderhoof would be pursuing his nefarious plans, whatever they were, and she could do nothing about it.

She needed a plan of her own.

When Patrick awoke, missed her, and went downstairs looking for her, he found her seated at his desk in the den, busily writing.

"You're up early, darlin'."

"What? Oh, Patrick. What do you want?"

"Have you had breakfast?"

"Yes. No. I do not know. Go away, I am busy."

His eyebrows rose nearly into his hair, but he went away. Finding Eileen in the dining room, he said, "Take Miss Hilda some coffee, please, Eileen. She's in the den, up to somethin' or other. Better take the pot. She looks like she'll be there a while. And if you see Andy, send him in here, will you?"

When the boy appeared, Patrick gestured to a chair. A little unsure of himself, Andy sat.

"Andy, I want you to stay here today instead of goin' to the store with me."

"Have I done somethin' wrong, Mr. Patrick, sir?"

"No. It's Miss Hilda who's worryin' me. She got up early and didn't eat her breakfast, and now she's shut herself up in the den, writin' away like the devil set her an essay. I don't know what she's up to, but she's in a mood to take it into her head to do somethin' foolish. I want you to keep an eye on her for me."

"Yessir. What do you think she might do?"

For a moment the two shared a look of the liveliest apprehension. Then Patrick raised his hands and eyes to heaven. "The saints alone know! But she might decide to go someplace to see somebody. I don't know where or who, but I don't like the idea."

"So you want me to stop her?" His tone implied doubt that such a thing was possible.

"If you can," said Patrick with a sigh. "But if you can't, I want you to go with her. I don't want either of you to get into trouble, and seems to me there's less chance of it if there are the two of you. I wish I could stay here, but—"

"But with Mr. Malloy still not feelin' so good, you've got to be at the store. I know, sir. Don't you worry. I'll see to things here." His twenty-five-inch chest swelled with pride and determination.

Hilda, oblivious to the machinations of her husband and protégé, sat at the desk, now with her pencil flying, now with her head tilted to one side reading what she had written and waiting for the next thought. A cup of coffee sat to one side; every once in a while she remembered to take a sip. Sheets of paper covered the rest of the desk. One was headed CLANCY, one VANDERHOOF, one FIRES, one TRAIN WRECKS, one BANKS, and one, the one in front of her at present, read UNIONS.

She frowned and chewed the end of her pencil as she read. No one else would have been able to read the hasty scrawl, written partly in English and partly, when she could not think of the English word, in Swedish. On the paper was written nearly everything she knew about unions, generally and specifically, and she had decided it was not nearly enough.

She knew the names of two big union men, Eugene Debs and Samuel Gompers. She knew, in a general sort of way, where Debs had been at the time of the Studebaker train wreck—but not where he had been a little earlier in June, when the Twentieth Century Flyer had been deliberately wrecked. She knew that Debs's particular interest was in railroads, that he had founded or at least was the moving spirit of the ARU. About Gompers she knew only that he was president of the biggest union of them all, the American Federation of Labor.

She knew that Studebaker's, the most important business in town, had never been unionized, and she was pretty sure the Oliver Chilled Plow Company had not. About Birdsell's factory, manufacturing clover hullers, she was less certain.

But now there were men coming around, acting strange, trying to organize a union at Studebaker's, or pretending to try. Hilda was quite certain it was only a pretense, a cover-up for— for what?

That was where she was stuck. Secret contacts with men in Sven's paint shop, secret meetings of bankers... She suddenly remembered to add a note to her BANKS page.

But what could meetings of bankers have to do with union activity? And train wrecks and fires?

An idea began to stir, sluggishly, uncertainly. Banks. Businessmen. Unions. Vanderhoof.

She touched the bell, and when Eileen came, she said, "More coffee, please, Eileen. This is cold."

"Yes, ma'am. And Mr. Patrick said as I was to make sure you ate somethin', or all that coffee's goin' to give you indigestion."

"It never did before!"

"You've never been nine months gone before, ma'am." Eileen left and closed the door smartly behind her.

That reminded Hilda. Making a face, annoyed at her situation, she made a quick trip to the downstairs lavatory. All that coffee had another effect, too.

When she got back to the den, Eileen had moved her papers aside and deposited a large tray with bacon and scrambled eggs and toast and jam and coffee and orange juice, and was standing in the corner waiting to make sure Hilda ate it.

"I am not hungry. I want only coffee."

"Yes, ma'am. Mr. Patrick said as I should watch you eat it, ma'am."

"I am *busy*, Eileen. Go away."

"Yes, ma'am. As soon as you've eaten your breakfast. Them eggs—"

"Those eggs."

"Those eggs is gettin' cold, and there's nothin' so nasty as cold scrambled eggs. I remember once, me gran said cold eggs were an abomination unto the Lord. I didn't know what she was talkin' about, but I knew I'd better eat me breakfast quick. That was back when there was eggs for breakfast. Later on it was just bread, when we were lucky enough to get it, or maybe an apple. I can remember when…"

She went on chattering until Hilda, in a frenzy of anxiety to be left alone with her thoughts and her notes, ate simply to get rid of her. Eileen smiled gently as she took the tray away. She was learning how to manage her mistress.

It took Hilda a few minutes to recover her thoughts of thirty minutes before, but when she did, she began to make notes again, slowly this time, as her brain began to work.

Vanderhoof (she had ceased to honor him with "Mr." even in her thoughts) was a businessman and a politician. He wanted to make money, and he wanted to have influence, and he wasn't overly particular about how he achieved either goal.

He had been interested in how Tammany Hall gained both wealth and power.

He had told Clancy to burn down Malloy's Dry Goods, and had killed him when he didn't succeed. (That was an inference, not a proven fact, but Hilda was sure she was right.)

Bankers were businessmen, also interested in making money. Bankers had held secret meetings with some of Vanderhoof's stooges. (Hilda liked that word.)

Trains had been wrecked. Trains were run by union crews, members of the ARU. Vanderhoof had some railroad interests. Railroad management didn't like unions.

And finally, a quotation from Patrick, barely heard at the time, but now burned into Hilda's mind: "That's what gives unions a bad name."

She looked at what she had written, and needed more coffee.

If what she suspected was true, this was wicked. This was greed and evil in its purest form.

"Pure evil," Aunt Molly had said. "He must be hunted down and stopped."

And how was she, Hilda Johansson Cavanaugh, great with child, how was she to stop him?

She had only her wits. She must try to outsmart him somehow.

She pulled herself to her feet and went into the hall to phone Aunt Molly. As the wife of an important businessman, she would know far more than Hilda about the ways of business, about how a businessman's mind worked.

Mrs. Malloy was not at home, Hilda was informed politely by Riggs. He believed she had taken another lady to a meeting of some of the Progress Club ladies. He could not say when she might be home. Certainly he would ask her to telephone Miss Hilda. No trouble at all, madam. Yes, thank you, Mr. Malloy was feeling quite well.

Hilda chewed at a knuckle, then picked up the phone again

and asked for Bell 264. "Mr. Williams? Oh, Colonel George, I am sorry. I did not recognize your voice. This is Mrs. Cavanaugh. Is Mrs. Clem at home?"

Mrs. Clem was not feeling well and was keeping to her room. Was there any way he could help her himself? Oh. And how was she feeling these days? Fine. No trouble at all, Hil—Mrs. Cavanaugh.

Frustrated, Hilda sat back on the chair next to the telephone. Colonel George was, of course, a businessman, one of the Studebaker vice presidents. But Hilda had never gotten along as well with him as with Mr. Clem, and she was sure he still thought of her as a housemaid.

Who, then? Who knew enough about business, and enough about sharp dealing, to give her some ideas?

Put that way, the answer was simple. John Bolton was the sharpest dealer she knew, and had driven Mr. Clem and Colonel George for years. He knew a lot.

She couldn't phone Tippecanoe Place again. Colonel George might answer again, and she didn't dare ask him to bring his coachman to the phone. There was no help for it. She went back to the den and rang for Eileen.

"I must go out, Eileen, and I cannot go dressed this way. The only decent dress I can wear is the black one you made. Help me upstairs, please, and help me into it. I feel foolish that I cannot do these things for myself—"

"Now, ma'am, you mustn't go out, and that's flat. Mr. Patrick said—"

"I do not care what Mr. Patrick said! I have had enough of what Mr. Patrick said. I wish to go out. You will help me, or I will try to do it myself."

"But, ma'am—" Eileen was almost weeping.

"Is there some trouble, Miss Hilda?" Andy peered around the edge of the door.

"Andy! Why are you at home? Why did you not go to the store with Mr. Patrick?"

"He said he didn't need me this mornin', and I could stay here and do whatever needed doin' around the house." He thought he hadn't better mention that he had been delegated to look after Hilda. In her present frame of mind, she would fly right off the handle, and that wouldn't be good for her or the baby. "So I wondered if there was somethin' you needed."

"There is nothing you can do, Andy, thank you. Eileen is about to help me go upstairs and dress."

Andy and Eileen, who had begun to establish a truce, exchanged glances. This was Hilda at her most willful, and neither of them was quite sure what to do.

"That dress you're wearin' is right pretty, Miss Hilda, if you don't mind me sayin' so."

"Thank you, Andy, but it is not appropriate to wear outside the house. I must put on my black dress. Eileen, help me up, please."

"Is there an errand I can run for you, Miss Hilda? It's gettin' kinda hot out there. You might not want to get out in it, 'specially dressed all in black."

"This is not something you can do for me. And you are not to be out alone. Eileen?"

She put out a hand, and Eileen, seeing no choice, helped her out of the chair and up the stairs.

It was some little time before Hilda was properly dressed. She came slowly down the stairs, holding up her dress with one hand while the other gripped the railing. Andy was waiting.

"Andy, have Mr. O'Rourke bring the carriage around, please. Tell him I wish to go to Tippecanoe Place."

Andy ran off, but returned immediately, panting. "Please, Miss Hilda, can I come along? I've never seen that house up close."

Hilda was so astonished she forgot to be either suspicious or protective. "Never seen the biggest, most important house in town?"

"Just from the street, miss. It ain't a place for the likes of me." He looked downcast.

"Do not be foolish. Have you never heard the saying 'A cat may look at a king'?"

"No, miss. What does it mean?" He was helping her to the door as they talked.

"It means—" Hilda paused for thought. "It means you will go with me to see Tippecanoe Place. Come and get in."

Andy helped Hilda into the carriage while a frowning O'Rourke stood holding the reins of the horses. Eileen had come out with them, and Andy winked at her before he climbed in himself. "It'll be all right," he whispered, and they drove off.

GENERAL STRIKE PROBABLE
Governor Altgeld has ordered the entire
First Brigade National Guard of five
regiments to Chicago.

   —South Bend *Tribune*
    July 8, 1894

30

T HE GREAT HOUSE basked in the late-morning sunshine, its gray stone walls looking almost golden. The rains all summer had turned the lawns to a brilliant green, and the gardener, Mr. Czeszewski, had mowed and rolled them until they were smooth and even as moss. Chrysanthemums bloomed in brilliant colors in all the flower beds, with rose-and-white asters for company. Overhead, the puffy clouds had already the indefinable look of autumn about them, a heaviness, a faint tinge of purple on their undersides.

"Gosh, miss!" As the carriage rolled up the drive, the house loomed larger than Andy had imagined. His pretended awe became real. This was, certain-sure, no place for the likes of him. "Um—maybe I'd better stay in the carriage and wait for you."

"We are going to the carriage house first, Andy. You will like that. You like horses, do you not?"

It was a foolish question to ask a fourteen-year-old boy. O'Rourke pulled the horses to a stop before the open carriage house doors, and John Bolton stepped out as Andy hopped down.

"It's young Andy, isn't it? And what might you be doing here?"

"Miss Hilda—I mean Mrs. Cavanaugh brought me, sir. I mean I came with her. Can I see the horses?"

"Nothing stopping you, is there?" John pointed through the door to the stalls beyond, and turned to the carriage. "I didn't expect to see you again for a while," he said, helping Hilda out.

"I need your help, John. Do you need to go out soon?"

"No. Mrs. Clem is feeling poorly, Mrs. George is out of town, and the colonel went to a meeting and said someone else would bring him back."

"Good. Is there a place where we can talk, privately?"

John grinned that wicked grin of his. "There was a time, dear lady, when I would have welcomed that suggestion. However... anyway, I don't want to make you climb the stairs to my quarters. They're steep and narrow. We could go around back. The chairs there are reasonably comfortable, and the lilacs make a screen."

There was, behind the carriage house, a secluded area which John had furnished with a couple of discarded wicker chairs and a low, somewhat battered wooden table. A lilac hedge provided complete privacy from the neighbors.

"But we must be very quiet, John. No one must hear us. And tell Andy where we will be. No, perhaps he should come with us."

John narrowed his eyes and gave Hilda a long look. "Has something happened?"

"He has been threatened, and followed. He is living with us for the present."

"I see." He put two fingers in his mouth and uttered a piercing whistle that brought Andy running. "You can spend some more time with the horses in a bit, lad. Right now Miss Hilda wants you to come with us."

"To the house?" Andy sounded both scared and eager.

"Not just yet, Andy. We need to talk, the three of us. We are going to sit behind the carriage house, where no one can see us, but we must talk very quietly."

Now he was just scared. "Yes, miss," he said with a gulp.

"And John, please tell O'Rourke I will not need him for a little while. He can go home and come back for us."

So the three of them made their way around the red brick building and sat down, and Hilda got straight to the point.

"I think I know what Vanderhoof plans to do, and I need your ideas about how to stop him."

John whistled again, long and low this time. Andy, sitting on the grass, made an odd little ducking motion as if he would like to burrow into the earth.

"And what do you think he's planning?" John's voice was low, and loaded with skepticism.

"I think—I am sure he plans to organize a disturbance on Labor Day." She waited for one or the other to question or object, but Andy said nothing, and John only nodded for her to go on.

"I have been thinking." John, for whom this was a familiar phrase, smothered a smile.

"I think what began it was when Patrick was talking about some of the things that have happened, the thefts and fires and other things at Studebaker's, and he said, 'That is what gives unions a bad name.' And I thought, what if that is what Vanderhoof wants to do? What if all these things—the train wrecks, the fires—have been planned to discredit the unions?" She was proud of remembering the phrase from Aunt Molly. That thought passed as soon as it came to her mind.

"And why would he want to do that?"

"Because he is a union-buster. I do not think that is good English, but that is what they are called, yes? People who try to stop the unions?"

"That's what they're called, all right." John frowned in thought. "And I have to admit, I can see Vanderhoof as a union-buster. They're sneaky, underhanded bas—crooks who would rather smash in a few heads than sit down and talk like honest men. And it's big businessmen who hire them. Do you think Vanderhoof is in this on his own?"

"I do not know, but I do not think so. He is not—not big enough, not important enough to cause some of these things to be done."

"The Twentieth Century wreck," said John.

Hilda nodded. "I do not think he was in back of—was behind that. But it was maybe then that he got his ideas, or decided how to make them work." She lowered her voice still further. "I think he has men pretending to be union organizers, stirring up the laborers. I think he will get them together on Labor Day, real union members and the ones who are just pretending and the ones he has bribed, and then—then I do not know. Something will happen, something that will make people hate the unions."

"A riot," said John thoughtfully, his head cocked to one side. "It's easy enough to get one started. Get a bunch of people fired up, make sure lots of free beer is available. Someone throws a punch, someone punches back. It isn't minutes till the Pinkertons are there, fighting back. The thing grows, heads are broken, property is damaged—and it all looks like the fault of the union men. Simple. But how does that benefit one Augustus Vanderhoof?"

"Augustus? Is that his real name? Patrick calls him Cornelius."

"Don't know. I'm not sure anybody knows his real name, except maybe his family. It just seems to fit him, the way he's so pompous and all. But as I said…"

"I am not sure, exactly, why he wants these things to happen. But I know that some businessmen hate unions. If Vanderhoof shuts down the unions in South Bend, or keeps them from growing, there are some businessmen who will be grateful. They will help him get elected, if he wants to run for office, or—I do not know."

This was the weak point in Hilda's scenario, and she knew it. She simply could not get her mind to work like the evil Vanderhoof's. Her instincts told her he wanted something important out of all this, wanted money or power or both, but she could not see how setting business management against the laborers would give him what he wanted. She bowed her head, in discouragement and weariness.

"Miss Hilda?" Andy's voice, a breath of a voice, hesitant, wary. "I heard some stuff at the hotel, just before I went to work for Mr. Patrick."

"Here, lad, come up and sit on the table. It's not much, but it's sturdy enough for that. And tell us what you know."

"It didn't make no sense to me at the time, but now—well, anyway, it was in the billiards room. A bunch of men was playin' and drinkin' and talkin' loud. And you know how the stairs run right past that room?"

Hilda did not. Her acquaintance with the Oliver Hotel was limited, and she had certainly never approached the billiards parlor. But John nodded.

"Well, I was showin' some people to their room, and I heard some men talkin' about Mr. Vanderhoof, only they said Cornelius—like you said, miss. And they was laughin' silly-like—you know how they do when they've had a little too much to drink?"

Again John nodded.

"So I slowed down a little, pretended I had to put down one of the suitcases and get a better grip on it. And I heard someone say, 'Protection, that's how old Cornelius will make his pile, no matter what he tries to pretend.' Or somethin' like that. And I wanted to stay and hear more, but the lady was tired and the gentleman gave me a poke and told me to hurry it up, so I had to move on."

"The protection scheme, by—by gum!"

Hilda laid a finger to her lips. "John! Not so loud. But tell me what is a protection scheme."

"Sorry I yelled. I was just mad at myself for being so stupid. Of course! And that's what the old son of a—gun—learned in New York, from Tammany. It all makes sense."

"But not to me," said Hilda. "And John, you will have to wait a moment to tell me. I will be right back." She lumbered into the carriage house. John looked blankly at Andy, who turned slightly pink.

"She drank a lot of coffee this morning," he muttered.

When she returned, she seated herself, not without difficulty, and said commandingly, "Now."

"The protection scheme. It's an old game, probably as old as crime. The way it works, you get a gang of thugs to start trouble. It can be anything. Say a store keeps getting things stolen, or its windows get broken, or little fires start, or ugly louts hang around and scare the customers away. The police can't seem to do anything."

"Why not?" asked Hilda indignantly.

"We'll get to that in a minute. Pretty soon the storekeeper is losing money left and right, and then a nice man comes to see him. He says how sorry he is about all this trouble, and he wants to help him out. For a small sum of money every month, he'll make sure the trouble stops.

"Well, the storekeeper is no fool. He knows he's dealing with extortion. He loses his temper and says—well, let's just say he turns down the nice man's offer and starts sleeping at the store. And then one night the windows get broken again, and the storekeeper jumps up ready to catch the villain, only there are three of them, with clubs, and by the time they're done with him he's lucky if the only thing broken is the window. So when the nice man comes around again, the storekeeper gets out his billfold."

"Danegeld," said Hilda.

John quirked an eyebrow.

"You are right, John, it is a very old crime, many centuries old at least. I learned of this from my father. When the Vikings— my people, I say to my shame—were raiding the lands of your people, the British, your kings decided it was easier to pay the raiders than to fight them. So they raised taxes from your people and used them to pay the Vikings to make them go away. The money was called Danegeld, Danish gold, but the Vikings came from all the Norse countries. And your kings paid some of the money to their armies, to defend the country, only the country did not need to be defended if the raiders were just paid off, so that was extortion, too."

"Nothing changes, really, does it? You asked why the police could do nothing to help the storekeeper? They were being paid by the nice man to keep their eyes shut to what was happening."

"And this you think is what Vanderhoof is going to do?"

"Sure. He'll convince the businessmen that the unions are violent, but that if they band together and hire him, he'll see that they're not troubled by the unions. And then, if he's really sharp, he'll go to the union men and say he's sorry about all the fuss there's been about them, but if they'll hire him, he'll make sure things stay quiet and the bosses don't start persecuting them again."

"And life goes well, and everyone is happy," said Hilda bitterly. "Especially Vanderhoof, who is making a lot of money for doing nothing except wickedness."

"But—but Miss Hilda. Mr. John. He ain't a man to keep his promises. Who's to say the trouble won't start again?"

John ruffled his hair. "This is a bright lad, Hilda. Mrs. George is looking for a new footman; Anton has taken it into his head to get married. I don't suppose you'd like to come to work here, would you, Andy? The Oliver's no place for an up-and-comer like you."

Hilda waited for his response.

"Thank you, Mr. John, sir, but I work for Mr. Patrick now, at Malloy's. He said I'm doin' a good job and he'll promote me soon. And I'm sorta fillin' in after work, helping out Miss Hilda at home. So you see…"

"I see." To Hilda he said, very quietly, "Rescuing strays again, I see."

Hilda pursed her lips but said nothing. Not in front of Andy. Later, though…

"Now, John. Andy. The thing we must decide is: What are we going to do about it?"

Make no little plans; they have no magic
to stir men's blood.

—attributed to Daniel Burnham,
   19th century

31

ILENCE FELL, while each thought about the problem. Then John opened his mouth at the same time as Hilda. He gestured a go-ahead.

"I'm thinking we need honest union men on our side."

"And I was thinking we need honest businessmen, who won't stand for this sort of nonsense."

"And I," put in Andy, "think we need to let everybody know what might happen."

"The press!" Hilda exchanged glances with John.

"A two-edged sword," he said dubiously. "Vanderhoof can claim libel and sue everybody in sight."

"Yes, but…" Hilda trailed off into thought. Finally she said, "I have an idea. We will need many people to help us, but I think it will work. Now listen. This is what I want you to do.…"

When they finally went home, Hilda thought she would be too excited to rest, but she fell into a deep sleep, not even waking for lunch. Patrick worked at the store through his lunchtime, so it wasn't until he came home for supper, hungry and tired, that he got from Andy and Eileen a report of Hilda's activities that day.

Andy was more than a little apprehensive, but he was a sensible boy. He distracted Patrick with a glass of beer, and a snack of bread and cheese, before responding at all to his questions about Hilda.

"She rested just fine this afternoon, Mr. Patrick, sir. She's just wakin' up now. She had a good breakfast—Eileen was really smart about gettin' her to eat it all—but she was too tired to want her lunch, so she'll be extra-hungry for supper, I expect."

"Workin' with those papers of hers all mornin', was she?" Patrick finished his beer.

"Well—no, sir. Not ezzackly."

Patrick sat up, all attention. "What d'you mean, not exactly?"

Andy faced it like a man. "We went out, sir."

"Where? Why? Did she get into more trouble? You went with her, or I'll skelp the both of you!"

"Yessir, and we didn't get into no trouble, we—"

"We went to talk to John Bolton, Patrick, and we had a nice visit, and I have solved our problems."

Hilda had come downstairs, and she was a vision. Eileen, with an afternoon free of her mistress's needs, and with Andy to help Mrs. O'Rourke, had run up a new wrapper for Hilda. Made of white lawn, it dropped straight from the shoulders to her feet, and was trimmed with small bows of pink ribbon. With her golden hair freshly braided and pinned into a halo atop her head, Hilda looked lovely, even if her shape did suggest a porpoise. She was rosy from sleep and her eyes were bright.

Patrick was disarmed. "Darlin' girl, I wish you'd stay home where you're safe."

"I was perfectly safe, Patrick. And did you not hear what I said? I have solved our problems. I know who has been making all the terrible things happen, and I know how to stop him."

"I helped!" said Andy proudly.

So over supper, Hilda outlined her plans.

"It will be on Labor Day. That is only a little over two weeks away, so we must work quickly. There will be a parade—"

"You found time to read today's paper? Because that was the first report I've seen—"

"No, I did not read the newspaper. I knew it would happen."

"She deduced it," put in Andy, bringing in a fresh pitcher of iced tea, "just like Sherlock Holmes."

"Yes. The laborers will march, and then the trouble will start. Except it will not, because we will stop it."

"Now look, me girl. I'm not wantin' to interfere, but in the first place you may not be goin' anywhere by Labor Day, and in the second place, even if you're still up and about, a parade where there might be trouble is no place for you atall, atall."

"Of course I will not be there, Patrick. What an idea! I will not need to be, because there will be many other people working to make sure there is peace."

Patrick blinked. Her mind had run ahead of his again. "But why should there be any trouble anyway? The unions in this town are peaceful, always have been."

Hilda, assisted by Andy (who had given up all pretense of serving), explained her elaborate theory.

"Hmm," said Patrick when she had finished. "Sounds pretty twisted to me."

"But that's the way he is, sir," said Andy. "Got a mind like a corkscrew, my pa says."

"Your father knows him?" said Hilda. "You did not tell me that."

"I forgot till this minute. And he doesn't know him, just knows about him. See, Pa's worked a lot o' places." Andy paused. Hilda saw the pain and embarrassment in his face. His father had a weakness for drink, and frequently got fired. But he was a good worker when sober, and a friendly, pleasant man, so he didn't usually find it too hard to get another job.

"Lots o' places," Andy went on. "And he keeps hearin' about Vanderhoof. He talks out o' both sides of his mouth, Pa says. Promises the bosses one thing and then turns around and promises the men somethin' else. Just like we was talkin' about earlier."

"You mean he goes to the factories himself?"

"Naw, he sends other guys. But everybody knows he's the one behind it all."

Eileen brought in the peach pie, the last of the season, and when she had gone back to the kitchen, Hilda and Patrick and Andy went on talking about Hilda's plans.

❧

Mrs. O'Rourke, having finished her cooking, and with two helpers to serve and clean up, was having her evening meal in the kitchen with her husband. "Sounds like she's at it again," said the cook. "Tryin' to run the world."

"Huh," said O'Rourke. "She's always tryin' to run somethin'. Can't see why he puts up with it. I'd teach her a lesson if she were my wife."

"Oh, ye would, would ye, O'Rourke? And how would ye be doin' that, if you don't mind my askin'?" Mrs. O'Rourke stood. She was taller than her husband, and weighed fifty pounds more. Her arms were strong from decades of kneading bread and lifting heavy roasts and, in the old days, carrying water. She placed her hands on her hips and glared down at him.

He finished her beer and stood. "I'll be off, then," he said briefly, and left at what was not quite a run.

Mrs. O'Rourke snorted. "Talks big, but that's all it is." She deposited her bulk back on the chair. "Eileen!" she called in to the scullery. "I'd be obliged if ye'd make me another pot of tea, girl."

Meanwhile O'Rourke, grumbling, walked down to the tavern on the corner, where his complaints about his know-it-all mistress and his bossy wife got a full airing.

Hilda stayed home from church the next day, her sheer size being enough of an excuse. "And there is no lavatory at the church," she confided to Eileen, "and you know I cannot be far from one these days." She had planned, at first, to talk to Sven after church and enlist his help in her scheme. But she decided that he would probably refuse to talk about it anyway. His views about profaning the Sabbath had grown stronger of late. When Patrick took Eileen with him to St. Patrick's, though, Hilda asked if he would go to Sven's house and ask him to call on her the next day. "Early, tell him, please. Before he goes to work. Say it is important, but do not tell him why."

"I'll tell him, darlin'. And yes, I'll tell your mama and everyone else that you're doin' fine, or you'll have the whole herd of 'em comin' here, thinkin' you're feelin' bad."

So Sunday was a peaceful day, at least for Hilda. She spent much of it lying in bed, alternately making plans and dozing, dreaming of a beautiful little blond girl she would dress in ruffles and bows and teach to speak a little Swedish.

Patrick spent much of the day in earnest conversation with Andy, planning and fretting. Hilda's plan was sound, as far as it went, but there were so many things that could go wrong. "I don't like dependin' on so many other people. If even one of them is crooked—"

"But we got to, Mr. Patrick. We got to have lots of help, 'cause there ain't enough of us by ourselves. And beggin' your pardon, sir, but we're not important enough. We got to get the important ones, the bankers and that, or nobody will pay attention. And we got to get the smart union men, and the honest ones, or—"

"I know, I know." He ran his hands up through his hair and left them there. He was developing a headache. "I just hope we can trust them all."

On Monday Sven came to see Hilda briefly, and was given his assignment. Patrick stopped at the Oliver Hotel on his way to work, and asked a few of the bellboys to come to the store when they got off work.

Hilda telephoned Aunt Molly, who listened carefully and promised action. She also confirmed Hilda's ideas. "Yes, dear, you're quite right. Mrs. Hewlitt spoke quite freely on the subject when we talked on Saturday. I had intended to come visit you today and tell you. She said that Mr. Hewlitt has met with others—"

"Those secret meetings at the bank!" Hilda said, interrupting.

"Yes, dear. And that most of the men there agreed that recent events, the train wrecks and fires and so on, were signs of union unrest, and that there could be trouble ahead for everyone unless the unions were put in their place. Those were her words, not mine, as I'm sure you'd know."

"Did she say which men agreed?"

"She did," said Molly with satisfaction, "after a little judicious prodding. I wrote the names down afterwards."

"Good. That means we will know who we can trust and who we cannot. Now, how can we persuade the honest bankers, and the businessmen, that they cannot trust Vanderhoof?"

"I wish Mr. Malloy were well enough to help, child, but he is not. Doctor McNamara is very pleased with him, but says he must not be upset until his heart has grown stronger. I will think about it, and then I, myself, will talk to some community leaders. Don't worry, Hilda. Worry isn't good for you just now, either, and it will be all right. You've done all the hard work now. It only remains to put a spoke in that scoundrel's wheel for good, and we'll manage that."

Hilda hung up the phone pleased both with her plans and her acquisition of a new English idiom.

Of the plans to put a spoke in *her* wheel she had, as yet, no knowledge.

The reports came in, slowly, steadily, all week. Sven had quietly enlisted the aid of ten of his most reliable men. They were keeping an eye on the unreliable ones, the ones who had taken bribes, and had promised to march next to them on Labor Day, keep them sober, and make sure they caused no trouble. The word was spreading to other parts of Studebaker's and to other factories, but quietly. It was understood that this was in the nature of a secret military operation and must not be broadcast.

Andy's friends at the Oliver slipped over to Malloy's whenever they got the chance, to report on the whereabouts and activities of Vanderhoof and his men. They were careful never to send the same boy twice, and had never been followed or threatened. They reported that, although the men were being more careful about where they met and how loudly they talked, the boys had a secret weapon. "Because Joe, see, he's got a brother who's deaf— and he taught him to read lips!"

Molly called on Hilda, bringing her some lovely cool grapes, for the weather had turned sultry again. She also brought news that she had had quiet talks with several businessmen and bankers, trustworthy men who knew a good deal more of Vanderhoof's background than some of the newer men. They had promised to help hold the line.

To Hilda fell the two most delicate tasks. When Sergeant Lefkowicz came to see her, at Patrick's request, she laid out the whole plan before him. "This is what is going to happen, Sergeant. Or this is what they think is going to happen. We want to stop it. I have brought in—have asked to come—"

"Recruited?" Lefkowicz suggested.

"Yes! I have recruited many people to help. There are sensible union men, and laborers who do not belong to the union, who will march along with the others and keep them quiet. There are businessmen who will help to keep things calm and quiet, by talking to the men before the march, and making speeches that day. There are even honest saloon-keepers who have promised to stay closed that day, and that is very noble of them, because they will lose business." Lefkowicz nodded in agreement.

"But I do not know anyone in the Pinkertons, and I am afraid. If they have orders to break up the march, will they maybe do it, even if there is no fighting to give them an excuse?"

"Some might. But, Miss Hilda, we've had word, the police have, that there might be trouble, and we're ready for it. Every man will be on duty that day."

"Yes, but from whom have you had word?"

He thought about that. "You mean Vanderhoof's spreading the word, so he can start a little trouble and it'll turn into big trouble because everybody's nervous and ready to fight?"

"Yes. Can you do anything about that?"

"I'm not a very big bug on the force, you know."

"But you are honest, and you know who the other honest men are. Are not some of them big bugs?"

The words sounded so funny in Hilda's accent that he had to stifle a laugh. "That they are. I'll do my best, Miss Hilda. We can't arrest a man for planning and thinking, you understand, but we can keep an eye on him, and on the Pinkertons. We don't want any riots in this town."

She wasn't completely satisfied with that, but if it was the best she could do, she would have to leave it at that.

Finally, she phoned Aunt Molly once more. "I need one more thing from you, please. You have done such a lot, but…"

"Nonsense. What is it you need?"

Hilda explained, and presently Eileen came into the parlor with a puzzled look. "There's a man wants to see you about time, he says."

"From the *Times*, he said maybe?"

"I guess."

"He is a newspaper man, Eileen. Show him in, and please bring us some lemonade."

He was, in fact, the editor of the South Bend *Times*. He would never, she knew, have come to see Hilda Johansson, or even Mrs. Patrick Cavanaugh. The niece of Daniel Malloy, however, rated at least a polite visit.

In two minutes, when Hilda had begun to explain, his manner of indulgent courtesy changed to the avid interest of a devoted newsman. When she had finished, he sat back and said, "Whew! How certain is all this?"

"What is planned is certain. We hope there will be no trouble. But if you could have a reporter there, and a photographer maybe…?"

"Either way it works out, this is news!"

"But there must be nothing in the paper ahead of time!"

"No, indeed, ma'am. If for no other reason, we don't want the *Tribune* getting hold of this."

So, feeling she had done everything she could, Hilda waited, with growing impatience, for the next few days to pass, for Labor Day to arrive and to depart, peacefully. And for practically the first time in her pregnancy, she hoped her own labor day would hold off until after September fourth.

...screw your courage to the sticking place...

—William Shakespeare, *Macbeth*

32

S UNDAY, SEPTEMBER THIRD. Hilda thought seriously about going to church, but the heat was bad again, and she could no longer fit into even the mourning dress Eileen had made. She could not sleep, though. She got up when Patrick did.

"You are going to an early Mass?"

"Couldn't sleep," he admitted. "Thought Mass might settle me down a little."

"You are worried, too?"

"Can't help it. Seems like we've got all the bases covered—"

"What does that mean?" Hilda asked with a frown.

"Oh. It's a baseball term. Means we've tried to think of everythin' that could go wrong. But still..."

"I know. I wish I could go to church, but I cannot. Perhaps you will say a prayer that all will be well tomorrow?"

"That I will, darlin'. I'm off."

Hilda's firmly Protestant mind was not certain that Catholic prayers would be effective, but it didn't hurt to "cover all the bases."

The day grew hotter. Clouds gathered and faint rumbles of thunder were heard now and then, but no refreshing rain came, only a heavy, oppressive feeling in the air that made tempers fray and tensions rise. Nobody wanted to eat, or read, or listen to music on the graphophone, or look at pictures on the stereoscope, and certainly nobody wanted to go for a walk or a ride, with the temperature in the nineties and the air so humid one could hardly breathe.

Hilda gave it up shortly after she had picked at the cold supper Mrs. O'Rourke had left ready to serve. They had come late to
the table, hoping for cooler air that would tempt an appetite, but
no relief had come. "I am going to bed," Hilda announced. "It is
too hot to sleep, but it is too hot to do anything else, either. I wish
tomorrow were over."

"Me, too." Patrick kissed her good night, somewhat absently,
and tried to read for another hour, but his nerves were stretched
tight. The wind howled round the house, and again there was the
distant rumble of thunder. When a gust of wind turned the pages
of his book and nearly slammed it shut, he decided it was time to
drop the pretense of reading.

He made the rounds of the house, checking the doors. It was
far too hot to close the windows, but he made sure the screens
were securely hooked, the gas stove turned off properly, and all
the lights out. He wasn't sleepy, but he might doze. He felt, he
thought wryly, a little like a child on Christmas Eve. Anything to
make tomorrow come sooner. Only in this case anticipation was
well mixed with dread.

He was on his way up to bed in the now-dark house when
he heard the tap. It was so quiet he might not have heard it, if he
hadn't been so keyed up. He froze, his foot on the bottom step,
his heart beating absurdly hard. The wind, he thought. A branch
knocking against a window.

It came again, this time unmistakably a tap on the back door,
a little louder than before.

Patrick found himself reluctant to turn on a light. There
was a candle on the table by the stairs, a holdover from the days
when everyone went to bed by candlelight. He struck a match, lit
the candle, and carried it somewhat unsteadily to the back door.
"Who's there?" he whispered, feeling foolish. Who could it be
but one of the O'Rourkes, coming back into the house for some
reason?

"For God's sake, let me in," came an unfamiliar voice. "And
don't light a lamp."

"Who is it?"

"Sam Black. Let me in, for the love of God!"

Patrick was never sure afterwards why he opened the door. He had never met Sam Black, but he knew very little about him that was good. To admit him to a house where his wife lay sleeping, with their unborn child, was imprudent, to say the least.

But there was true desperation in that voice.... Patrick unlocked the door, opened it a crack, and held up the candle to see the man's face.

"Quick! Close the door and put out that candle." The wind blew it out before the words left Sam's lips, and then he had slipped through the door and closed it behind him.

"What are you doin' here? What d'you mean, bustin' into a man's house in the middle of the night?" Patrick said in a furious whisper.

"Please," said Sam. "Please listen to me. I know what you think of me, and you have every right to throw me out, but I beg of you, listen to me first."

Patrick wished he owned a gun. The man sounded harmless enough, and scared right out of his mind, but he was Vanderhoof's man, and he'd been present when Clancy was killed, even if he hadn't done the killing—and Patrick was still of two minds about that.

"Why should I trust you?"

"No reason in the world."

He sounded beaten, and at the very end of his strength. It was that aura of defeat that decided Patrick. He led the man into the kitchen, closed the windows, pulled the curtains tightly closed, and then lit the candle and put it on the kitchen table. Then he opened a drawer and pulled out a ball of twine and a pair of scissors.

"I'll listen to what you've got to say, but I'm goin' to tie you up first," said Patrick grimly.

Sam nodded, and sat quietly while Patrick secured him to the kitchen chair, his hands bound at the wrists, but in front of him, not behind. He was dripping with sweat, the acrid sweat of fear added to the heat-sweat of the sultry night. Patrick had taken a good look at him, and doubted the man had an ounce of fight left in him. Nevertheless, Hilda was upstairs. He intended to be careful.

"Now. Say what you have to say."

"I came to warn you. Vanderhoof's out to get you and your wife. He's going to make sure his scheme works tomorrow, in spite of everything you've tried to do to stop him. And then he's sending men to kill you."

When Patrick could breathe again, he said, "How do you know? How do you—how does *he* know anythin' about it?"

"Somebody blabbed. I don't know who. Maybe one of your servants?"

Patrick opened his mouth for an indignant denial, and then remembered O'Rourke, fond of his beer, not always discreet.

"Anyway, why should I believe you? You're Vanderhoof's man."

"I was." Sam's head had been sinking lower and lower, but suddenly he raised it. The candle flickered. "I never reckoned on killing! It was just union-busting. That's what he said. I hate unions. They killed my business, them and the banks between them! I'd do anything to get rid of the damned unions. And he paid me pretty well. I needed the money, damn it! No work, no decent home, no wife—she left me, you know, when everything went bad. But murder—that wasn't in the deal." He lowered his head again, and his voice, which had become loud with passion. "I didn't kill Clancy, Mr. Cavanaugh. On my oath, I didn't."

"Who did?" Patrick's voice was passionate, too, but he kept it low.

"I don't know! As God is my witness, I don't know. Clancy was coming to my house to hide out. He was afraid his father was dead, and he'd be blamed. And he knew that stupid bank clerk was dead, though he didn't mean to kill him, just to damage the store. He knew everybody was after him—the police, Vander-hoof, everybody. So he sent me a message, and I agreed to let him in. But somebody got to him first." He paused. "And now some-body will get me, too. Vanderhoof doesn't let rats get away. But as long as I'm going to die anyway, I had to warn you. Maybe if you get out of town quick enough—"

"Patrick?" It was Hilda's voice, and it was her footfalls on the stairs. "Patrick, I heard voices. Who are you talking to?"

Patrick reached for the candle to blow it out, but it was too late. He had left the door to the hall open, and Hilda had seen the light. She switched on the hall light and padded into the kitchen.

Patrick moved quickly. He pulled out a chair for her and said, "Now, darlin', don't worry. Everythin's fine."

She looked at the man tied up in the chair. "Is he a burglar?" she asked.

"No, darlin'. I'll explain everythin', but let me just turn out the light first."

He explained as briefly as he could, leaving the man's name until last, and then looked anxiously at Hilda. She was remarkably calm.

"Sam Black. You are in the middle of all this, are you not?"

"I was, Mrs. Cavanaugh. Not anymore. I've had enough."

"Did you kill Clancy Malloy?"

"No, I did not. If you'll bring me a Bible I'll swear it."

"Andy said not. I believe you. But what do you think we must do?"

"I told Mr. Cavanaugh. You'd best get out of town, just as fast as you can. If I were you, I'd get your carriage hitched up and get in it and ride hell for leather to—"

"Yes. To where, Mr. Black? Vanderhoof knows many people in many places, does he not? And as you see, I am not in a condition to ride the way you suggest. I have a better idea, but we will need your help. If you are brave enough." There was some doubt in her voice. This sorry specimen of humanity before her did not appear particularly brave.

He sat up straighter and lifted his head. "I was brave enough to come here. They could have killed me on the way. It's only this damned—this dratted wind, forgive me, ma'am—this wind that kept me safe. There's so much noise they couldn't hear me, and it's so blamed dark they couldn't see me, either. If I'm a dead man anyway, I might as well do one good thing before they get me. What do you have in mind?"

"If you do it properly, you will not die. You may go to prison, though."

"I'm not afraid of that. It'd serve me right, I reckon. And I'd be safe there, anyway."

"Good. Then listen carefully."

After she had given him precise instructions, she made a telephone call. A sleepy butler answered.

"Riggs, I am so sorry to wake you, but this is very important. I must speak to Aunt Molly at once."

"She's only just got to sleep, Miss Hilda. I don't know whether—"

"I would not ask if it were not important. Tell her I am so sorry, but there was no one else to help."

Molly came to the phone remarkably lucid for someone awakened out of her first sleep. She listened in silence, and then said, "Leave it to me," and hung up.

All's well that ends well…

—William Shakespeare

L
ABOR DAY DAWNED bright and hot, with a haze over the sun that only made it feel hotter. The Cavanaugh household rose early. Sam Black had spend the night in the small back bedroom with Andy, who was very surprised indeed when he woke and saw a strange man sleeping in his armchair, and even more surprised when he recognized him. Sam had been told that Andy was to be trusted, so Sam explained, and the two discussed the day's altered plans and came down to breakfast satisfied that each knew his duties.

Sergeant Lefkowicz was at the door just as they all left the breakfast table. "Mrs. Malloy phoned early this morning, ma'am, and told the chief she wanted to see me. But I guess it was really you I was supposed to see?"

"Yes. I did not want to call myself. Sergeant, we have a guest." She stood aside and let him see Sam, who was somewhat white and shaking a little. "I know you may need to arrest him later, but not now. Let me explain."

Meanwhile Patrick was on the phone to the South Bend *Times*, a brief call that was apparently satisfactory, for he hung up smiling.

"All right, darlin', he said a few minutes later. "We're off. You behave yourself, now."

She nodded gravely. "Doors locked, answer to no one. But oh, Patrick, come home soon!"

He gave her a quick hug and kiss, and suddenly serious, made the sign of the cross on her forehead. "Don't mind it, darlin'," he whispered. "I want you safe. Both of you."

Hesitantly, she repeated the sign on his forehead. Then she straightened. "I am glad my mother cannot see me," she said tartly. "Popish foolishness, she'd say."

Patrick laughed and headed out the door with Andy. Sam, dressed in a coat of Patrick's in a dull gray-green that would blend in to almost any background, waited by the back door to creep into the carriage when O'Rourke's back was turned. Sergeant Lefkowicz shook his head as he watched them go. "If anything goes wrong, it's my badge, you know, ma'am."

"Nothing will go wrong." I hope, she added silently. "Now go, and try to make sure no one sees you near this house."

Then she and Eileen closed all the windows and curtains, shooed Mrs. O'Rourke to the carriage house saying that Hilda had a dreadful headache and could not bear noise of any kind, double-locked all the doors, and sat by the telephone in front of an electric fan to wait.

Patrick and Andy, with Sam Black crouched uncomfortably on the floor of the carriage, rode to the assembly point of the parade, just to the south of the courthouse. A crowd had already gathered; it wasn't hard for Sam to slip out of the carriage and mingle with them. His coat blended in; Patrick lost sight of him in moments.

An unusual number of police were on the streets. Patrick saw uniforms everywhere. They were acting friendly, though, talking and laughing with the laborers as they assembled, helping with a heavy banner until it was reasonably stable in the wind. At one point Patrick spotted Sven Johansson talking earnestly with a small group of men, who then fanned out and joined other groups. The mood was relaxed. Everyone seemed to be in a holiday mood, despite the oppressive weather.

No, not everyone. Patrick saw a knot of men with heavy scowls on their faces. They were looking around, scanning the crowd for someone they couldn't find. They had just broken up when a trumpet sounded somewhere nearby, along with a roll of drums.

The crowd quieted, looking for the source of the trumpet call. This was not a normal part of the parade.

Two men were standing on the courthouse steps. With satisfaction, Patrick recognized one of them as James Oliver, of Oliver Chilled Plow works. He was in his eighties but still strong and hearty. The other was John M. Studebaker, president of the Studebaker Manufacturing company. As owners of the two huge companies, both with world-wide distribution, both with enormous payrolls, between them they held the reins of power in South Bend manufacturing. Patrick climbed down from the carriage, but motioned Andy to stay put.

Oliver stepped forward. "Men of South Bend!" he roared between cupped hands. The crowd stilled further.

"What the hell!" muttered someone behind Patrick. He didn't turn to look.

"Men of South Bend," Oliver continued. "And ladies, of course."

The crowd chuckled at that.

"You didn't expect to see me here today, did you?"

At that they roared. A doughty Scotsman, Oliver was known to be an opponent of organized labor. He had in fact once been rumored to have shot a gun into the air to quell a union demonstration at his factory.

"Well, I'm sure you'll be happy to know I don't intend to make a long speech." Chuckles again, and some applause. "I'm just here to tell you I'd back South Bend workers against any other labor force, anywhere in the world. I'm proud of you, and grateful for all you've done to build my company, and John's here, and all the other businesses in South Bend. Congratulations to you all, and if you want to come back to the factory—either of 'em—" gesturing to Studebaker "—after you've done marching, we've got a little party laid on for you."

A roar of surprised applause, and then quiet again as Studebaker stepped forward.

"I can't talk as loud as James, here, and anyway he stole what I wanted to say." Chuckles. "But I want you to know that we realize, all of us in business in South Bend, that we couldn't have done any of it without you. Two of my brothers started a tiny business here a little over fifty years ago, and you men, yes, and women too—thank you, James—all of you workers have made Studebaker's what it is today, and while I'm proud of you, you can be prouder of yourselves. Have a good time today!"

Prolonged cheers. The marchers began to form into orderly lines, the men in front of each group carrying banners. A band started to play.

Patrick went back to the carriage and gestured to Andy, who slipped out and was gone in the crowd in a moment. Patrick strolled up to the courthouse steps, where Oliver and Studebaker stood conferring. "Thank you, gentlemen," he said quietly. "And Uncle Dan thanks you, too."

"Glad to oblige," said Oliver. "Anything for the Malloy family, even if you are a bunch of Irishmen. But should you be up here, showing yourself? I understood there might be a question of some roughhouse."

Patrick almost smiled. "Some roughhouse" was a mild way of interpreting a death threat.

"I think we'll be all right, sir. Do you see some of the policemen, talking to those men on the corner?"

"By heaven, that's Hewlitt! And John, isn't that Goodman with them?"

"It is," said Studebaker grimly. "It's almost enough to make me change my politics."

Oliver laughed at that, and the two shook hands and strolled off, leaving Patrick in sole command of his vantage point. He watched and waited.

There was a scuffle in one of the marching units! But no, it was just that someone had stumbled. Someone else helped him up. Patrick breathed again.

The watching crowd was having a wonderful time. Yes, it was hot and muggy. But that made the ice cream vendors happy, and their customers, too. Patrick scanned the scene to see if he could spot the Pinkerton men. Yes, surely that was one, marching along with one of the units, keeping his eye on a belligerent-looking man near the rear.

So far, so good. But it wasn't enough that the parade finish without incident. There would still be the chance for it all to be done over again—and there was still the threat to him and his family. He kept his watch.

There was Andy! He was heading down the Washington Street hill, toward the river. Looking in the direction he was going, Patrick could just see, ahead of him, a gray-green back. And coming up the hill, about to meet up with both of them, a portly figure in a white linen suit.

Vanderhoof.

Patrick's every nerve tightened. He ran down the steps, waited impatiently until the next unit went past, and then headed down the hill.

Where were they?

Ah, there was Andy, just getting up. He had knelt to tie a shoelace. He barely glanced at Patrick, jerked his head to his right, and strolled nonchalantly back up the hill to watch the rest of the parade.

Patrick edged into the alleyway Andy had indicated. A few yards away, there was Black and a furiously angry Vanderhoof.

"What the hell went wrong? Oliver and Studebaker were supposed to be out of town, not standing up there making damn-fool nice-nice speeches. And what about the parade! It's all looking like a bunch of milk-and-water let's-play-pattycake. Where's the riot? Where are the Pinkertons to keep things stirred up? And I've been looking for you for hours, you lily-livered bastard. You've wrecked months of planning, and you're going to find out what happens to a traitor!"

He reached into a pocket. Patrick was halfway down the alley when two men stepped out of a doorway.

"Mr. Vanderhoof, I arrest you on a charge of carrying a concealed weapon, of threat to commit bodily harm, and of conspiracy to disturb the peace." Lefkowicz smiled gently as he pulled out a pair of handcuffs.

"Oh no, you don't, you little pipsqueak. Just wait till the super finds out about this, you—"

"Very interesting, Mr. Vanderhoof," said the second man. "John Stoll, South Bend *Times*. Am I to understand that you think the superintendent of police would stand behind you on these serious charges?"

Vanderhoof looked from one to the other, his face turning redder and redder. He turned to run up the alley, but Patrick stepped in his way. "I'm thinkin' I owe you a debt, sir," he said, and launched a large fist at his eye.

❧

"The sergeant could have arrested you for assault," said Hilda, bandaging Patrick's hand.

"He had his hands full," said Patrick. "*Ouch.* Anyway, I think he closed his eyes just then."

"There. That will hurt for a little while."

"Not as long as old Vandy's black eye," he said with satisfaction.

"Is it really over, do you think?" She handed Eileen the bandages and bottle of iodine. "I cannot wait to see the morning paper."

"It should make good readin'. And it's over—for now. Old Vandy was the brains of the outfit, and the bankroll. He's goin' to be in jail for a good long while, I'll bet, and without him to pay off all his stooges, it'll all die down. Of course it'll spring up again. A crook's born every minute or so. But for now, it's over. And all because of you, darlin' girl. You're a wonder, you are."

"No. It was everyone. Especially you. You are a hero! I could do nothing but sit at home."

"You could 't'ink.' Your specialty. And you could get everyone else to help defeat the lion, all the 'mice.' You're my own darlin' Sherlock, you are. And you'd best get to bed, or Kevin'll have a fit."

On with the dance; let joy be unconfined…

—Lord Byron,
"Childe Harold," 1816

34

ON SEPTEMBER 12, what was to be the last bad thunderstorm of the season broke in fury shortly after midnight. Hilda, awakened from an uneasy doze by a deafening thunderclap, thought at first that she was trembling with fright.

But did fright produce stomach cramps?

She woke Patrick, who woke Eileen and then sent O'Rourke for Aunt Molly. It was Eileen who had the sense to phone the doctor.

The labor was as easy as such things can well be. To Patrick it seemed endless. He paced the floor downstairs, listening anxiously to muffled groans and hurried footsteps. When morning came, he had finally fallen into a restless sleep in the big chair in his den.

Footsteps on the stairs. He started, leapt to his feet. Only half-awake, he saw Aunt Molly come into the room, a blanket-wrapped bundle in her arms. "Patrick, meet my new grandson, Kevin Cavanaugh."

He stared in awe at the tiny red face, its eyes screwed tightly shut. With a tentative finger, he touched the rose-petal cheek. Kevin turned his face toward the finger and began working his mouth.

"Well, look at that, will you?" he whispered. "Smart little fellow, isn't he?"

"And look at this," said Eileen, entering the room with another bundle. "Do you not also want to meet Kristina?"

He looked from one bundle to the other. "Two?" he said, bewildered.

"Two," said Aunt Molly. "You're the proud father of twins."

"Twins," he repeated obediently. "Kevin. Kristina. Twins." Pause. Patrick blinked, rubbed his eyes, and suddenly woke up. "By all the saints—twins!"

He bounded up the stairs two at a time to congratulate Hilda on her astonishing achievement.

Afterword

SAM BLACK WAS given a short prison sentence, in recognition of his help to the police in apprehending Vanderhoof. Black never returned to South Bend.

Eustatius Vanderhoof (his real first name had the singularly inappropriate meaning of "peaceful"), on the other hand, was given a long prison term, as were those of his associates who could be proven to have committed the crimes of murder, arson, and malicious damage. Vanderhoof served less than three months of his sentence. His apoplectic fury at a prison guard led to a true apoplexy, which proved fatal.

Eugene Debs ran again for president in 1908—and lost again.

Author's Note

WHEN I BEGIN to plot a book in the Hilda series, I always start by scanning the local newspapers for interesting events that took place in the period in which the book will be set. While working on this book, I came across several intriguing headlines. Some were about labor unrest, first in Russia—the horrifying riots in St. Petersburg—and then in Chicago—the confusing events following upon the Montgomery Ward strike of 1905. The other headlines that caught my eye had to do with train wrecks, of which there were a good many that year. The Twentieth Century Flyer really was wrecked in June, with loss of life and limb, and it was (apparently) caused deliberately. These two constellations of troubles combined in my scheming mind to make a plot.

That being said, I stress that none of the events in South Bend that I relate here ever happened, and the historical persons I have mentioned did none of the things I have suggested or attributed to them, with the exception of Eugene Debs, whose participation in the formation of the IWW is well documented. In particular, the Labor Day Parade was very nearly rained out, and certainly there were no untoward incidents.

The full story of Vanderhoof and Clancy Malloy and their involvement with Hilda, Patrick, and their families can be found in *Green Grow the Victims*, published in 2001.

Mary Ivancsics

About the Author

Jeanne M. Dams was born and raised in South Bend, Indiana, and has lived there virtually all her life. She was completely uninterested in history throughout her schooling, but was captivated by it once she realized that history was just a story about people—who are endlessly fascinating. Her formal education was from Purdue and Notre Dame universities, but most of her real knowledge is self-acquired through voracious reading.

Of Swedish descent through her mother, Dams has been nominated for the Macavity, and has won the Agatha Award. She welcomes visitors and e-mail at www.jeannedams.com.

MORE MYSTERIES
FROM PERSEVERANCE PRESS
💀 *For the New Golden Age* 💀

JON L. BREEN
Eye of God
ISBN 978-1-880284-89-6

TAFFY CANNON
ROXANNE PRESCOTT SERIES
Guns and Roses
*Agatha and Macavity awards
nominee, Best Novel*
ISBN 978-1-880284-34-6

Blood Matters
ISBN 978-1-880284-86-5

Open Season on Lawyers
ISBN 978-1-880284-51-3

Paradise Lost
ISBN 978-1-880284-80-3

LAURA CRUM
GAIL MCCARTHY SERIES
Moonblind
ISBN 978-1-880284-90-2

Chasing Cans
ISBN 978-1-880284-94-0

Going, Gone
ISBN 978-1-880284-98-8

Barnstorming *(forthcoming)*
ISBN 978-1-56474-508-8

JEANNE M. DAMS
HILDA JOHANSSON SERIES
Crimson Snow
ISBN 978-1-880284-79-7

Indigo Christmas
ISBN 978-1-880284-95-7

Murder in Burnt Orange
ISBN 978-1-56474-503-3

JANET DAWSON
JERI HOWARD SERIES
Bit Player
ISBN 978-1-56474-494-4

KATHY LYNN EMERSON
LADY APPLETON SERIES
**Face Down Below
the Banqueting House**
ISBN 978-1-880284-71-1

**Face Down Beside
St. Anne's Well**
ISBN 978-1-880284-82-7

Face Down O'er the Border
ISBN 978-1-880284-91-9

ELAINE FLINN
MOLLY DOYLE SERIES
Deadly Vintage
ISBN 978-1-880284-87-2

HAL GLATZER
KATY GREEN SERIES
Too Dead To Swing
ISBN 978-1-880284-53-7

A Fugue in Hell's Kitchen
ISBN 978-1-880284-70-4

The Last Full Measure
ISBN 978-1-880284-84-1

MARGARET GRACE
MINIATURE SERIES
Mix-up in Miniature
(forthcoming)
ISBN 978-1-56474-510-1

WENDY HORNSBY
MAGGIE MACGOWEN SERIES
In the Guise of Mercy
ISBN 978-1-56474-482-1

The Paramour's Daughter
ISBN 978-1-56474-496-8

DIANA KILLIAN
POETIC DEATH SERIES
Docketful of Poesy
ISBN 978-1-880284-97-1

JANET LAPIERRE
PORT SILVA SERIES
Baby Mine
ISBN 978-1-880284-32-2

Keepers
*Shamus Award nominee, Best
Paperback Original*
ISBN 978-1-880284-44-5

Death Duties
ISBN 978-1-880284-74-2

Family Business
ISBN 978-1-880284-85-8

Run a Crooked Mile
ISBN 978-1-880284-88-9

HAILEY LIND
ART LOVER'S SERIES
Arsenic and Old Paint
ISBN 978-1-56474-490-6

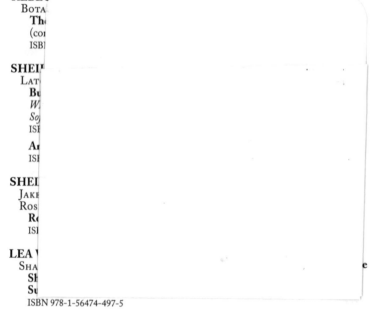

**Available from your local bookstore or from
Perseverance Press/John Daniel & Co. at (800) 662-8351
or www.danielpublishing.com/perseverance.**